randall
& hopkirk
{deceased}

GHOSTS FROM THE PAST

randall
& hopkirk
{deceased}

GHOSTS FROM THE PAST

GRAEME GRANT

BOXTREE

First published in Great Britain 2000 by Boxtree
an imprint of Macmillan Publishers Ltd
25 Eccleston Place London SW1W 9NF
Basingstoke and Oxford

www.macmillan.co.uk

Associated companies throughout the world

ISBN 07522 2346 1

1 3 5 7 9 8 6 4 2

A CIP catalogue record for this book is available
from the British Library.

Typeset by Blackjacks

Printed by Mackays of Chatham plc

prologue

The man in gold walked towards the bar, where the depleted remains of another man was talking at the bartender. The latter was polishing a glass and listening with that plastic smile people wear when they're trying not to scream. As discreetly as he could, the other man raised a gold-clad arm in the air. But the bartender failed to notice. The man bit his lip. It was crucial that he attract his attention in the next few minutes. Because from now on, every second counted. Every tiny ticking of the clock meant the passing of a vital moment.

The languid brunette further down the bar was watching as well. One hand toyed with a glass of Bourbon. With the other she twirled a lock of hair in a gesture that was at once suggestive and innocent. The customer with her leered and declared an interest in the suggestion, not the innocence. The girl's sultry smile belied the fact that she barely registered his existence. Other men occupied her thoughts. One was the man in gold. The girl looked at her watch. The rest would be here soon. She pulled her scrap of mink over her bare shoulders, leaned towards the salivating man and whispered something in his ear. The rosebud lips touched his lobes. Then she giggled, put a talonlike finger to his mouth and slid elegantly off her barstool.

Then the foyer doors burst open, a phalanx of armed men appeared at the balustrade and swarmed down the horseshoe staircase – and the shooting began.

The guns triggered pandemonium as well as death. Women began to scream, people stampeded to the back of the club and, in the middle, a wall-eyed, reptilian man with stacks in his heels was swamped by an army of minders. They, too, were armed, and as they edged their charge out of the fray, their indiscriminate fire peppered every corner of the club, its invaders, its walls, its ceiling – and its customers.

A man hurled himself behind the bar and covered his ears with his hands. Ricocheting bullets slammed into the optics above him, shattering bottles and drenching him in liquor. Intent on self-preservation, he edged himself further under the counter. Even there, the air was leaden and pungent with cordite.

The screaming mass of humanity flooding towards the staircase came off worse. Caught in the cross-fire, they fell bleeding and writhing to the floor. But the volley of bullets wasn't the only danger. People tumbled from the balustrade – one of them, alive but bleeding from a gash near his mouth, was the man who had headed the raid.

As the mayhem continued, great shards of glass came scything down from the ceiling as the giant chandelier was peppered with a salvo of bullets. And then, foreshadowed by an ominous lurch, the chandelier itself plunged thirty feet to the floor, flattening those beneath it. Pinned to ground, several were killed instantly, while the rest were condemned to writhe in a bloodbath until the breath left their bodies.

Among them were the wall-eyed reptilian man with the stacked heels and three of his minders. The man in gold was nowhere to be seen. Nor was the girl with the scrap of mink and the sultry, sensuous smile.

chapter
one

'So what does this woman want, then?'
'I think she said something about protection.'

'Oh, God.'

'Why "Oh, God"?'

Jeff looked over at Jeannie. Her expression, like her question, was one of genuine surprise. A few months ago, a client seeking protection would have been like a mental abrasion; salt in a psychological wound. Tears would have welled. Now, instead, curiosity was aroused. Jeff supposed that he ought to be glad that the idea of personal protection no longer prompted in Jeannie an immediate recall of the circumstances of Marty's death. Her grief was no longer raw.

Then he noticed that her curiosity had given way to understanding, and that she was looking at him with sympathy. But it was sympathy tempered, he suspected, by mild irritation. He was right.

'Jeff, look, I know it still hurts…God knows I know. But we can't let Marty hang over us like…like some sort of spectre. We have to move on. I mean, of course we'll never forget, but we have to move forward. And if that means protecting a woman then we'll do it without reopening old wounds.' Suddenly Jeannie grinned. 'Think of Marty differently. Think how he would have hated us to be miserable every time we had a case that reminded us of him.'

But even as she spoke, Jeannie realized this wasn't quite true. A little voice in the back of her head told her that the word 'Marty' was synonymous with 'me, me, me'. The thought made her grin again, as she recalled Marty's larger than life presence.

Jeff didn't need a little voice to remind him. And he wasn't grinning. In fact, he was looking slightly apprehensive. Marty had a habit of gate-crashing Marty moments, of eavesdropping when the conversation turned to one of his favourite subjects. Jeff was anticipating Marty's larger than life presence any second.

For the moment, though, his fears were unfounded and they remained alone in the office. After a while, he said, 'You're right,' without much conviction. 'Onwards and upwards, eh?'

'Mmm. And while we're at it,' said Jeannie, 'don't you think we should spruce this place up a bit? It's looking a little...a little faded. We need an injection of new life. Freshness. Plants.'

'Plants?'

'Yes, plants.' Fuelled by sudden enthusiasm, Jeannie jumped up from her desk and began pacing the room, pouncing on various objects with disapproval. 'This, for instance,' she said, brandishing the orange lamp. 'What does this do for our image?'

'Well, it's got a certain...a certain timeless charm,' tried Jeff.

'It doesn't have any charm at all.'

No, thought Jeff, but it's Marty's. Life wouldn't be worth living if Marty descended to find a lampless

11

office. 'Er…it was Marty's,' he said hopefully. 'I know we're moving on, but I think we should keep the odd memento.'

'It's a *very* odd memento, Jeff.'

'Well, I like it,' he said in desperation. 'It reminds me of…of you.'

'*Me?*' Jeannie turned, aghast, to her partner.

Jeff swallowed. 'Ye-es, it's got…it's got its own style. It might not be…well, the conventional idea of perfect beauty' – Jeannie's expression told him he was skating on thin ice, trespassing and in danger of being shot, all at once – 'but I like it. I *really* like it.' He met Jeannie's gaze straight on. 'It's irreplaceable.'

Jeannie didn't reply. Then, with an inscrutable look on her face, she replaced the lamp with great care on the filing cabinet. When she turned to face Jeff again she was smiling. 'I think,' she said, 'I'll go and buy a plant.'

Jeff sat quite still for a long while after Jeannie's departure. He was still half expecting Marty to materialize, but his deceased partner was seemingly engaged elsewhere. He was, Jeff realized, increasingly engaged elsewhere; his visits were becoming less and less frequent. Perhaps it really *was* time to move on. Perhaps it was even time to make a move on Jeannie. They both knew the attraction between them was mutual, that decorum as much as anything else was holding them back and that it would be an insult to Marty's memory to turn their friendship and their partnership into a relationship of a different kind.

Then Jeff sighed. He was not the kind of person to dishonour Marty's memory. He was a decent man and he knew it. He also knew that he wasn't the most dynamic man in the world, that he lacked

Marty's charisma and energy. But he was a fundamentally decent bloke who had never wittingly done anything wrong. So what on earth, he wondered, had he done to deserve the fate of being haunted by Marty Hopkirk until the day he shuffled off his mortal coil and departed to a world that, if Marty's stories were anything to go by, was as turbulent and fraught with mishaps as the realm of the living?

Marty had been dead for nearly six months and, as Jeff had pointed out on numerous occasions, he hadn't even had the good manners to allow Jeff a reasonable period of mourning before he had come back to haunt him. True, he had been a man with a mission, a ghost with a grouse, when he had first reappeared. He'd been allowed back to solve his own murder. But the solving part had proved rather complicated and time-consuming, and Marty had outstayed his time back on earth. Like a man without a passport, he had been detained at Customs, belonging to neither one place nor another. Lurking in limbo, he was not allowed to consort with the truly dead or to share space with the living. His only consolation – and that, as he was fond of telling Jeff, was more often a curse than a consolation – was that he could appear to Jeff, his 'chosen one', at any time, in any place, for a limited period. Marty's interpretation of that state of affairs was that he was a godsend; that Randall & Hopkirk (Deceased), Security Services, would have become Randall & Hopkirk (Ceased) were it not for Marty's other-worldly input into solving their cases. The opinion that Jeff voiced to Marty was slightly different: he acknowledged that Marty, being invisible to everyone else and possessed of certain useful powers, was handy for business. But he was also adamant that

Marty was more of a burden than a blessing, having a slightly dodgy grasp of his powers, failing to appear when he was most needed and, worst of all, interfering in Jeff's personal life.

In other words, their relationship was exactly the same as it had been when Marty had been a permanent presence on earth.

Jeff sighed, nudged himself out of his reverie and reached into his desk drawer for a file. The drawer opened to reveal a state of chaos – a microcosm of the office at large. He thought of chaos, the place where, according to Greek mythology, troubled souls milled about. He made a mental note to ask Marty about that. Then he mentally crumpled up the note and threw it away. Marty didn't use his time in the other world to brush up on mythology – brushing up against Marilyn Monroe was more his thing.

Smiling, and tempted for only a fleeting moment by the bottle of whisky winking at him, Jeff extracted a blank file and closed the drawer. He reached across for a pen and, in his neat, precise hand, wrote across the top of the file the words 'Personal Protection'. Then he sat back, chewed the end of the pen and allowed himself to fantasize about the enormous sums of money this new client would pay him.

Five minutes later, the fantasy gave way to reality. Jeff had been lost in his musings when the client walked into the outer office, and he realized he was no longer alone only when she knocked tentatively at the door of his inner sanctum. Startled, he jumped to his feet. And he very nearly slumped back down into his chair again when he saw the woman in the doorway. She was tall, whippet-thin and had a deathly pale face, matched in tone by her almost luminous hair. She was clad entirely in white.

'Oh, God!' was Jeff's greeting.
'Yes,' came the reply. 'I've come to haunt you.'

chapter two

'Would you like a glass of water?'

'Er…yeah. Yeah. That would be great, love. It's just there. No, not in the fridge. In the tap.'

'Well, just you sit there for a moment. We'll have you back on your feet in a moment. I must say,' she added with a tinkling laugh, 'I knew I'd get some sort of reaction from you, but I didn't expect it to be that extreme.'

Jeff remained slumped in his seat. He was aware that his head seemed to have shrunk between his shoulder blades, but it was a posture that suited his mood. He felt humbled, belittled and decidedly foolish. In his line of business he met all types of people…probably every sort there was…even the sorts that didn't exist. And so he stayed slumped, ashamed that he of all people should make a fool of himself in front of a ghost.

He raised himself into a rather more dignified position when she proffered the glass of water. 'Thanks,' he said ruefully. 'And…er, sorry about the fainting. I just wasn't expecting…' He trailed off into silence and took a sip of water. 'I wasn't expecting…well, you know.'

'I do know. It must have come as something of a shock.'

'Yes.'

'Clearly you weren't expecting me.'

'No. Clearly.'

'And,' she said with a gentle smile, 'I look different.'

'Yes. Yes, you do.' She looked very different from mortal souls. Jeff made a mental note to ask Marty if they all wore white up there. It must, he reflected, be a very clean place.

'I've learned a lot over the past few years, you know.'

Jeff nodded. If she'd been dead for years, that would explain why she was more adept than Marty at worldly things. Like pouring a glass of water without dropping the glass; like sitting on the chair opposite him without disappearing through it as Marty sometimes did.

He smiled at her. She smiled back. They faced each other across the desk. Smiling.

This wasn't, he thought, getting them very far. He cleared his throat. 'So,' he began, in what he hoped was a businesslike manner, 'haunting me. Is it really necessary? It's not that I particularly *object* or anything. It's just, well, I've got rather a lot on my plate in that area...'

'Oh? So I'm not the first to come back to you?'

'Well, apart from Marty, yes, I suppose you are.'

His visitor dismissed that with what seemed a relieved smile and an impatient wave of her hand. 'Oh, but I don't count Marty. After all you'd been through together, it was obvious you'd stick with each other whatever happened.'

'Was it? Oh, well...yes, I suppose it was.'

The woman looked around the room. 'Where is he anyway?'

'I don't know. Actually I haven't seen him for a while. He just drops in now and again.' Jeff cast a quizzical look at the woman. 'Why, did he say he'd be here?'

'No. No. I haven't spoken to him. Anyway,' she continued, 'it was really you I wanted to see.' She leaned a little closer. 'I'll always have a soft spot for Marty, but he's not the most reliable of people, is he? A little volatile, don't you think?'

As he always did when other people criticized Marty, Jeff sprang to his defence. 'Unreliable? Absolutely not. And I think volatile's going a little far. He may be a little over-enthusiastic sometimes, but he's always focused. We have to be in this business.'

'Good.' The woman opposite him smiled again. 'Because I need focus. I need you to focus very clearly. And I'll pay you handsomely for doing so.'

'Oh, right.' Then Jeff looked at the woman through narrowed eyes. There wasn't any money where she came from. Dead people didn't need chequebooks. He leaned closer. 'Um, may I ask where the money's coming from? I don't want to be rude or anything, but under the circumstances...'

Again she laughed. 'You're sharp, aren't you? No, it's a fair enough question. I kept back some of the money I made all those years ago. I suspected it might come in handy one day.'

'Very far-sighted, I must say. But let's just get this clear. The money will come via a third person then?'

'Always one step ahead, aren't you?'

If Jeff were the sort of person who blushed, he would have blushed. Instead he squirmed. 'Well,' he said eventually with a self-deprecating little nod, 'I like to think I'm prepared. Focused.'

'Quite. And before you jump the gun about the money being legitimate, don't worry. Just because I don't need it where I am now doesn't mean I've become cavalier about where it comes from. We pride ourselves on honesty, you see.'

This was news to Jeff. Marty had told him he'd never seen such a bunch of thieving bastards: 'Just as well nothing's real,' he had said. 'They'd have had the place cleaned out years ago.' But perhaps this one really was different. She certainly had a pious air about her.

'So,' said Jeff, 'what exactly is it you want me to do? Personal protection?' he added doubtfully.

'Not yet. That'll come later. Maybe.'

'Good, 'cos that would be more Marty's area really.'

'I want you to find someone.'

'Someone here?'

'Now he is.' The woman pursed her lips. 'He's just been released.'

'Oh. Does Marty know him?'

'Well, yes. And so do you.'

Jeff brightened. 'That should make it easier. Who is he?'

The woman stood up, suddenly a magisterial presence about to deliver a stinging blow. 'Dave Day,' she hissed.

No longer stunned, Jeff was now completely nonplussed. Slowly, he rose from his seat until he was facing the woman across the desk. He knew he had to be careful with his response; had to compose his thoughts and control his demeanour. For a moment he just stared. Then, expressionless, he repeated the name in a flat monotone: 'Dave Day.'

'Yes,' she replied. Then she reached into her bag – a strange affair with little flaps that looked like wings – and extracted a card that, like everything else about her, was crisp and white. 'Here,' she said. 'My number.'

Without uttering a word, Jeff took the card.

'Will you call me when you've found him?'

Jeff nodded.

'Good. We'll take it from there.' And with that, Jeff's ethereal visitor turned and walked out of the room, through the outer office and away into another world.

It was a world where peculiar things happen, where fact is often stranger than fiction, where reality meets illusion – and where Tallulah Joplin ran into Jeannie Hurst in the corridor outside the office.

'Hello,' said Jeannie. 'Can I help you? Were you looking for someone?'

'I found him,' said Tallulah with a smile. 'Jeff Randall. He was,' she finished, 'a little surprised to see me.'

Jeannie cast a covert glance at the woman's attire. 'Yes,' she drawled, 'I can imagine he would have been.'

'And it wasn't just because I was early for my appointment.'

'No, I don't suppose it was…Oh!' Suddenly something clicked. Jeannie looked at the woman with renewed interest. 'You mean you had the three o'clock? You're…'

'Tallulah Joplin.' The woman let out a peal of tinkling laughter and walked towards the stairs. 'A ghost from Jeff's past!'

chapter three

'What a very odd woman.'

Jeff was slumping again and barely registered Jeannie's presence.

'Jeff? Are you all right?'

'What? Me? Yes...No. No, I'm not.' Jeff hauled himself upright in his seat and stared balefully at Jeannie.

'What's wrong?'

'I think I must have had a turn.'

'A turn?'

'Yes, a turn. I get them sometimes.'

Jeannie stared at him. 'You're not seeing things again?' she asked quietly.

Jeff wasn't quite sure how to reply to that one. Months ago, shortly after Marty's death, he had told Jeannie that Marty was haunting him. Being a rational human being, Jeannie had taken the pragmatic approach and bundled Jeff into a health farm. The results had been rather more dramatic than either of them had bargained for and had included, among other things, the incarceration and subsequent death of the owner of the farm, Jeff's seduction by a nymphomaniac and a fairly substantial hole in Jeannie's sister's bank account. As regards the haunting, the visit had been a mixed blessing. Jeff, like it or not, had conclusive proof that he was inextricably tethered to Marty. And Marty, while still a pain, had proved that being dead positively boosted his powers of detection. He had been invaluable in getting Jeff out of a hole – invaluable and, if Jeff's sanity were to be preserved, unmentionable to anyone else. To spare Jeannie's feelings and maintain his own equilibrium, he had determined never to bring up the ghost of Marty in conversation.

'Jeff?' prompted Jeannie. 'I asked if you were seeing things again. You really *do* look as if you've seen a ghost. Mind you,' she added, 'I'm not entirely surprised. That woman would be enough to spook anyone.'

'What woman?'

Jeannie gestured to the outer office. 'The one who's just left. The woman in white.'

In a passable imitation of a dead fish, Jeff gawped at her. Then, in a tremulous voice, he stammered, 'You…you *saw* her?'

'Yes.'

'Let me get this right. You met that woman in the corridor?'

'Yes. Jeff, for heaven's sake, what's wrong?' Then, giggling suddenly, Jeannie answered her own question. 'You thought she was a ghost, didn't you?' Leaning forwards, she teasingly poked Jeff in the ribs. 'You really thought you'd been visited by a ghost. Oh, Jeff, you *are* sweet…'

The tips of Jeff's ears turned pink. 'Well…' He shrugged. 'You know how it is…working too hard, bit tired…that sort of thing.' Trying desperately not to meet Jeannie's eye, he fiddled with the file on his desk. Then, grinning, he looked up again. 'You know how I'm always telling you we have to be precise and organized, how we can't leave out any details?'

'Yes.'

'Well, I forgot to ask her her name.'

Jeannie burst out laughing. Then, remembering her conversation in the corridor, she frowned at Jeff. 'But she said you knew her.'

'Did she?' Jeff's mind went into overdrive. Snatches of the elliptical conversation he had had with the woman in white came back to him and, belatedly, he reached the obvious conclusion. She had clearly assumed he knew who she was and had attributed his rather extreme reaction to her reappearance in his life. Marvelling at (and rather regretting) his over-active imagination, he started to chuckle. Then, like Jeannie, he frowned. 'So what *was* her name?'

'Tallulah Joplin.'

The words seemed to have the effect of an electric shock on Jeff. He sat bolt upright and stared at Jeannie. '*What?*'

'Tallulah Joplin.' Jeannie perched on the edge of Jeff's desk and looked at him in concern. 'Jeff, what's all this about? Who or what *is* Tallulah Joplin?'

Jeff was still reeling. 'Well, I'm not sure what she is any more, but I know what she used to be. She was a nightclub singer.'

'Good God! She looks more like she used to be a nun.'

'Mmm.'

Jeannie was intrigued. 'Is that why she said she was a ghost from the past?'

'She said that?'

'Yes. She seemed to find it rather amusing.'

'Well, I don't.' Jeff was adamant. 'Tallulah Joplin was very bad news.' Suddenly aware that he still had her card in his hand, he looked down at it. There was no name; just a telephone number. 'I wonder,' he said in a half-whisper, 'what she wants?'

Jeannie was aghast. 'You mean you didn't ask her?'

'Well, no...I mean, yes. Yes, I did ask her. I was just feeling a bit peculiar when she came in so...so...' Jeff trailed off into defeated silence.

'So what did she want?'

'She wants us to find Dave Day.'

'Who's he?'

Jeff didn't respond immediately. Then, miserably, he summoned the courage to look into Jeannie's eyes. 'I haven't the faintest idea.'

'This is ridiculous.'

'I know, I know.' Jeff shifted uneasily in his chair. 'I'm sorry, Jeannie.'

Jeannie sighed in exasperation. 'I mean, why didn't you *say* you didn't know who he was?'

Jeff was beginning to develop a headache. His brain, he felt, had suffered a triple assault. Or possibly a quadruple assault. It had been comprehensively mugged. Why, he asked himself, hadn't he asked the woman who Dave Day was? Then it came to him: it was because of Marty.

Jeff reluctantly met Jeannie's inquisitorial gaze. 'I didn't ask her because she seemed to think Marty was still alive and I sort of, well, forgot that he wasn't.'

Jeannie frowned. 'That doesn't make sense, Jeff.'

'Yes, it does. I pretended that I knew who Dave Day was because she's going to pay us great wads of cash to find him.'

'That still doesn't make sense.'

'Yes, but it was quite clear that Marty knew who he was. I didn't want to look stupid. Because of the way she was talking, I sort of forgot Marty was dead. I sort of…well, I thought we could ask him later.' Jeff was having difficulty holding Jeannie's gaze. He lowered his head and opened his desk drawer. 'Would you like some whisky?'

'No.' Jeannie swung her legs over the corner of the desk and jumped to her feet. 'Acting like someone who has just given himself a frontal lobotomy is an odd way of trying to be clever.'

'I know, I know,' groaned Jeff.

'Still, all is not lost.'

'Isn't it?'

'No. You tell me everything you know about Tallulah Joplin and, hopefully, there'll be a connection somewhere to this Dave Day person.'

Oh God, thought Jeff. This is getting worse. He watched as Jeannie walked over to her desk, leaned down, extracted something from a large paper bag and slammed it with unnecessary force on to the filing cabinet. It was a spider plant, its fragile leaves quivering in protest at Jeannie's treatment.

Jeannie sat down and looked across the office. 'Now, Tallulah Joplin.'

Jeff took a deep breath. Jeannie wasn't going to like this at all. And he wished she hadn't bought a spider plant. It conjured up images of a distant web of corruption – and some very unwelcome ghosts from the past.

It was, of course, all the fault of that present-day ghost, the much-needed and very absent Marty Hopkirk.

chapter four

Marty had always had an extremely low boredom threshold. Had he ever paused to analyze the matter, he would have realized it was the bane of his life. But pausing had never been his thing. Instead, he had rushed around, blaming other people for his ennui – and then becoming bored by their reactions.

Death had proved a revelation. The shock of dying had temporarily raised that low threshold, and the subsequent thrill of being a ghost saw him embracing his new half-life with enormous zeal. Then reality – or what passed for reality – had struck. Being a ghost wasn't, for the most part, terribly convenient. A proper life on earth was denied to him, and while Jeff was alive he couldn't get on with the business of being dead and graduate past limbo. And limbo certainly wasn't all it was cracked up to be. The inhabitants, as he had told Jeff, were a pretty tedious bunch. Boring. Now he was beginning to understand why.

He was taking out his frustration, as was his wont, on the only person who would listen: the man who had eased his passing from the mortal world, enabled him to reach limbo and who, to Marty's enormous relief, was always willing to lend a sympathetic ear. Or rather, nearly always. Today, Marty was trying Wyvern's patience as never before.

'I mean,' pleaded Marty, 'can't I just have one look? A little peek?'

Wyvern sighed. Again. 'Marty, Marty...I've told you before. It simply isn't in my power. I can't get you into the Celestial Firmament. *I* can't even get there.'

'Can't you?' Marty was sceptical. 'Oh, come on, surely you can get a day pass? Some sort of reward for what you do here?'

'The doing,' explained Wyvern with a pious air, 'is a reward in itself. Look at you, for instance. You were in a terrible state when you arrived.'

And that, he thought, was putting it mildly. He considered the big man sitting opposite him. Marty had been a challenge. There was no doubt he was bright, but his intelligence was matched – and hampered – by his wayward tendencies. Keen to learn, his mastery of a subject was thwarted by his eagerness to move on to the next one before he was ready. His powers of concentration needed developing. There was, Wyvern had pointed out, no point in being a ghost if you couldn't concentrate. You'd end up as one of those sad creatures who wrapped themselves in sheets, floated about in an aimless sort of way and went 'woo, woo'. A few of those had slipped through Wyvern's net, but not many.

Wyvern was in the business of turning his lost souls into powerful, sophisticated ghosts about town. And, by and large, he had succeeded with Marty. The boredom factor was, however, another matter.

'What about,' he suggested, 'popping down to see Jeff? You haven't been there for a while.'

Marty waved a dismissive hand. 'Jeff hasn't had a case in ages. Last time I went down I was so bored I was reduced to rattling cups and saucers all day.'

'But, Marty, you should think of that as an achievement. When you started, you couldn't rattle anything without breaking it. You never break things now.'

Marty shuffled in his seat and developed a pressing desire to examine his shoes.

'Oh dear.' Wyvern rolled his eyes. 'How many?'

'Only one.'

'Marty, Marty...you really must concentrate more.'

'How am I supposed to concentrate if I'm bored?'

Marty placed his hands between his knees and looked mutinously at the ground. He looked, and felt, like a little boy who was refusing to tidy his room on the grounds that he hated the ice lolly he was being offered as a reward. After a moment's silence, he also looked, and felt, rather stupid. A man not normally given to introspection, he was beginning to realize that his petulant stance wasn't working. He straightened up in his chair and looked slyly at Wyvern.

'I couldn't haunt someone else, could I? Just for a little bit?' He held up a hand and extended his thumb and forefinger. 'Just for a tiny, weeny little—'

'No.'

'*Please.*'

'No. You know the rules. You can only haunt Jeff.'

'But,' countered Marty, 'I can possess other people.' He looked suddenly haughty. 'I'm rather good at that.'

'You know perfectly well you can't possess them

on a whim. It requires a great deal of willpower. And,' finished Wyvern, 'it's extremely dangerous for the host.' As he spoke, he cast his mind back to the pigeon episode and looked pointedly at his companion.

Marty knew exactly what the look meant. 'Well, it was ill. And old. Ill and old. I probably did it a favour.'

'That's not what I've been told. I had to pull a lot of strings to get that one sorted out.' Wyvern paused. He had also broken a few rules, but he wasn't going to elaborate on that to Marty. 'Just don't, *ever*,' he warned, 'try to possess a weasel.'

'A weasel?'

'It's a long story. Mark my words, Marty. Stay away from weasels.'

Keen to change the subject, Wyvern stood up and stared at the 1960s-style table in between them. As he concentrated, it turned into a Louis XIV writing desk.

Marty barely reacted. 'Never liked all that Renaissance stuff,' he mused. 'Reminds me of that dismal woman in limbo.'

'What woman? And it's Baroque, by the way.'

'Well, it's still foreign. So's the woman. Nasty German accent. She's always bleating on about how boring it is to take off her head every day and go and sit on a park bench.'

'Oh, yes.' Wyvern knew all about her. 'Versailles.'

'And then she starts wittering on about how difficult it was being a queen when all she really wanted was to be a milkmaid.'

'Well, we can't always have what we want, Marty.'

'Don't I know it.'

Wyvern looked in concern at his companion. It was becoming increasingly clear that Marty had a serious case of the glums. Something would have to be done.

'Look,' he said, 'I think you ought to give limbo another go. Some people have a lot of fun up there.'

'If moping about's their idea of fun, I'd rather take off my head and sit on a park bench.'

Wyvern cupped his chin in his right hand and looked pensively at Marty. An idea was beginning to form in his mind. 'What about,' he suggested, 'providing the fun yourself?'

'What d'you mean?'

'Well, didn't you once tell me you used to be an entertainer of some sort? Before you were a private detective.'

Wary, but with a glimmer of interest, Marty nodded. He hadn't, in truth, thought seriously about that for years. He had mentioned it in a fleeting sort of way, enjoying giving the impression that he used to be a hugely successful singer and dancer before becoming bored with fame and adulation. The truth had been slightly different.

'Well...yeah.' Marty tried – not very hard – to look bashful. 'I was a nightclub singer and tap-dancer.' He looked at his feet again and, quite involuntarily, they began to twitch. 'In fact,' he added, 'I was a pretty ace dancer. A damn good singer as well.' As he warmed to his theme, the glimmer of interest became a flame of passion. 'God, you should have seen it, Wyvern. The applause was deafening – and that was even before I'd started. Soon as I began the old routine, they'd start screaming at me.'

'Screaming with enthusiasm?'

But Marty missed the raised eyebrow and teasing tone. 'God, yeah. They couldn't get enough of me. I was brilliant.' Marty was really getting into his stride – literally. He was now on his feet and executing a slightly ponderous yet, thought Wyvern, quite promising tap routine. 'Hey!' he said, more to himself than to Wyvern. 'It never really goes away, does it? It's like riding a bicycle. It's like…ouch!'

'Ye-es.' Wyvern looked on as Marty tumbled to the floor. 'It's not *quite* like riding a bicycle, Marty. You have to concentrate a bit more. Especially,' he added helpfully, 'now that you're dead. You have to decide whether to dance round the table or through it. You can't do both. You'll end up…on the floor.'

Marty glared at him as he rubbed his knee with vigour. 'Thanks for pointing that out. Any other tips?'

'Yes. A little practice might not go amiss before you resume your old career.' Then, genuinely interested, he walked closer. 'Why did you pack it in anyway? Nightclub entertainer to private detective isn't really a natural career progression.'

'It's a long story, Wyvern. A very long story. Let's just say there was more to the nightclub than met the eye.'

'Ah. Criminal classes.' Wyvern nodded. 'The old gangster routine, eh?'

Marty shot Wyvern a rather nasty look. 'What makes you think that?'

'Oh, nothing. It just seemed logical, that's all.'

It did indeed seem logical to Wyvern that Marty would blunder into some sort of criminal set-up. And he wouldn't have been at all surprised if Marty had become enmeshed in a complex scenario, tried to sort it out himself, turned to Jeff for help – and ended up as Jeff's partner. Wyvern nodded to himself. That would definitely have been the case. With the addition, naturally, of a sultry vamp somewhere along the line. Marty's CV just cried out for a sultry vamp.

Marty now seemed distinctly uneasy. Wyvern sometimes had a way of looking at him as if he were an easily digestible book and, worse, one that contained a few unsavoury little passages. Marty had styled himself as many things, but potboiler wasn't one of them. He determined to propel the conversation into the future.

'OK,' he said, standing up and brushing out the creases in his white suit, 'so you reckon that with a bit of practice I'd be up for entertaining the troops in limbo?'

'I don't see why not. As you said, they do spend rather a lot of time moping about.'

Marty looked excited – then hesitant. 'They're…well, they're a pretty critical bunch.'

'So you'll have to practice a lot then.'

'Yes. Yes, I think I will. And it would give me something to do, something to work towards. You know, Wyvern,' he finished, as he drew himself to his full height, 'I reckon I'm really going to make something of myself this time. I'll become a star. Hey! A star. Geddit? I'm only halfway to the heavens and already I'm a star! Whaddya think about that?'

Wyvern's only response was to roll his eyes and send a silent prayer up to the heavens. But Marty didn't notice. He was preparing to head earthwards. Finally he had something new to share with Jeff.

'Hi, Jeff.'

'Marty! Christ, Marty, where the hell have you

been? I've been *desperate* to see you. I've been sitting here willing you to come. What on earth have you been up to?'

'Nothing at all on earth. Ha ha!'

As usual, Marty had shimmered unannounced into the office. But this time, to Jeff's irritation, he didn't pause for the usual chat. Instead, he began dancing about the room, concentrating on his footwork rather than on Jeff.

'Marty! For God's sake! Listen, will you? We've *got* to talk.'

'Why talk when you can sing?' said Marty, immediately launching into an excruciating rendition of a Fred Astaire number.

Jeff watched in silence. This was vintage Marty, but, under current circumstances, a little puzzling. Since his demise he hadn't had much to sing about.

Then, slightly breathless, Marty paused for the first time since he had entered the room and looked at Jeff. 'I'm going to be a singer again, Jeff! And a dancer! And this time I'm really going to make a name for myself.'

This wasn't just puzzling, Jeff thought, it was insane.

'Oh, well, that's really sensible,' he said. 'I'll be your manager, shall I? I'll go to the clubs and say, "Look, I've got this really great guy. Voice like an angel. Niftiest footwork this side of the Styx. Only trouble is, he's invisible to everyone but me." That'll have the punters stampeding all over the place.'

Marty laughed. 'No, no, little man. You don't understand. I'm going to conquer limbo! I'm going to be the classiest act they've ever had. I'm going to be...Hey, Jeff, get this – I'm going to be a limbo dancer!'

Delighted with his little joke, Marty readopted his Fred Astaire mode and began to dance around again.

'Marty,' pleaded Jeff. *'Please…'*

'Maybe I could even form a group,' mused Marty. 'Marty and the Martinets? Or I could—'

'Marty!'

'I could get a partner. Yeah. That would be more like it. The new Fred and Ginger.' He punched the air with a fist. 'Yeah! That's it. Only one problem…' He began to pirouette as he deliberated. 'Who would be the new Ginger?'

Jeff took a deep breath. 'How about,' he suggested, 'Tallulah Joplin?'

Marty's pirouette began to fall apart. He spread out his arms to balance himself, remained deathly still for a moment and then, with one foot still off the ground, turned to face Jeff.

'Now that wasn't nice, was it? That *really* wasn't nice, Jeff.' He stared nastily at his partner. 'We don't talk about Tallulah. In fact, we agreed that Tallulah never really happened. Whoosh!' he said, flapping an arm in the direction whence he had come. 'Tallulah vanished a long time ago.'

'Until,' said Jeff in measured tones, 'she walked through this door a few days ago.'

Silence. Then, almost imperceptibly, the temperature in the room seemed to cool. And Marty, Jeff noticed, was suddenly having trouble with his ectoplasm. It had happened before in times of stress. Marty needed energy to maintain his presence. He shimmered slightly.

'Don't you dare disappear on me,' Jeff seethed. 'I need you, Marty. I really need you.'

'Yeah,' said Marty. 'I s'pose you do.' Gingerly, he

lowered himself into the seat opposite Jeff's. Only when he was confident of not falling through it did he give Jeff his full attention. 'So, Tallulah Joplin. Fancy that, eh?'

'I didn't fancy it at all, Marty. Especially the way she looks now.' Jeff grimaced, leaned forward and proceeded to tell Marty about Tallulah's strangely spectral appearance.

Marty was intrigued. 'But she used to be a *vamp*. Black fishnets and...God, Jeff, the things she could do with those stilettos. And all that raven hair. She was pretty foxy, Jeff, let's face it. Foxy to the point of scary. A creature,' he continued in awed tones, 'of the night.' Then, unable to resist, he lowered his voice. 'A Creature of the Ni-i-i-i-ght...'

Jeff shot him a distinctly unfriendly look. A look that was tacitly understood. Now was not the time for *Rocky Horror Show* impersonations.

'So why,' asked Marty, 'has she gone all white?'

'I don't know. But she seemed to be under the impression that I knew what she was up to nowadays. Seemed to think I knew all about her.'

'Strange. What did she say?'

With great reluctance, Jeff steeled himself and recounted the entire Tallulah episode to Marty. The memory of the encounter still made him cringe with embarrassment. But, anxious to get to the nub of the matter, he gave Marty the concise version. 'The upshot of the whole thing,' he finished, 'was that she wanted me to find someone. Someone who, again, she thought I knew.'

'Oh, yeah? Who?'

Jeff studied Marty's face very carefully. 'Someone called Dave Day.'

Unskilled in the art of hiding his feelings, Marty

desperately tried to adopt a variety of expressions to disguise the only one that fitted: shame.

'Ah,' was all he said.

Jeff had suspected as much. He sighed again and reached for a pen and paper. 'There was something you didn't tell me all those years ago, wasn't there?'

Marty nodded. Then he found his voice. 'It really wasn't much, Jeff. Nothing sinister. I was just...'

'A little economical with the truth?'

Marty was beginning to look distinctly miserable. 'You could put it that way, I suppose.'

'Well, you'd better tell me everything now. Tallulah is going to pay me a lot of money – great wads of the stuff – if I can find Dave Day for her.'

Marty was extremely surprised. 'I wonder why?' He leaned forward. 'I mean it, Jeff. There was really nothing sinister, nothing special even, about Dave Day.'

Jeff chewed the end of his pen. 'Tallulah said he'd just been released. I took that to mean...Well, it doesn't matter what I took it to mean, but she obviously meant from prison. Why'd he end up there?'

'Heroin,' said Marty. 'He got ten years for dealing in heroin.'

'That's quite special.'

'Yes, but it doesn't explain why Tallulah would want him now, does it?'

'No.' A vision of Jeannie suddenly appeared in Jeff's head; a memory of her words to him about Tallulah. 'Look, Marty,' he said. 'You're going to have to tell me everything you know about Dave Day. Everything. That way we might get to the bottom of this.'

Marty was wearing a new expression: one as apt as his shame of a few moments previously. He was sulking. 'You won't tell Jeannie, will you, Jeff?'

'I'll have to,' said Jeff slowly. 'Just like I had to tell her all I knew about Tallulah.'

Marty fell through his chair.

'*Gentlemen.*' *The tall man pressed his hands together, nodded to the right and to the left and then invited his audience to sit down. Like automatons, they lowered themselves into the high-backed leather chairs. 'First, I must thank you for your patience. I'm not just talking about the last few weeks, but the several years during which, from afar, you have pledged your involvement. And, of course, your money.'*

Each of the twenty men ranged on either side of him allowed himself a little smile at the mention of money. Between them, they were worth several billion pounds. It wasn't difficult to smile about that – even easier to smile in anticipation of the untold sums they would soon be worth. And they were gathered here today, from all over the world, in anticipation of that very near future.

'I thank you,' continued the tall man, 'for all that you have contributed. You will not be disappointed at the results. You will be seeing them shortly. But before that, I would like you to join me in a toast to the success – the imminent success – of our project.'

The remark, as he knew it would be, was greeted with puzzlement. The vast expanse of table was quite empty. Nothing, not even a speck of dust, lay on the glittering black surface. And there were no bottles and no glasses anywhere else in the cavernous room. Then, as a few of the men began to look at their host with varying degrees of doubt – and one with a flicker of suspicion – twenty-one tiny, hitherto unseen sections of the table slid silently sideways and glasses of chilled champagne rose from the void below. Each was perfectly placed at the right-hand side of the men at the table. Except one. The left-handed delegate from Manchuria marvelled at the meticulous planning and reached for his glass.

The tall man stood up and raised his glass in salute. 'To our project,' he announced.

'To our project!'

'In the thousands of years of what historians laughingly call civilization,' continued the host, 'there have been whole races who struggled – and perished – in their attempts to fulfil the dream. Mongol hordes–' He waved a dismissive hand. 'Assyrians, Persians...'

The delegate from Iran paused mid-sip. Then he remembered he shouldn't be sipping at all and dismissed the idea of a protest. Best, he reckoned, to keep a low profile.

'Babylonians. And what did any of them leave? A few fragments of pottery. Was that their dream?' The tall man smiled. 'No. Of course it wasn't. If they had fulfilled their dreams we wouldn't be here today.' This, he knew, was pure theatre. His enraptured audience was loving every minute. 'Macedonians?' he offered with a sneer. 'Oh, yes. Alexander the Great. But we all know about him, don't we? What was his legacy?' He paused theatrically and leaned towards his audience. 'Homosexuality,' he spat.

The French delegate shuffled uncomfortably and looked into his glass.

Still the tirade continued. 'Aztecs. A fearsome, warlike people, they thought they could enslave the world. But what did they achieve? Nothing. Nothing, I tell you. They withered and died and left piles of stone. What use, I ask you, are piles of stone? How did the Egyptians affect the world with their piles of stone? Well, I'll tell you what they gave the world.' Again he paused and leaned forward. 'Tourism. Mass tourism. That's what they gave the world. Thousands of oiks wearing sandals and gawping at pyramids. Is that what we want?' He looked around before banging the table and continuing, 'No! We want to conquer the world! And we shall conquer the world!

'In recent times,' he added quietly, 'we've seen pure evil trying to conquer the world. Hitler,' he snarled with palpable distaste. 'Hitler was evil. He visited monstrous carnage and unforgivable sin on this world – and what happened to him? He perished, engulfed by the flames of his own fanaticism. But he deserved to die. We don't – and we won't.

'Why? I'll tell you why? Because we've learned the lesson others failed to learn. We are not sinful. We are not warlike. We have no axe to grind against the less fortunate in this world. Unless,' he conceded, 'you count the poor.' Then he raised his voice and looked imperiously at the other men. 'But why should you? What have the poor ever contributed to this planet? Nothing! Nothing except dirt, squalor and over-crowding! And poverty. Think about it, gentlemen. If there were no poor, there would be no poverty! Do we want dirt, squalor, overcrowding, poor people and poverty? No! We want to rule the world!'

Again the magnificent orator lowered his voice. 'And how shall we rule the world? I'll tell you. We shall rule the world by our religion.'

A ripple of unease flowed through the room. He had expected that.

'No! Not the religions that have scourged human-ity since the dawn of time! Not these conflicting creeds which preach peace, love and understanding, yet force mankind to worship at the altars of strangeness and taboo. No. Because what has been their legacy apart from war, privation and, let's face it, some pretty dubious myths? I'll tell you what these

"religions" have given us.' He pressed his hands together in a gesture of supplication. 'Buildings. They've given us buildings. Great big whacking buildings! Temples, forts and churches; abbeys, monasteries and shrines. Millions of them. Littering our planet. Oh!' he added with another dramatic gesture towards his audience. 'Buildings have their uses. This building,' he all but whispered, 'has its use. And we all know what that is, don't we?' He reached for his glass and raised it into the air. 'It enables us to practise the only true religion. Gentlemen, I ask you to be upstanding and to join me in a toast to that religion!'

The rather sudden conclusion had the desired effect. Every man in the room rose to his feet with alacrity.

The tall man looked at each one of them in turn and then inclined his head.

'Gentlemen, I give you...money!'

And as they drank their toast, the only sound in the room was the gentle tinkling of the wind chimes in each corner. They were the only decorations in the vast, domed expanse of this cathedral to cupidity.

chapter five

At this time of year the garden of the Old Rectory was at its spectacular best. The sweeping lawns rushed from the house in lush, regimented stripes. The ancient beeches bent like stooping dowagers, draped in all their finery. At the side of the house, severely clipped box hedges formed a protective ring round the powerfully scented herb and knot gardens. Elsewhere, sinewy paths wound their seemingly aimless yet carefully orchestrated way round borders ablaze with colour. Gorgeously groomed pathways led enticingly towards the hidden tennis court, the sunken pool and, in a triumph of artifice, the perfectly coiffed and scented wilderness below the orchard.

It was beautiful, and Jeannie loathed it.

It didn't usually bother her. She enjoyed being outdoors, relished being in the country and, in the normal course of events, went into the garden to play tennis, to join the others for tea on the south lawn or to meander up and down the pathways, chatting to her sister. She benefited from the glories of the garden, but she didn't normally notice them.

Today was different. Jeannie was in a foul mood and the artificial, over the top and contrived nature of the garden, rather than soothing her, was making things worse. She glared at the lavender, cowering between the serried ranks of box. It should be free, she decided, at liberty to grow anywhere, not trapped by the geometry of convention. Then she looked away from the house at the pristine 'Georgian' folly with its cunningly disguised concrete pillars and realised, for the first time, how terribly twee it was.

A noise from behind her made her look back at the rectory. It was Wendy striding towards her, a beaming smile on her face. Jeannie smiled in return – until the ivy covering the mellow bricks of the house caught her eye. She frowned at the blameless foliage. It, too, was a victim of rigorous cultivation: tendrils were allowed only to waft suggestively over windows; errant ones that threatened to obscure the views hacked to death.

As Wendy approached, Jeannie stopped glaring. The garden might have committed countless offences, but Wendy could never share its guilt. Angus was the culprit.

'Look,' said Wendy as, slightly breathless, she stopped beside her sister. 'Do stay to dinner. *Please*. I know I don't normally press you, but, well, this time...'

'This time I'm in a bit of a state and you really think I need sorting out.' The words sounded far harsher than Jeannie had intended. As soon as she had spoken them, she reached out instinctively for Wendy's arm. 'Oh, God,' she said with an apologetic grin, 'I didn't mean to sound like such a cow. I know you're doing your best but, honestly, I don't want pity.'

'Well, I do,' countered Wendy.

'What?'

A mischievous glint came into Wendy's eye. 'I need rescuing.'

'Ah. Boring people of Angus's?'

Wendy bit her lip. She hated being disloyal to her husband, even in front of Jeannie. She adored Angus. And the parts she didn't adore she could put up with – but those parts didn't include his business friends.

'Well,' continued Jeannie, 'd'you really think I'm the person to rescue you? I can handle Angus, or rather,' she said when she saw the look on Wendy's face, 'Angus can handle me. He seems to have accepted that I'm a bit odd. But his friends? The last ones I met thought I came from a different planet.'

'That's probably because they were jealous.'

Jeannie was dumbfounded. 'Of me?'

'Yes. They thought you were a free spirit. Not hidebound by, well...' She trailed into silence and the hand that had been raised in a sweeping gesture to encompass 'all this' dropped to her side.

Jeannie didn't reply at first. It was a tacit convention of theirs that they refrained from discussing the startling differences between their lifestyles. The good sister had always embraced the conventional life into which she had been born; she had even done the correct thing and married into it. Jeannie, on the other hand, had rebelled – 'In spades, but she'll get trumped in the end,' as Angus was fond of saying in his patronizing way. Yet while their lives had always been utterly different, they remained extremely close. They discussed everything – except whether one or the other was happy with her chosen path.

They avoided that subject because both of them knew that, despite Marty's death six months previously, Jeannie was the happier of the two. Or at least she had been until Jeff's revelations about Marty's past and the circumstances that had brought the pair together.

Wendy misinterpreted the sudden look of doubt on Jeannie's face. 'Oh, come on,' she said. 'It'll be fun.'

'No, it won't.'

Wendy took her arm and began to propel her towards the house. 'All right, then, but we can have a good giggle afterwards. And a very large gin and tonic now.'

'That,' said Jeannie, 'is definitely the best idea I've heard in a long time.'

Nursing her second gin and tonic as she dressed for dinner, Jeannie began to feel that perhaps she had overreacted. Was it really so terrible that, years ago, Marty had had a long-standing affair about which he hadn't told her?

No, she decided; it wasn't terrible. Just disappointing. But then, had she told Marty absolutely everything about her own past? Again, no. A half-embarrassed smile played at the corners of her lips. She had told him most things, but if she had omitted to mention the Argentinian polo player it had been purely – well, almost purely – to spare Marty's feelings. Her intuition had told her that Marty wouldn't have welcomed tales of swarthy, bronzed equestrian heroes. And the Juan episode had anyway been a long time in the past. Just like the Tallulah episode.

No, thought Jeannie as she fastened the strap of her black leather cocktail dress, she didn't really

mind so terribly about the existence of Tallulah.
What she did object to was the fact that Marty had
known perfectly well that Tallulah had been firmly
attached to someone else at the time; someone, she
now knew, who had been up to his eyeballs in drug-
smuggling, money-laundering and, probably (for she
didn't doubt that Jeff, in retelling the story, had tried
to spare her feelings), murder. And Marty had
known all about it. He should, she felt, have blown
the whistle as soon as he had found out.

Jeannie frowned and cast her mind back to her
conversation with Jeff. He had, as usual, been at
pains to defend his friend while at the same time
trying to spare her any pain. All he had succeeded in
doing was to tie himself up in knots.

'But, Jeannie,' he had protested, 'Marty *did* try to
blow the whistle.'

'Then he should have gone to the police. That's
what normal people do.'

'But he was frightened for his life!'

Jeannie had reached over and touched Jeff's arm.
'I don't mean to be rude, Jeff, but I can't see how
going to you instead would have made him feel any
more secure.'

Jeff had wondered about that one as well.

'The thing is, Jeannie, Marty was in a real pickle.
He wanted legal advice before he took any action.
That's fair enough, isn't it?'

'I suppose so. And what legal advice did you give
him?'

Jeff looked away. 'To…er, to go to the police.'

'So why didn't he?'

'Because,' sighed Jeff, 'he persuaded me – rightly,
I think – that if they raided the joint they would
catch everyone except the one person responsible for

the whole set-up. You know what it's like, Jeannie. They always get the stooges and the scapegoats, never the man at the top.'

'Cedric Tipton?'

'He preferred to be known as Don Carlos.'

'Ye-es, I suppose he would.' Jeannie sat down and fixed Jeff with a not altogether friendly look. 'So, let me get this clear. Marty persuaded you – a solicitor – to help him set up Tipton?'

'Yes.' Jeff knew exactly what Jeannie was thinking. He spread his hands in a half-pleading, half-defensive gesture. 'I was *bored* of being a solicitor, Jeannie. It was really boring.'

Jeannie could identify with that. Angus was a solicitor.

'But,' she replied, 'it didn't bother you that you might get struck off?'

'It didn't occur to me. We planned it really well, Jeannie.'

Jeannie remained silent for a moment, mulling over everything Jeff had told her. She had always known that prior to setting up Randall & Hopkirk, Jeff had been a solicitor and Marty a nightclub singer. Both men, however, had been a little vague about exactly how, when and why they had abandoned their previous careers. Now she was beginning to understand the reason. 'So,' she said at length, 'you were in the club, engaged in supposedly casual conversation with Tipton, when the raid took place.'

'When we *organized* for the raid to take place,' corrected Jeff. 'I told you – we planned it really well.'

'And Marty was out the back, spiriting away our blameless little moll?'

'She *was* blameless, Jeannie. Tallulah was terrified of Don Carlos. She was desperate to get away. She really needed our help.'

'Mmm. And she was so grateful for Marty's help that she thanked him by dumping him and vanishing into thin air? That's really sweet, Jeff.'

Jeff looked down at his hands. 'Well, all right then, Tallulah used Marty. She wasn't really a very nice girl.'

Again Jeannie pondered. 'But, ten years later, she has no compunction about swanning back into your life and asking you to look for someone you've never heard of? That's really weird, Jeff.'

'I admit that the swanning back part's a bit strange but, well, I dunno. Water under the bridge? It was all a long time ago. I've changed a lot. Marty's...well, Marty had changed by the time he died. And Tallulah's changed beyond all recognition. I can still hardly believe it was her. She used to be so, well...' Jeff swallowed the rest of his sentence. It somehow didn't seem right to use the word 'sexy' in front of Jeannie. He changed the subject. 'And it's not at all weird that she asked me to look for this Dave Day character. Remember, she thinks Marty's still alive.' Suddenly animated, Jeff leaned across the desk towards Jeannie. 'Marty obviously knew this bloke. Presumably he was part of the nightclub set-up. And then he went to prison. Now he's out and Tallulah's frightened he'll try to find her. It's all quite simple really. Deduction, Jeannie,' he finished with a confident smile. 'It's part of the detection process.'

'And how exactly are we to deduce who Dave Day is?'

'Well, that's simple as well. All we have to do is...Oh!' Again Jeff checked himself. 'Yes, I see what you mean.'

'Tallulah,' said Jeannie, 'is the key. And nothing you've told me sheds any light on what she's up to now. She's our only lead, Jeff. Somehow, we have to get to Dave Day through her.'

'Yep. You're absolutely right.'

They faced each other across the table, resolute in decision, united in their mission – and totally divided as to how they were going to accomplish it. It pained Jeff that he couldn't share his *modus operandi* with Jeannie; it reminded him of the eternal, unbroachable gulf between them. And it pained Jeannie that however hard she tried to think professional thoughts, she couldn't dismiss the demon in her head that was fanning the flames of an unfamiliar emotion: jealousy.

Now, in her bedroom and preparing to descend for dinner, she realized that her efforts to rationalize her emotions were in vain. She was still jealous of Tallulah Joplin. And the only way to kill the demon was to concentrate on finding out all there was to know about the woman. Familiarity, hopefully, would breed contempt.

Closing the bedroom door behind her, Jeannie walked across the landing and down the stairs. Her movements were instinctive and unconscious; her mind was still miles away, mulling over the series of unanswered questions posed by the unwelcome arrival of Tallulah in her life.

It was her own arrival in the drawing room that nudged her back to reality.

Wendy saw her first. 'Jeannie! How lovely. We've been waiting for you.' Her smile was jolly but her eyes were reproachful. Jeannie wasn't sure of the nature of the reproach: the delay in her appearing –

or the nature of her appearance? She remembered,
too late, that a dinner party at Angus and Wendy's
was invariably rather formal. Black leather cocktail
dresses with orange straps were not quite the thing.
They did, however, emphasize another difference
between the two sisters: both were highly attractive,
but while Wendy had the robust good looks and long
silken hair of the healthy country-dweller, Jeannie
had cropped blonde hair and a doe-eyed, elfin beauty
that suggested fragility as well as urban chic. But
'fragile' was the last word anyone would use to
describe Jeannie's personality, and the dress duly
implied that its owner was possessed of a steely
determination.

She returned her sister's greeting with a
tentative smile and looked around the room. Her
heart sank.

'Jeannie!' Angus sprang across the room. He was
sporting a hugely expensive dark suit, sombre tie
and, as he looked at Jeannie, a rictus grin. He put
his arm round her shoulders and drew her close to
him. The gesture was not one of affection but of
slight desperation. It was as if he were hoping his
own tailored jacket would spawn a clone that would
crawl all over Jeannie and transform her into something decent.

'You haven't met, have you?' he said as he
gestured to his guests. Pulling Jeannie forward, he
proceeded to introduce her to the five guests, who
were, Jeannie didn't doubt, extremely important but
whose names she forgot as soon as they were
mentioned. Yet mindful of Jeff's advice about
detection, she quickly deduced who belonged to
whom. It wasn't difficult. The two beautifully
dressed but strained-looking women were obviously

attached to the men who, until her arrival, had been standing chatting as far as was decently possible from their wives. That meant the man in the black suit in front of her wasn't a husband. She suppressed the desire to turn and flee from the room. She had been set up.

The man noted her fleeting panic. 'Forgotten something?' he asked.

'Um...no. No. I just...' Jeannie sank miserably into silence. In any other situation, she *would* have fled. But here, in her sister's house, the decorum and good manners that had been instilled into her from an early age automatically reasserted themselves. She couldn't embarrass Wendy in front of her husband's colleagues, however dreary they were.

Then she noticed that the man was smiling. And it didn't appear to be out of politeness. He seemed to find her discomfort highly amusing. Worse, he didn't appear to be in any hurry to smooth over the situation with polite conversation. He just stood in front of her, smiling.

Jeannie quelled a wave of irritation. She had hoped to be given the opportunity to confirm the undoubted boringness of his conversation by listening with a glazed expression. Instead, she had nothing to listen to. In the end it was she, not he, who paved the way with conventional chit-chat. 'Well,' she said, 'what brings you here?' She cursed herself even before she had uttered the words. *Nul point*, she thought, for originality.

'My wife,' replied her companion, 'is a friend of Wendy's.'

To her intense annoyance, Jeannie felt the blood rise to her cheeks. 'Oh,' she said after another embarrassed pause. 'How...er, where is she?'

She looked around the room, not so much for the wife as for help. Wendy, however, was deep in conversation with the strained women and Angus had joined the men.

'She's in bed,' came the reply. 'With flu. She was hoping to make it but had to cancel at the last minute. You know what these bugs are like. One minute you feel fine, next thing you know you've got a raging temperature.'

'So what are you doing here then?' Again Jeannie cursed herself. This time for her appalling, involuntary rudeness.

But the man just burst out laughing. 'Well,' he said after he had treated Jeannie to a great guffaw and a set of startlingly white teeth, 'I had rather hoped I was coming for an enjoyable dinner in convivial company. Perhaps I was mistaken.'

'No. Look, I'm sorry. I thought…Well, I thought…'

'You thought you were being set up?'

'It was that obvious?'

'Mmm.'

'And you just stood there grinning. Enjoying my embarrassment.'

'Mmm.'

'That wasn't very gentlemanly.'

The man took a sip of his drink and looked at her over the rim of his glass. 'No, it wasn't. But you don't look like the sort of person who's easily embarrassed.'

Damn, thought Jeannie. This is all going horribly wrong. The wretched man is flirting with me and I'm responding. 'What,' she asked pointedly, 'does your wife do?'

'She's an interior designer.'

'Oh.' Jeannie looked around the room again. 'Did she do this?'

'No. But she's hoping to.'

'I didn't know they were going to have a make-over.'

The man leaned closer. 'Nor, I think, does Angus.'

'Ah.' Enough had been said. This man and his wife were Wendy's friends, invited to help diffuse the difficult people. She wondered why Wendy hadn't told her. Then she remembered his last-minute singleness and her own aversion to the species. That, of course, was why. Jeannie looked impishly at her companion. 'Now that we've cleared up that little misunderstanding, can I ask you something?'

'Yes. It's Martin.'

'What?'

'My name.'

Jeannie flushed again. 'How on earth did you know I'd forgotten it?'

'You never even took it in. I saw your eyes glaze over as soon as we were introduced.'

Mistress of the barbed remark, Jeannie was very rarely lost for words. She stood staring at Martin, desperately trying to dredge up a cutting reply. She failed. 'You are,' was all she could manage, 'the most appalling man I've ever met.'

'Aha,' said Martin as he nodded in the direction of the other male guests. 'I think that's about to change. You haven't talked to them yet.'

It changed rather sooner than Jeannie expected. Two minutes later Wendy announced dinner and they trooped through to the dining room. Jeannie wasn't remotely surprised to find Martin on one side of her and one of the husbands on the other. She identified the corresponding wife by the brittle little glare thrown at her from the other side of the table. 'I know what you are,' it said. 'You're a minx.'

The husband was clearly hoping this would be the case. 'So,' he said as he turned and looked down her dress, 'you're Wendy's little sis? Angus told me about you.' Then he winked. 'Said you were one of life's free spirits.'

'Did he?' Jeannie reached into the middle of the table for a bread-stick and deftly snapped it in half. Then she turned to the husband and sank her teeth into one of the halves. 'I wonder why?'

'Well,' he said with a leery grin, 'perhaps because you are.'

'No, actually, I'm not. I'm a private detective.'

This was absolutely not the response her companion was expecting. He stared at her, totally nonplussed, and then looked across the table. 'Jemima, darling, pass the bread, would you?'

Beside her, Jeannie sensed Martin shaking with suppressed laughter.

Meanwhile, relieved since the idea of being both a minx and a private detective was, in her book, impossible, Jemima began to warm towards Jeannie. 'A private detective,' she trilled. 'How thrilling!'

'Not really,' replied Jeannie. 'A lot of it's just hard slog. Surveillance, that kind of thing.'

'What sort of people do you keep under surveillance?'

'Oh, you know, errant husbands and all that. We get a lot of wives keeping tabs on their husbands. And vice versa.'

Jemima pursed her lips. 'Oh. I see. How very... messy.'

A short but rather awkward silence descended.

'Do start, everyone,' said Wendy, leaping into the

breach, grabbing her fork and spearing a slice of smoked salmon.

Palpably relieved, the man beside Jeannie took a large swig of Chablis and proceeded to attack his own fish with vigour. Jeannie kept her eyes firmly fixed on the plate in front of her as she squeezed a slice of lemon over the pink flesh. Angus, she knew, was glaring at her from the head of the table. If she was going to survive the meal, she was going to have to lower her profile.

It wasn't until they had started the *boeuf en croûte* that the subject of her career came up again, this time from Martin. 'What,' he asked, 'are you working on now?' He too seemed to have withered somewhat after a strained conversation with Georgina on his right.

Remembering her resolve to pursue every avenue in her investigation of Tallulah, Jeannie decided there would be no harm in telling him about their strange, ethereal visitor. 'Well, it's really peculiar. This woman appeared at the office, asking us to find a missing person.'

'Doesn't sound weird to me.'

'No, sorry, *she* was weird. She was all wispy and dressed from head to toe in white.'

'That doesn't sound particularly weird either,' laughed Martin. 'I'm dressed from head to toe in black.'

Jeannie looked him up and down. 'True, but you don't have a black face and black hair. She was white, Martin. *Totally* white. It was almost as if it were some sort of uniform.'

'Maybe it was.'

Jeannie pondered that one. It wasn't a bad suggestion. Maybe it *was* a uniform. 'Yes,' she said, thinking aloud. 'That might explain it.'

'Explain what?'

'The fact that she seemed to think we knew where she'd come from.'

Suddenly Jemima leaned towards her. 'Did she have a handbag?'

Jeannie hadn't been aware that Jemima was listening to their conversation. She looked reflectively at the other woman, trying to visualize Tallulah. 'Ye-es,' she said tentatively. 'I think she did.' Then, with more certainty, 'Yes. Definitely. She had a sort of shoulder bag with bits on it.'

Jemima shot into overdrive. 'Bits? What sort of bits?'

Jeannie frowned. 'I don't know. Decorations, I suppose. Come to think of it, they looked like wings.'

'Ha! I knew it.' Jemima's triumphant squawk silenced the other conversations around the table. 'She's an Angel!'

'I beg your pardon?' said Jeannie.

'An Angel,' said Georgina in slightly wistful tones. 'How utterly fascinating! I've been reading all about them. I must say I've been dying to see one.' She turned to address Jeannie. 'Are they everything they're cracked up to be, or are they just a bit silly? Do tell, I'd love to know.'

All eyes were now focused on Jeannie. Everyone, with the exception of the bemused Martin, was awaiting her answer with a polite, questioning air. No one seemed to think, as Jeannie did, that between the fish and the meat courses the entire party had somehow contrived to move to a different planet. Feeling slightly desperate, she looked to Wendy for assistance.

'Go on then,' urged her sister. 'We're all dying to know.'

Jeannie fought to quell her mounting panic. 'Look, I don't know what you're talking about. This was a woman, not an angel. She was just a perfectly normal...well, apart from the white bit...but she was—'

'My dear,' drawled Jemima. 'You really *don't* know, do you?' Her eyebrows seemed to develop a life of their own and curved upwards into a supercilious arch. 'Not very impressive for a private detective.'

'I...I...' stammered Jeannie.

It was Henry, Jemima's husband, who sought to enlighten her. He turned and looked, not unsympathetically, into her troubled face. 'My dear girl, it's all perfectly simple. The woman you saw was an Angel with a Broken Wing.'

chapter six

'I have *never*,' announced Jeannie, 'felt so stupid in my life. Can you imagine?' Wincing at the memory, she glared at Jeff. 'Jeannie Hurst, investigator extraordinaire, didn't even know of the existence of the most talked-about modern phenomenon.'

'Well,' said Jeff, 'it's not really your sort of thing, is it? Crisp?' he added, proffering the bag.

'I'll have one,' interjected Marty.

'No! There aren't enough for you!'

'Then why did you offer?' Jeannie sighed in exasperation. 'If you ate properly, Jeff, you wouldn't need to guzzle crisps all the time.'

'I do eat properly!' protested Jeff, glowering at Marty.

'No, you don't,' snapped Marty.

'And you're a fine one to talk,' said Jeff.

Jeannie sighed again. 'I know, I know. I'm too thin. But I've always been thin. It doesn't matter what I eat, I'll always be thin. I ate like a horse at Wendy's. Smoked salmon, beef wellington...didn't put on an ounce.'

'Oh, God.' Marty looked as if he would faint. 'Food. Succulent, glorious, fattening food. It's not

58

fair, Jeff. This is torture. I want food!'

'I wish,' seethed Jeff in a whisper, 'you'd just go away.'

'What?' said Jeannie from across the room.

'Nothing. A file's gone astray, that's all.'

'Oh.' Still smarting from the humiliation of dinner at Wendy's, Jeannie looked into the mid-distance. 'Angels with Broken Wings – I still can't believe we'd never heard of them.'

'Well,' said Jeff, 'maybe they're not as well known as Wendy's lot seemed to think.'

'Oh, yes, they are.' Jeannie gestured to the pile of newspapers and magazines in front of her. 'They're mentioned in practically every publication you can think of. Even, for God's sake, the financial press. Pompous Henry was right. They appear to be the latest hot investment.'

Jeff frowned. 'I don't really understand. Why would anyone want to invest in a bunch of nutcases having therapy?'

Jeannie grabbed the magazine on the top of the pile. 'They're not nutcases and it's not therapy. It's "the new way to live in the new millennium". It's about getting back to community living without having to swear allegiance to some bizarre cult. It's about stemming the disastrous tide of people living on their own and contributing to a fragmented society.'

'As I said,' mused Jeff, 'a bunch of loonies having therapy.'

'*You*,' said Jeannie, 'weren't at that dinner party. I'd be inclined to agree with you if I hadn't witnessed a bunch of rational, sane people – including my own sister – waxing lyrical about them. No, Jeff,' she said with conviction, 'they're for real.'

'Well, why are they all women? That doesn't seem very forward-thinking, does it? And how's that going to solve the problem of a fragmented society? It's not as if women can...well, procreate on their own.' Why, he asked himself, am I embarrassed talking about procreation in front of Jeannie?

'Careful,' warned Marty. 'She's mine.' Jeff ignored him.

'Ah,' said Jeannie, 'but they're opening men's ones now. The idea, apparently, is that people find it easier to learn about relationships by bonding with their own sex. Only when they feel really confident about doing that can they form lasting, loving relationships with the opposite sex. I admit,' she continued, 'I'm still pretty sceptical about it, but I've never had much time for these how-to-lead-your-life theories. I don't know why people can't just get on with it.'

No, thought Jeff, I don't either. 'The point,' he said, in a determinedly businesslike manner, 'is that Tallulah Joplin is now an Angel. And from what you say, she's obviously been one for years.'

'Yes. The original one was set up for girls who wanted to atone for their murky pasts. And Tallulah's past was, let's face it, pretty murky.'

'It wasn't that bad!' protested an indignant Marty. 'She was just a little misguided.'

'She was more than a little misguided,' corrected Jeff.

'Ye-es,' said Jeannie. 'I suppose you could put it that way. But – and in the light of all the evidence, it's a pretty big but – she's a reformed character. She has to be, Jeff. Angels with Broken Wings is quoted on the Stock Exchange, half the celebrities in the country have been there and it's even, for God's sake, the subject of all these "lifestyle" articles.' And, she could have added, it's the talking point at all the smart dinner parties. Instead, she looked pointedly at Jeff. 'We're not going to get to Dave Day through Tallulah, Jeff. We have to find another route.'

'Aha!' Jeff crumpled up his crisp bag and threw it towards the bin. It missed. 'That's what I was about to tell you. I've remembered who he is.'

'What?'

'I've remembered who he is.'

Jeannie was aghast. 'But you thought it was more important to sit there munching crisps than to tell me about it?'

'No,' said Jeff with a lopsided grin. 'I've been trying to tell you, but since you marched in this morning all you've done is mouth off about Angels with Broken Wings.'

Jeannie looked contrite. She had, she realized, been doing exactly that. She looked wearily at Jeff. 'I'm sorry. I suppose I just feel...Well, I suppose I know how they feel. The modern world is proving too much for me. I feel as if my wings are damaged, Jeff,' she finished, not altogether jokingly.

'Don't you dare,' warned Jeff, 'enrol in that place. I need you here. I really need you to help me find Dave Day, Jeannie.'

Jeannie felt a warm glow engulf her from within. It wasn't often Jeff told her she was needed. 'So,' she said. 'Shoot.'

'I beg your pardon?'

'That's what they say, isn't it? Shoot – tell me all about him.'

Jeff stood up. 'It's a long story. What about some coffee while I tell it?'

'Mmm. That would be lovely.'

Jeff glared at Marty, inclined his head towards the outer office in a 'follow me or else' gesture, and left the room. Marty dutifully accompanied him.

'Look, Marty, I really don't need you hanging around like this.'

'Oh, I *see*.' Marty loomed uncomfortably close to Jeff. 'You don't need *me*. Oh, no. I've served my purpose, haven't I? I've told you all about Dave Day.'

'It might have helped,' countered Jeff in mild rebuke as he switched on the kettle, 'if you'd told me ten years ago.'

Marty wisely chose not to follow that particular route. 'You don't need *me*, but you really need Jeannie. "I really need you to help me find Dave Day, Jeannie",' he whined. Then he cocked his head to one side and pressed his face against Jeff's. 'Is it need, Jeff, or is it want? You really want Jeannie, don't you?'

'For Christ's sake, Marty! I really want her to help me find Dave Day! What's wrong with that? She is my *partner*, after all.'

'She's *my* fiancée, Jeff.'

Jeff glared at the taller man. 'She *was* your fiancée, Marty. It may have escaped your notice, but there's a fairly fundamental barrier to that relationship now.'

'And what's that?'

'The fact that you're dead.'

'Oh.' Marty recoiled as if from a slap in the face.

'Look, Marty, you've got to let go some time. I mean, I realize how you feel and that it must be a little frustrating not to be able to eat, sleep or, well, enjoy the sort of things that normal people enjoy, but...'

'Aha!' Marty all but shouted. 'So now I'm not normal, is that it?'

Jeff *did* shout. 'Marty, you're DEAD! Being dead is not normal.'

'What?' cried Jeannie from the inner office.

'Nothing…Er, coffee's dead, that's all. We've only got de-caff, not normal. Sorry.'

'That's all right,' replied Jeannie distractedly. The article she was reading was far more interesting than coffee anyway. "An Angel at My Table", it was a sample of Angels' recipes, written, she was intrigued to note, by an Angel called Serenity Blush. She made a mental note to cut it out and give it to Wendy.

'You've got to get used to the fact,' said Jeff in the other room, 'that things change.'

'So I've noticed,' pouted Marty. 'You've bought a plant.'

'No. *Jeannie* bought a plant.' Jeff poured boiling water into two mugs. One of them suddenly started to sway from side to side. 'Stop it, Marty!'

'I don't,' said Marty through gritted teeth, '*like* spider plants.'

Jeff picked up the mugs. 'Marty, I'm getting really, really tired of this. If you can't think of anything better to do then I can't stop you being here, but *please*, for once in your life, can't you just sit down and shut up?' And with that he walked back to Jeannie, leaving a very deflated Marty in the outer office.

Jeff *never* shouted at Marty; he never really raised his voice. He must be very annoyed, thought Marty. Shoulders hunched, he slunk after Jeff, said not a word and perched himself on top of a filing cabinet.

'Thanks,' said Jeannie, reaching for her coffee. 'So, Dave Day. What made you remember?'

Marty looked smug.

Jeff ignored him. 'Oh, y'know…these things just come back to you if you think hard enough. Time plays funny tricks on your memory, doesn't it, Jeannie? You only recall the things you want to remember.' He looked briefly and not nicely at the filing cabinet. 'And you "forget" the inconvenient things. Dave Day,' he continued as he focused on Jeannie, 'worked at the Terrapin Club.'

'I'd rather guessed that, Jeff.'

'Yes, but there's more.' Jeff frowned and cast his mind back to what Marty had told him.

How much easier this would be, he reflected, if Marty could tell Jeannie himself. And how much more convenient it would be if Marty were to absent himself from this particular conversation. But Marty was firmly ensconced on the filing cabinet, as eager as Jeannie was to hear what he had to say about Dave Day.

'I only went to the Terrapin a couple of times,' he said. 'And it *was* ten years ago, but I'm pretty sure that Dave Day was a mate of Marty's. Not a great mate, but…well, Marty didn't have many friends there and—'

'You bloody liar!'

Jeff studiously ignored the protest. 'And he and this Dave bloke used to pal around a bit. When we tipped off the police, I remember Marty said that he was going to warn Dave there would be a raid – he didn't want Dave to be caught with the rest of them.'

'Why?'

'Be very careful,' warned Marty. 'Be very, *very* careful.'

'Because,' sighed Jeff, 'they'd done a trade-off. Dave was the only person who knew Marty was having an affair with Tallulah. He also knew that

Don Carlos would kill Marty if he found out. And Marty...um, Marty knew something about Dave.'

'And what exactly,' asked a slightly cool Jeannie, 'was that?'

'Be economical with the truth,' urged Marty. *'Please*. I don't want Jeannie to think I was involved in anything grubby.'

'Dave,' continued Jeff, 'had this little scam going with customers' credit cards. It was pretty nifty, actually. He wasn't daft. He didn't fleece them on the spot or anything like that. He took their card numbers and entered them into some sort of program he had invented.'

Despite his resolution to ignore Marty, Jeff looked over to the filing cabinet. Marty nodded back.

'So,' explained Jeff, 'weeks or even months later, small sums would appear on their statements. Nothing drastic – just a few quid here and there – and always debited from a pretty likely-looking source. You know...if the customer was a gambler or a drinker, then it would look as if he'd spent money at a gambling or a drinking club. And because the sums were so small, no one ever questioned them. I mean, if you had a vice, you wouldn't be too inquisitive about the money you spent on it, would you?'

'No,' said Jeannie. 'I suppose not. But if I'd been abroad and my card was debited to somewhere in this country I'd be pretty suspicious.'

'If you'd been a regular at the Terrapin,' said Jeff with utter certainty, 'you wouldn't have been the sort of person who went abroad.'

'Oh.' Jeannie smiled at Jeff. But the smile disappeared as something else occurred to her. 'Marty was taking backhanders from this Dave person, wasn't he?'

'No!' protested Jeff and Marty in unison.

Jeannie fixed Jeff with a steely glare.

'Well…'

On top of the filing cabinet, and unnoticed by Jeannie, the spider plant began to wobble.

'No!' shouted Jeff.

Jeannie's glare intensified. 'I think he doth protest too much,' she mused.

'Look,' said Jeff, 'I don't know. I just don't know, Jeannie. He might, he might not have. He didn't tell me.'

'That's right. He didn't tell you.'

'I might have had my suspicions, but—'

'Careful!'

'I never voiced them. Let's face it, Jeannie, Marty was a pretty honest bloke. Yes, he could be annoying – *really* annoying – but he was a fundamentally decent bloke. And if he did something dodgy ten years ago…well, it's all in the past, isn't it?'

Jeannie sighed. 'Yes…Yes, I suppose it is.' Looking vaguely perturbed, she stared, unseeing, at the filing cabinet. 'But it's just a little odd to think that the man I loved was involved in something so…so grubby.'

'Oh, Jeannie,' pleaded Marty. 'Don't think badly of me. Please.'

'If Marty were still alive,' said Jeff in a quiet voice, 'would you forgive him for anything he might not have told you about? Would you believe that if he'd been economical with the truth, it was because he wanted to spare your feelings?'

Jeannie pondered that one while, on the filing cabinet, Marty held his breath. 'Yes,' she said at length. Then, with more conviction, 'Yes. I would. Definitely.'

Hugely relieved, Marty released his tension with a deep sigh and the papers on Jeff's desk wafted in the sudden breeze. Jeff leaned on them. 'Good,' he said from his new and highly uncomfortable-looking position, 'so now can you *please* shut up?'

'Jeff!' Jeannie was stunned. Jeff never spoke like that.

'Don't you dare,' snarled Marty, 'speak to my girl-friend like that.'

'I wasn't speaking...I mean...what I meant to say was...' Jeff removed his elbow from the far side of his desk and assumed a more dignified posture. 'Sorry, Jeannie. What I meant was, can we please move on? We're supposed to be discussing Dave Day.'

'OK.' Jeannie, too, changed into business-mode. 'So, in exchange for Dave keeping quiet about his affair with Tallulah, Marty arranged for Dave to be warned about the raid?'

'Yes.'

'But, if Tallulah is to be believed, Dave has just been released from prison.'

'Correct. What Marty didn't know was that Dave had several grand's worth of heroin among his possessions. The old bill found it and he got well and truly nicked. Ten years.'

'Hmm.' Like Jeff before her, Jeannie found that rather strange. 'For a man who was clever enough to hack into computer databases,' she said, 'leaving heroin lying around is a remarkably foolish thing to do.'

'That's exactly what I said to Marty!' Jeff was thoroughly animated now and, as it appeared to Jeannie, in the grip of total recall of a years-old conversation. 'But Marty, you see, didn't *know* about Dave's habit, or his drug-dealing. All he knew about was the credit card fraud.'

'So,' said Jeannie, 'when Marty warned him that a raid was about to take place, they were talking at cross-purposes?'

'Eh?'

'Presumably Dave thought Marty was telling him to get rid of the drugs, but Marty was under the impression that he was warning him about the credit cards.'

'Er, yes.' It began to dawn on Jeff that he wasn't quite as *au fait* with the situation as he would have liked to be.

'So,' continued Jeannie after a pensive sip of coffee, 'why did it all go wrong? Presumably Dave had enough time to get rid of the drugs.'

Jeff scratched his head. 'P'raps it took him longer than expected to get rid of the credit card evidence?'

'No! You've got it all wrong!' Exasperated and no longer able to contain himself, Marty leapt off the filing cabinet and began to pace the room. '*I* got rid of the credit card evidence for him!'

'But that still doesn't explain about the heroin,' protested Jeff.

'Doesn't explain what about the heroin?' asked a puzzled Jeannie.

Jeff held out a hand in protest. 'Wait! Let's just stop for a minute. I need to think about this. It's buried in here somewhere,' he said, tapping his head. 'Just let me think it over.' With that, he placed his elbows on the desk and cupped his chin in his hands. To Jeannie, he appeared to be deep in thought.

'Duh!' said Marty in disgust. 'Don't you *ever* listen? Let me spell it out for you.' He went on in a voice that suggested he was addressing a tiny child:

'Marty knows about the raid. That's because clever Marty *organized* the raid, aided, it now appears, by someone without a brain.' He cast a scornful look in Jeff's direction and continued pacing. 'So while Mr Brainless engages the nightclub boss in delaying conversation, Marty tells Tallulah to skip the joint before the police get there. Then Marty tells Dave to do the same. But Dave is in the middle of serving customers and can't just skedaddle without arousing suspicion. So Dave hands clever Marty the keys to his computer and tells him to wipe the computer. Clever Marty does what he's told.' Marty stopped pacing, bent down to Jeff and tapped him slowly on the head. 'Got it? Has it sunk in or shall we try a third time?'

'No, no, I've got it,' said Jeff, raising his head and glaring at his irate, deceased partner. 'But that *still* doesn't explain about the heroin.'

'Jeff!' Jeannie was as exasperated as Marty had been. 'That's what you call "thinking it over"?'

'Dave,' sighed Marty, 'didn't want me to know about the heroin. He knew I hated the stuff. He reckoned that our deal would be off if he told me about it. So *that*, little man,' he finished with another, rather more vigorous tap on Jeff's head, 'is why he asked me to wipe the computer. He thought it would give him time to flush the stuff down the loo or whatever you do with thousands of pounds of drugs.'

'The only logical answer,' said Jeff, looking through Marty to Jeannie, 'is that Dave just didn't have time to get rid of the drugs.'

'Correct,' congratulated Marty.

'I suppose so,' said a rather doubtful Jeannie.

'It *does* make sense,' urged Jeff. 'And it's the only

conclusion we can draw. What I can't make sense of is why, ten years later and on his release from prison, Tallulah Joplin wants to keep tabs on him.'

'No,' said Marty, 'that doesn't make sense to me either. They barely knew each other.'

'Not,' sighed Jeff, 'very helpful.'

'Don't beat yourself up, Jeff,' said Jeannie with a slightly wistful smile. 'It's not your fault. None of us knew we'd have to go raking over the past like this. If Marty...well, if Marty were here, he might have been able to shed further light on the situation, but—'

'I wouldn't be so sure about that.' Jeff couldn't help himself. Far from shedding light, Marty was muddying the waters. Jeff glared at his ex-partner. Marty stuck his tongue out.

Jeannie, however, was a little miffed by Jeff's lightning – and negative – response. 'That's not fair, Jeff. Marty *worked* at the nightclub. He'd be bound to remember a link between Tallulah and Dave.'

Silence – noncommittal on Jeff's part and embarrassed on Marty's – greeted her protestation.

'As it is,' she continued after a moment, 'we're on our own with this one.'

'And no further forward,' added a gloomy Jeff.

'Oh, I don't know.' Jeannie picked up the card on which Tallulah had written her mobile phone number. 'At least we know all about her present whereabouts.' Suddenly resolute, she reached across her desk. 'I'm going to phone her, Jeff. See if I can find out more about why she wants to know where Dave is.'

'OK.' Jeff cast around for a useful occupation. 'I'll just sit here and...twiddle my thumbs.'

'No, you won't. You're going to go to the only place that might lead to Dave Day.'

'Prison?'

'No.' Jeannie leaned over and handed him another card. 'The Terrapin Club. I checked. It's still going strong.'

Again her remark was greeted by silence. At least it was silence as far as Jeannie was concerned. Jeff's ears were assaulted by a gleeful cry from the dead man in the white suit.

'Wow!' yelled Marty. 'The Terrapin Club! Still going after all these years. Whaddya think about that, Jeff?'

Jeff cast his mind back ten years, to the first time he had become involved with the Terrapin Club. 'I think,' he said slowly, 'this might lead us into trouble.'

'Trouble,' replied Jeannie as she dialled Tallulah's number, 'is our business.'

*T*he tall man was beginning to find the stillness unnerving and oppressive. The adrenaline that had fuelled him over the past few days had vanished; it had eloped with its handmaiden, euphoria, leaving him drained, exhausted and alone but for the demons of impending disaster.

He was in trouble and he couldn't see a way out. The delegates, he was sure, hadn't suspected anything. They had believed every word of his glorious rhetoric. And why not? The rhetoric had been a reflection of their own glory, a testament to their own vision and intelligence, a glowing commendation of their commitment, drive and ambition.

This was an acceptable way of saying that they were dull little people with inflated egos who had nothing to contribute except money. Staggering amounts of money.

It was a delicious irony that a great deal of the money had been spent in pandering to their egos. The construction of the magnificent building, he reflected as he absent-mindedly stroked the scar on his chin, had been largely unnecessary. The monumental edifice was, in reality, a façade. Utterly pointless. The great, cathedral-like central hall; the sumptuous suites equipped with every luxury known to man; the grottoes and waterfalls – all had been constructed on a giant artifice.

But the tall man was an expert in the psychology of megalomania. Individuals whose vaunting ambitions had already propelled them into the arena of vast wealth were, by definition, different. They needed to be kept apart from the seething masses of humanity who toiled at the tail end of the scale of wealth. They needed hymns sung to their greatness. And they needed to be cosseted in great, gilded cages wherever they went.

So he had built a cage of towering magnificence when, in fact, he could have run his empire from a grubby little office. Or at least he could have done before everything started going horribly wrong.

With an enormous effort, he hauled himself to his feet and dragged the burden of his trouble across the hall and into the little room at the back. The only sound as he did so was the familiar tinkle of the wind chimes escorting him into the darkened office: the epicentre of his crumbling universe.

chapter seven

Tallulah had been extremely friendly on the phone. Because Jeannie was still suspicious, she had assumed Tallulah would, in turn, be suspicious of her. It was only as she had confirmed their appointment and replaced the receiver that she remembered Tallulah had no reason to be suspicious. Jeannie's innate distrust of the woman had nothing to do with her transformation from vamp to Angel; it was entirely due to another previous incarnation – that of Marty's girlfriend. Having so publicly embraced the concept of goodness, Tallulah was presumably on the fast track to heaven, but she was surely still human enough to sense that basest of emotions: jealousy. Unless she had absolutely no idea that Jeannie had been engaged to Marty.

As Jeannie drove through the meandering country lanes, she realized that must be the case. Tallulah was ignorant of her relationship with Marty. The thought came with an unwelcome jolt that forced her to confront her true feelings: her jealousy of Tallulah stemmed at least partly from the fact that Tallulah wasn't jealous of *her*. Jeannie had always considered herself far too sensible to entertain such petty notions. Feeling uncharacteristically small, humbled by her frailty, she unconsciously tried to compensate by switching the Stag into over-drive and roaring past the hedgerows that lined the long, straight stretch of road ahead.

Ten minutes later she passed the pub that had featured in Tallulah's detailed instructions. 'It used to be called the Princess of Wales,' Tallulah had said, 'but the new owners changed it. They thought,' she had added with a giggle, 'it would be good publicity for them, but it's even better for us!'

The turning she had been told to take, Jeannie reminded herself as she began to slow down, was about 200 yards past the Sign of the Angel. Sure enough, as she changed down into third she saw an elegant wrought-iron sign with an arrow pointing to the left. It bore the now familiar legend 'Angels with Broken Wings'. Jeannie deftly switched into second and accelerated into the driveway.

Several of the articles Jeannie had read had carried pictures of the building she was heading towards. But none of them had done justice to the magnificence of the grounds. In stark contrast to the carefully contrived garden of Wendy's house, these sweeping acres were the real thing. The languorous park undulated on both sides of the driveway; aristocratic oaks reached proudly to the skies; to the right a great lake shimmered into the distance; and each bend in the drive provided a tantalizing taste of another delightful vista. Jeannie thought it magnificent and marvelled at the fact – and her own acceptance of the fact – that what had been carefully contrived two centuries ago now qualified as 'natural'.

The last stretch of the drive was as straight as an arrow and led to the exquisite house that Jeannie had seen in the magazines. From the very first glimpse, the house seemed sublimely yet inexplicably right. Designed, she had read, by a contemporary of Sir John Soane, it had managed to resist the embellishments of subsequent generations and was even mercifully free of Victorian trickery. No expert in architecture, even Jeannie could spot a gem when she saw one. Yet her admiration of the building and its surroundings didn't close her mind to issues more pertinent to her role as a detective. As far as she could see, two aspects of her arrival were peculiar. The first was that there was no evidence of any security system, no visible monitoring of arrivals and departures from the place. The second was the total absence of people and activity. Were it not for the fact that the house and surrounding parkland were so beautifully maintained, the property could, for all the world knew, be empty.

The next surprise, as Jeannie pulled up in front of the shallow steps that led to the front door, was that the person who rushed out to greet her was Tallulah Joplin herself. She was dressed in almost exactly the same manner as on her visit to the office. Minus the winged handbag that had proved to be the key to her identity.

'Jeannie!' she exclaimed as she pulled open the driver's door of the Stag. 'Welcome to Angels!'

Feeling ambushed by the woman's enthusiasm, Jeannie smiled a tentative smile as she alighted from the car. She hadn't quite known what to expect. A hushed air of reverence? People wandering around in quiet contemplation? A uniformed flunkey to greet her? The last thing she had anticipated was to be greeted by Tallulah in the casual 'welcome to my country house' manner.

'Hi,' she said.

'I'm so glad you wanted to come and see me,' continued Tallulah. 'I have to confess I was a little worried by Jeff's reaction when I came to your office.' She shot Jeannie a curiously intimate look. 'I expected him to be a little...well, surprised by the fact that I'd become an Angel, but I really wasn't counting on him going into some sort of catatonic trance.'

'Oh, that's Jeff,' said Jeannie with a lame shrug. 'He...he's not really one to show his feelings. He tends to don a mask of inscrutability when he's feeling pressured.'

Tallulah looked worried. 'I didn't mean to *pressure* him—'

'Sorry,' interrupted Jeannie. 'Not pressured. Surprised.'

Tallulah smiled again. This time rather sadly. And, as they climbed the steps, she put a gently restraining hand on Jeannie's arm. At the same time she turned to survey the parkland in front of the house, obliging Jeannie to do likewise.

'It's sad, really, that people are so surprised,' she said as she looked, unseeing, at the gorgeous vista. 'I can't pretend to be a saint, Jeannie – I suppose you know all about my past – but it's a shame that people are so resistant to accepting the fact that I've changed. I mean, what do I need to do to convince them? Become a nun?'

'Oh, I don't think so,' said Jeannie. 'An Angel's probably good enough.'

'An Angel,' corrected the other woman, 'with a Broken Wing. That's what people forget. We don't claim to be perfect. We're just as fallible as the next person.'

Jeannie was becoming increasingly intrigued by Tallulah. Rather ungenerously, she had been prepared to abandon suspicion and jealousy for another emotion: pity. She had been revving up to dismiss the woman as irredeemably silly. Now she realized she was talking to a sentient, thoughtful human being.

'All this,' she said, gesturing towards the grounds and then looking pointedly at Tallulah's all-white attire; 'what's it really all about? Is it about wearing your fallibility as some sort of talisman? Isn't it a sort of "Look at me, I'm a damaged person sharing other people's pain" declaration? I mean, can't you just say, "OK, I screwed up in the past, now I'll just get on with normal life"?'

Tallulah eyed Jeannie for a long moment before answering. 'But what is "normal life"? Living on your own in a poky flat, struggling from one work day to the next?'

An image of Jeff, his struggles and his poky flat flitted through Jeannie's mind.

'Or is it being married with children? Or is it working in a nightclub, operating on the fringes of society, one step removed from the underworld?' Tallulah sighed. 'That was normal for me at one point, Jeannie. I tried the poky flat bit, I was even tempted by the marriage and kids at one point. But this is normal for me now. Is that so wrong?'

'No.' Jeannie looked away. 'It just seems...well, a little contrived. A bit unreal.'

Tallulah smiled. 'Would it be easier to accept if I were part of some sort of sect?'

'Aren't you?'

'No. I thought you would have known enough about us to realize that we're a viable organization; a decent business proposition even. Come.' Tallulah touched Jeannie's arm again and gestured towards the house. 'Let me show you what we're all about.'

With that, Tallulah led Jeannie up the steps, through the great front door and into a grand marble hall.

'One of the reasons why people have invested in us,' she explained, her words, like their steps, echoing in the vastness, 'is because we don't have any specific aims. We don't claim to be able to cure anyone of anything, we don't preach at anyone, and we don't promise anything we can't deliver.'

Jeannie was half intrigued, half amused. 'So what *do* you do? Forgive me if I sound sceptical, but presumably people pay a lot of money to come here. You must give them *something* in return?'

Tallulah's response surprised her. 'What have you got since you've been here?'

'I've only been here two minutes.'

'I know, but what are your impressions so far?'

'Well…' Jeannie paused to reflect on the last few minutes. 'It's beautiful. Stunning, actually. I was thinking that as I drove through the park. And…well, yeah. That's it.' Feeling slightly foolish, she smiled uncertainly at Tallulah.

Tallulah laughed: the twinkling, musical sound that Jeannie remembered from the office. 'Well, that's not bad, is it? After only two minutes.' Then she turned abruptly and headed towards the double doors at the far end of the hallway. 'Follow me!'

Feeling as if Tallulah had somehow stolen a march over her, Jeannie scowled. Yet if she didn't want to appear even more foolish, she had no option but to obey instructions.

'This,' announced Tallulah with understandable pride, 'is the drawing room.'

Jeannie followed her into the huge, perfectly proportioned Georgian interior. Despite its grandeur and size, it somehow contrived to be both warm and inviting. Massive sofas littered with comfortable-looking cushions shared space with ornate ormolu tables, and chaises-longues, while on the walls glittering pier-glasses hung alongside great gilt-framed paintings. The overall effect was of light, ease and quiet dignity. Jeannie felt that if she kicked off her shoes and sprawled on one of the sofas she would be doing exactly the right thing. This was a room to be enjoyed as much as admired.

'It's beautiful,' she whispered. 'Really lovely.'

'Glad you like it,' said Tallulah briskly. 'I'm very fond of this room.' She turned to Jeannie and flashed her an unnerving smile. 'Would you like to see round a bit more before we get down to business?'

'Yes. Yes, that would be nice.'

'Good. I love showing people round.' Tallulah escorted Jeannie out of the room and back across the echoing hallway. 'A lot of people are surprised that we live in such grand surroundings, but why shouldn't we? Broken Wings, you see, is really a synonym for damaged pasts. We try to make the present so much more pleasurable.'

Reaching the opposite end of the hall, she threw open another set of doors, this time to an elegant, formal dining room. 'This doesn't get used much, to be honest. A bit *too* grand. But the shareholders love it. They need that sort of spoiling, don't you think? Great formal black-tie dinners – makes them feel terrifically important,' she finished.

'Er...you entertain the shareholders here?'

'Yes, of course. And we hold the AGMs here...quarterly conferences as well. You have to remember, Jeannie, this is a business.'

'Yes, I know. I don't know why, but I was under the impression that the business side of things was separate from the residential side.'

'Oh, no.' Tallulah closed the doors to the somewhat austere dining room and led Jeannie towards a corridor under the delicate cantilevered staircase. 'Most of the Angels who live here are permanent. Most of us, in fact, are founder members and so we're very much at the hub of the—'

'You're a founder member?'

Tallulah appeared amused. 'Yes. Working at a nightclub wasn't such a bad training ground, you know. OK, it was slightly seedy, but I learned a thing or two about business – and about people.' Suddenly she winked at Jeannie. 'And let me tell you, some of the people who come to be Angels are every bit as strange as those who worked at the Terrapin Club.'

Noting Jeannie's somewhat shocked reaction, Tallulah laughed and reached out for her arm. 'There! You think I'm being disloyal, don't you? Well, I'm not. If we preached anything – which, of course, we *don't* – it would be tolerance. Live and let live, that's what I say.' She strode off down the corridor, an increasingly bemused Jeannie in her wake.

A moment later they reached what had presumably, in a previous era, been the family wing. The rooms, as Jeannie discovered, were smaller, with less intricate plasterwork, less grandeur.

'This is the residential bit,' said Tallulah. 'Those of us who are permanent have apartments here. The east wing's much the same, although it's mainly single rooms for visitors.' Then, momentarily thoughtful, she put a hand to her mouth. 'I'm just wondering who might be here for you to meet...'

Before she could come up with an answer, a tall, rather severe-looking woman appeared from a doorway to Jeannie's left. 'Ah!' beamed Tallulah. 'The very person! Emma, this is Jeannie – Jeannie, Emma.'

Jeannie extended a hand. 'Hello.'

'Splendid,' said Emma, grabbing Jeannie's hand with a vice-like grip. 'Visiting, are you? Or are you staying?'

'Visiting. Just visiting.'

'Ah, well,' replied the older woman. 'Maybe you'll come and stay one of these days.' Then, taking Jeannie by surprise, she leaned forward and scrutinized her. 'Yes. Yes, you really ought to. You're looking a bit peaky, my dear. Too much time spent cooped up in an office, I'd say. I'm right, am I not? Tell me I'm right?' Her cut-glass vowels scythed through the air, leaving Jeannie feeling like a naughty schoolgirl.

'Yes,' she said weakly. 'Yes, I suppose you're right. I could do with a bit of a break, but I really don't think I could afford—'

'Ah,' interrupted Tallulah. 'But we have all sorts of different rates, you see. Depending on the wing-damage.'

'I beg your pardon?'

'It's a hangover from when we started, from when all the Angels were girls with, shall we say, *racy* pasts. Not,' added Tallulah with alacrity, 'that I'm casting any aspersions on *your* past. It's just that wing-damage has become a pseudonym for...for—'

'For determining how much a girl needs a new

injection of life – regardless of her bank balance,' finished the no-nonsense Emma. Then she raised a hand in salutation and walked briskly down the corridor. The words 'so much to do and so little time!' floated back towards the other women.

'Emma,' explained Tallulah in a whisper, 'is of the old school. Very well connected. Very efficient. But don't let the accent fool you. She's a tough cookie. Black belt in judo.'

'Is she?' Jeannie looked at the retreating figure. The woman had to be in her fifties, she mused, but her figure was that of an athletic youngster. Just as well, thought Jeannie. It wasn't often a woman with half a century behind her could get away with a white leather catsuit. 'Is she a founding Angel?'

'No. Well…sort of,' said Tallulah. 'She's been here since the beginning. She's the housekeeper.'

Jeannie bit back a startled response. 'Oh,' was all she said. A different impression of Tallulah and the Angels was beginning to form in her mind. They weren't to be regarded as suspicious at all, she thought. They didn't have a strange, hidden agenda. They were just mad.

The next person she met confirmed her suspicions. Tallulah led her into a beautiful, sun-drenched conservatory at the end of the corridor, explaining that some of the girls sometimes sat here to catch the afternoon sun. 'Patience is often here,' she said, more to herself than to Jeannie. Then, in an even quieter voice, 'Poor Patience.'

Poor Patience was indeed there, half hidden behind an enormous, threatening-looking plant. She was sitting at a wrought-iron table, concentrating all her energies on the task before her – dealing tarot cards.

Like the other Angels, she was clad entirely in white, yet in contrast to Emma's skintight catsuit Patience's outfit was a long, voluminous kaftan, with, Jeannie was intrigued to note, playing-card motifs stitched on to it.

'Patience,' said Tallulah, 'I'd like you to meet Jeannie.'

Patience didn't look up. 'The Queen,' she said in a slightly breathy voice.

'No, not the Queen. *Jeannie*,' sighed Tallulah. Her expression informed Jeannie that this sort of response was par for the course for Patience.

Still Patience didn't look up. Instead, her long white hands peeled another card from the pack and laid it on the table. 'The Grim Reaper,' she announced. 'Death comes to us all in the end.'

Tallulah sighed and steered Jeannie away. 'God,' she said, rolling her eyes. 'And here I was, trying to persuade you that we're all perfectly normal.' She lowered her voice. 'Patience is a bit of an exception. She's, well…' Tallulah put a finger to her temple and looked knowingly at Jeannie. 'She's not quite all there. Mind you, can't say I blame her really. She had a really horrible time a few years ago in Jamaica.' Tallulah bent her head towards Jeannie. 'Voodoo,' she whispered.

'Ah!' Totally baffled, Jeannie nodded in understanding.

But Tallulah was now racking her brains, trying to think of someone 'normal' to introduce to Jeannie. 'I know!' she exclaimed. 'You must meet Rosa.'

'Tallulah, it's really sweet of you to want to introduce me to all these people, but I don't have much time and, well, I really came here to discuss business.'

'Yes, I know. Dave Day. Sorry.' She looked contrite. 'Didn't mean to sound so dismissive. It's just…well, it's just a bit painful for me to rake up the past. I know you want to know more about him, although heaven knows why Jeff and Marty couldn't have told you more.'

'It was a *long* time ago, Tallulah.'

'Yes, I know. Look,' she added, almost imploringly, 'indulge me. Come and meet Rosa – she's one of our success stories. You'll love her. And then I'll tell you more about Dave. Promise.'

Jeannie was beginning to feel vaguely uncomfortable. Tallulah was undoubtedly hovering on the cusp of a different planet. By turns fey, sensible, enthusiastic, serious and completely impenetrable, she was beginning to get on Jeannie's nerves. All Jeannie wanted to do was discover why Tallulah wanted tabs kept on Dave Day. She certainly didn't want to meet Rosa. Or fall in love with her.

There was no chance of the latter. Tallulah led Jeannie up a winding staircase to the first floor of the west wing, knocked on the first door she came to and then, when there was no response, yelled at the top her voice, 'Rosa! Rosa! I've got someone who wants to meet you! *Rosa!*' As she spoke she began to hammer on the door. Then she turned to Jeannie. 'Rosa's a little deaf,' she explained.

'Really?'

'Yes. Not surprising, I suppose. She must be in her eighties. Still, she's a game old bird really. And to think what she's been through…'

Jeannie didn't really want to know what the deaf, game octogenarian had been through, but realized with a sinking heart that she was probably going to find out.

Tallulah opened the door and ushered her over the threshold. 'It's always a bit hot in here,' she said as a blast of hot air all but knocked them over. 'Rosa feels the cold, you see, even though she comes from Russia.'

'Russia?'

'Oh, yes. There are no borders or boundaries for Angels with Broken Wings. We come from all over the place.' Tallulah peered into the sombre depths of the room. 'Rosa likes to keep the blinds drawn because...Ah! There you are!' With a beaming smile, she pulled the unwilling Jeannie towards the old crone sitting in a chair by the fire.

The first thing Jeannie noticed about her was the bright-red wig sitting askew on what was clearly a bald pate. The second was that Rosa was intensely ugly.

'Rosa!' trilled Tallulah. 'This is Jeannie. She's come to visit us – to find out all about the Angels.'

'Hello,' said Jeannie. She took one look at the gnarled, wizened hands clasping the arms of the chair and decided that she could do without a tactile greeting.

'*Dosvedanya!*' barked Rosa.

'Now that's not very nice, is it?' scolded Tallulah. 'What did she say?'

'She said goodbye. Poor old thing, she does get a little confused sometimes.' Tallulah bent closer to the old lady. 'Say something nice to our visitor, Rosa.'

'*Pashol na hkuiy!*' The words were accompanied by a glare of such intense ferocity that Jeannie found herself taking several steps backwards. Rosa noticed and lashed out with one tiny foot. The kick was futile, but it made Jeannie look down at – and notice

– the woman's odd footwear. She was sporting what appeared to be men's brogues with extra-thick soles. In contrast to the woman's ill-fitting white dress (and red wig), they were black.

'I...um...I don't think she likes me very much,' said Jeannie.

'Oh, I wouldn't worry. She's just a bit temperamental, that's all. It's a shame she's not being more forthcoming. She has some remarkable tales to tell.'

'*Espion!*' spat Rosa.

Jeannie looked questioningly at Tallulah. 'That means "spy", doesn't it?'

'Yes. But she's obsessed with spies, poor old thing.' Tallulah bent further towards the chair. 'Jeannie isn't a spy, Rosa. She's...a friend.'

Again the foot shot out – this time narrowly missing Tallulah's shapely calf.

Tallulah sighed and moved away. 'Oh, well, we tried. Perhaps "friend" wasn't quite the right thing to say. Rosa's never really had any friends. Still, as I said, she's one of our success stories. She wasn't *at all* nice when she arrived.'

Jeannie followed Tallulah out of the room, heartily glad that she hadn't met Rosa when she wasn't at all nice. Neither she nor Tallulah heard Rosa's last words as the door closed behind them.

'*Smersh!*' she screamed at their retreating backs. '*Espions!*'

Jeannie had had enough. If Tallulah really thought that Rosa was normal and that the entire Angels set-up was perfectly sensible, then she was severely and possibly dangerously deluded. That didn't worry her unduly. What surprised her was that otherwise sane businessmen – including, for heaven's sake, pompous Henry – thought Angels an admirable enterprise and a sound investment.

Tallulah unwittingly addressed that issue as soon as they were back on the upstairs landing. 'I think I got a bit carried away,' she said with an apologetic and endearing shrug. 'I suppose I thought…Well, I'd forgotten that you didn't see these women years ago, when they first came to us. I'm sorry, Jeannie. All I think I've done is convince you we're all mad.'

Jeannie rummaged around in her brain for a suitable response. She couldn't find one.

'The people who invest in us,' continued Tallulah, 'don't usually see our…veteran members. They're pretty keen on balance sheets and so on. On the Angels who pay to stay and those who earn money through good work.' Again she shrugged. 'You can't blame them, can you? After all, as I said, we're a business.'

'Yes.' Jeannie looked pointedly at her watch. 'And it's business I'd really like to discuss, Tallulah.'

'Of course you would. Come on. We can talk in the privacy of my apartment.'

In contrast to the stifling heat and shadowy gloom of Rosa's room, Tallulah's apartment on the top floor was a triumph of light and space. Being predominantly white, it also matched Tallulah. Yet it didn't flatter her. Jeannie noticed that the clean lines of the place showed up something she hadn't noticed about Tallulah – her wrinkles. For someone who paid so much attention to her attire and her surroundings, it was odd that she didn't seem to bother about make-up.

'Would you like something to drink?' asked Tallulah as she gestured towards a deep sofa.

'No. No, I won't, thanks. As I said, I'm quite keen
to—'

'Get down to business? Yes, I know.' Looking
weary and slightly pained, Tallulah sighed and sank
into the sofa beside Jeannie. 'This is a bit...well, a
bit embarrassing for me, Jeannie.'

'Oh. Why?'

'Because I'm an Angel. I know I said we don't
claim to be perfect, but on the other hand, we're
not really supposed to go around hiring private
investigators.'

'Mmm. I can see that.' Tallulah's words reminded
Jeannie of something Jeff had said about Tallulah's
method of payment. 'Is that why you're paying us
through a third party?'

'Yes.' Tallulah looked slightly sheepish. 'It's not
illegal or anything. Just...convenient.'

Jeannie thought it was time for a spot of reassurance. 'Look, Tallulah. You don't need to feel embarrassed with me. We're used to dealing with, shall we
say, the uncomfortable aspects of life. And I can
assure you that helping an Angel out of a spot of
trouble is hardly the worst scenario we've ever had
to deal with.'

As she spoke, Jeannie again experienced a sense
of unreality. Here she was, the deeply pragmatic
Jeannie Hurst, talking about helping Angels. She
fought back a desire to laugh out loud. Then she saw
Tallulah's expression and the desire disappeared.
She was now looking deeply troubled.

'Why,' asked Jeannie in measured, sympathetic
tones, 'do you want us to find Dave Day? We need,'
she added, repeating the words she had uttered over
the phone, 'more information about him.'

'I know, I know. I suppose I just sort of hoped that

Jeff and Marty would…oh, I don't know.' Twisting her fingers in her lap, Tallulah looked miserably at Jeannie. 'In the old days, Marty always seemed to have the answers to everything.'

'Yes,' whispered Jeannie. 'I know.' Then, mentally, she checked herself. He might have always had the answers, but not necessarily the *right* answers. 'We'll find Dave Day, Tallulah. Don't worry. But we really need more information. I assume,' she continued, 'that you think he's out to get you?'

Tallulah nodded.

'But why?'

'I don't think Marty ever knew about Dave,' said Tallulah. 'Not really.'

'*What* about Dave?'

'His habit.'

'Drugs habit?'

'Mmm. Marty *hated* drugs – and Dave knew it.'

Jeannie mulled that one over for a moment. 'But *you* knew about it?'

'Yes. He was up to his eyeballs in the stuff. Dealing, trafficking, using…oh, you name it.'

But Jeannie still couldn't understand why Tallulah was so upset. From what Jeff had told her, the entire Terrapin Club had been founded on the stuff. And if anyone had been up to his eyeballs, it had to have been Tallulah's boyfriend.

As if on cue, Tallulah sniffed and asked Jeannie if she knew about Don Carlos.

'Yes, I do. And forgive me if I sound a little harsh, but I gather he wasn't exactly squeaky clean himself.'

Tallulah smiled. 'No, poor Cedric, he wasn't. But you know, Jeannie, he wasn't very keen on the drugs business himself.'

'Oh?'

'No. He was drawn into it through his other activities.'

Poor little Cedric, thought Jeannie. 'And what were those other activities?'

'Gang warfare,' said Tallulah brightly. Then, with a fond smile, 'He wasn't really responsible for that either. He was just doing his duty.'

'*Duty?*'

'Oh, yes. It was the family business you see. He inherited it.'

Jeannie suppressed the wave of nausea that threatened to overcome her. 'Right,' she said. 'But let's get back to Dave.'

'We have to go back to Cedric first.' Tallulah relapsed into her earlier sadness and looked, doe-eyed, at Jeannie. 'You know what happened to him?'

'Yes. He died in the shoot-out on the night of the raid.'

'Yes. So he couldn't defend me.'

Jeannie mentally added another adjective to the bewildering collection that described Tallulah: selfish. 'No,' she mused, 'I suppose he really wasn't in a position to do that. But...er, defend you from what?'

'From Dave's accusations in court.'

'Ah.' At last they appeared to be getting to the nub of the matter. 'What did he accuse you of?'

'That's what I thought Jeff and Marty knew.'

'Well, they didn't,' snapped Jeannie.

But the snap was lost on Tallulah. She took a deep breath. 'Dave Day accused me...*me*...of planting the heroin that was found in his possession.'

Jeannie wondered if Tallulah was aware of just how irritating her 'poor little me' act was becoming.

'And did you?' she asked.

'*No!* Of course not. I hated drugs too.' Tallulah rummaged in her pocket and extracted a pristine handkerchief. 'Can you imagine?' She sniffed. 'The humiliation!' Then she smiled again. 'Luckily there was absolutely no evidence to link me with his horrible heroin and he was banged up for ten years.'

'And now he's out – and he wants revenge?'

'Yes,' said Tallulah in a small voice.

'But how do you know that?' asked Jeannie. 'He may be a reformed character. After all, that's what prison is supposed to do, isn't it? Reform you?'

'That's what I was hoping as well.' Tallulah sighed, stood up and walked to a small bureau in the corner of the room. 'I prayed for his salvation, you know.' As she spoke she opened a small box and extracted a piece of paper. 'But it was not to be.' Walking back to Jeannie, she handed her the paper. 'Dave Day is out to get me.' Her prognosis was corroborated by the inelegant scrawl in front of Jeannie. 'Dave Day,' it read, 'is out to get you.'

'I see,' said Jeannie. She read the bald statement again and turned the paper over. As she suspected, there was nothing written on the back. 'Yes,' she murmured, 'it would appear that he hasn't reformed.'

'But I have!' Tallulah gestured to the room at large. 'All this!' she shouted. 'I've worked so hard for this. Angels is such a success…We've helped so many people…So many people believe in us.' Tallulah stepped closer. 'We're *good*, Jeannie!' She lowered her voice to a theatrical whisper. 'And if Dave Day murders me it will look bad.'

There was no denying that one, thought Jeannie. 'I can't let that happen,' continued the other woman. 'I don't care about *me*, Jeannie. I care about all this.'

The inconsistency of this woman, thought Jeannie, is truly baffling. Then she remembered she'd already decided that Tallulah was mad. Insanity and constancy were not easy bedfellows. She stood up.

'Right. Let's work on the information we have. Dave Day has been released from prison, he's still smarting because he thinks you set him up and he's out to get you.'

'Yes.'

'But we don't know his whereabouts?'

'No.'

Jeannie bit her lip. 'But we do have a clue.'

'Do we?'

'Well, if he hasn't reformed, he's probably going to be dealing in drugs again, isn't he?'

'Mmm. I hadn't really got that far.'

'And if he's doing that, he's probably going to go back to where he left off.'

'You mean...'

Jeannie grinned. 'Well, it's worth a shot, isn't it?'

'Gosh,' said Tallulah. Then, more to herself than to Jeannie, 'the Terrapin Club. I wonder what it's like nowadays?'

'And,' added Jeannie, 'if he's planning to get at you, he's going to need help.'

'Is he?'

'Well, he can't just walk in here and shoot you, can he?'

'No.' Tallulah shot a sly look at Jeannie. 'You're not stupid, are you?'

A smile hovered at the corner of Jeannie's mouth. 'Given the amount of publicity Angels has had, I can't believe there's no security.'

'You're right,' said Tallulah. 'There's masses of it. About fifty hidden cameras on the driveway alone.'

Jeannie nodded in approval. 'Good. But we have to assume Dave isn't stupid either. He'll try and get you when you're out and about.'

'I don't go out and about all that much. There's not much need if you live in a place like this.'

'You came to see us.'

'True. But I wasn't alone. I had Archangels in the car.'

'Archangels?' This was a new one for Jeannie.

'Yes. Bodyguards.'

'Oh.' Jeannie didn't quite know what to say to that. She knew, however, that she had had quite enough of Angels – and indeed Archangels – with Broken Wings for one day. If she stayed any longer Lucifer would probably pop out of the cupboard. More to the point, she had all the information she was going to get out of Tallulah. 'I think,' she said, 'it's really time I was off.'

'Oh. Must you? You won't stay to tea? Have a drink?'

'No. Really. Thanks so much for…well, for everything. It's been…'

What had it been? Bizarre was the word that seemed to fit the bill. Jeannie settled for 'fruitful'. It hadn't, she reflected, been particularly fruitful on the Dave Day front, but it had been a real eye-opener as regards the Angels.

'I'll show you out then,' said Tallulah. 'Can't have you getting lost among the hosts,' she added with her high, tinkling laugh.

'Hosts?'

'Of Angels.'

'Of course,' said Jeannie through gritted teeth. 'Silly me.'

Tallulah was back in full flow as they walked down the corridor towards the staircase. 'I can't help remembering Jeff's face when I walked into the office,' she tinkled. 'It was so funny. He really *did* think I was a ghost.'

'Well, you do look a bit...white.'

'I know. And to think I used to be all darkness. I was what they call a vamp, you know. Marty thought...' But whatever Marty thought, Tallulah was evidently going to keep it to herself. 'Oh, well,' she finished with a shrug, 'that was a long time ago.'

'Yes.'

'I suppose,' said Tallulah as they reached the staircase, 'Marty would get a shock if he could see me now.'

'I think that's probably a safe bet.'

Tallulah bit her lip. 'I suppose it's just vanity or something but, well, I'm a little surprised that Marty didn't want to come and see me.'

'Come and see you...when?'

'When I hired you to do this job.'

Jeannie wondered if she had misunderstood. She cast a covert look at the other woman. Tallulah's wistful expression merely served to confirm her horrified suspicion.

'Tallulah?'

'Mmm?'

Jeannie held out a hand to halt Tallulah's descent. 'I...I think there's something I'd better tell you.'

'Oh?' Tallulah looked vaguely puzzled. 'What's that?'

'Marty *can't* come and see you.'

'Why?'

Jeannie took a deep breath. 'Because he's dead.'

'What?' Tallulah recoiled as if from a slap. Then, like Jeannie before her, she decided she had misheard. She shook her head. 'For a moment I thought you'd said...'

'I did. Marty's dead, Tallulah.'

'Marty...is...dead?' Tallulah's legs gave way and she collapsed on to a step. With disbelief still written all over her face, she looked up at Jeannie. 'What? How? Why didn't you tell me?'

Jeannie crouched beside the distraught woman. 'I thought you knew,' she sighed. 'Everybody knows. It even says on the office door that—'

'But I didn't know!' wailed Tallulah. 'How was I supposed to know? Oh, God! This means that the whole thing's...Why didn't Jeff tell me?' To Jeannie's amazement, Tallulah's last words were spoken in anger.

Jeannie shrugged. 'I suppose I'd assumed he did tell you.'

'But this is appalling!'

'I know. It was a tragedy for all of us.' As Jeannie spoke, she turned her head away from Tallulah. She didn't want the other woman to read her emotions. She failed, therefore, to notice the conflicting emotions that danced across Tallulah's face. Outrage, anger, fear and shock fought an involuntary battle. The anger won. Then, as Jeannie turned back to face her, Tallulah recovered enough to compose her features into an appropriate expression of grief.

'How *awful*,' she whispered. 'How did it happen?'

'In a car crash.' As always, Jeannie dispensed with the details. The fact that Marty was dead was enough.

'God,' said Tallulah. 'When?'

'About six months ago.' Jeannie was looking straight ahead now and missed Tallulah's pursed lips and the brittle look in her eyes.

'Well,' said Tallulah after a moment's silence, 'that's terrible. Terrible for you of course,' she added, patting Jeannie's arm in a gesture that was supposed to suggest sympathy but only conveyed disinterest. 'But...well, it does rather have a bearing on this case.'

'Does it?'

'Yes. You see, Jeff didn't know Dave Day. And Dave didn't know Jeff. Dave wouldn't...well, he wouldn't...'

'Wouldn't what?'

Tallulah lapsed into an anguished silence. She knew exactly what Dave wouldn't do, but she could hardly tell Jeannie.

'Oh, I don't know. He just—'

'He would, however,' interjected Jeannie, 'remember Jeff.'

'He would?'

'Yes. Jeff met him at the Terrapin Club. So don't worry about him not knowing what Dave looks like. Jeff,' she added with a half-smile, 'has a brilliant memory.' Well, she told herself that was true. He had remembered an astonishing amount about the events of ten years previously once he'd put his mind to it.

'Yes, but...'

Jeannie turned to face the distraught woman. 'Look, I understand that you...well, that you're trying to make amends for...whatever happened in the past.'

Tallulah bowed her head to hide her look of alarm.

'I realize that you wanted Marty to be the one to bury the ghosts, that, in the end, you came back to him for help. He would have appreciated that, Tallulah. Really he would.'

Tallulah breathed deeply. 'Yes. Yes, I was trying to atone for what I'd done. It's been bothering me for years. I thought if I hired Marty...'

'But hiring me and Jeff is the next best thing,' consoled Jeannie. 'We'll find Dave and put a stop to his threats. Believe me, we will.' She pulled herself to her feet and reached for Tallulah's hand. 'And anyway,' she said with conviction, 'Marty is still with us in spirit.'

*W*hen Jeannie's yellow Stag had disappeared down the drive Tallulah turned back into the house. The last few minutes had been something of a strain as she had struggled to contain her fury and to murmur unhurried sympathies while battling against a sense of mounting urgency. She reckoned it had paid off, that she had succeeded in disguising her true feelings from Jeannie.

Now there was no need for pretence. She hurried through the front door, into the great hall, and headed towards a door she hadn't opened for Jeannie. Behind it was the library of the house: a room quite as beautiful as the other state rooms and equally sumptuous in furnishings. Bookshelves displaying leather-bound volumes dominated three walls, while the fourth was almost entirely covered by a massive painting. Art connoisseurs would have immediately recognized it as a copy of Guercino's The Liberation of St Peter by an Angel. *The far right of the painting depicted a sleeping guard, blissfully unaware of the angel behind him who was pointing the way to freedom. The angel's feathered wing crowned the picture, its whiteness counterbalancing the surrounding darkness. And in the centre lay the semi-somnolent figure of St Peter, his square bulk resting upon massive forearms. Looking at the angel, he appeared uncertain as to whether this was a dream or reality.*

But there was no uncertainty about Tallulah as she approached the picture. She reached forward and touched one of the links of St Peter's chains. As she did so, Peter's right arm slid silently sideways, revealing a small passageway behind the picture. She stepped into the space and, seconds later, the arm reverted to its normal position and the library *resumed its peaceful air of dignified refinement.*

Things were quite different on the other side of the wall. The passage that Tallulah hurried down was faced in stainless steel and ended in a double doorway of the same material. Tallulah pressed a little button at the side of the doors. She stepped forward and a moment later she pressed another button. The doors closed behind her and the lift began its silent and rapid descent into a different world.

When Tallulah emerged, she, too, was different. She had removed the white wig, peeled off the thin layer of latex that had covered her face and given her the air of ethereal innocence and she had unzipped her white outfit. The Tallulah who appeared from the lift was raven-haired, heavily made-up and clad entirely in black.

And the cavernous room into which she stepped was totally at odds with the neo-classical architecture of the building above. Down here, all was modernity, epitomized by the clean, cold lines of minimalism. To Tallulah's left, a waterfall gurgled enticingly, to her right was a vast seating area and directly in front of her was a great domed room dominated by an enormous table and twenty-one chairs.

Apart from the waterfall, the only noise in the cavernous underground palace was the soothing sound of the wind chimes.

chapter
eight

'Beware the angel with the broken wing
And the siren song she loves to sing.
She'll sing like a dove
From the heaven's above,
But the reality is she'll stong.'

Marty paused, mid-tap. 'Stong?'
Yes, thought Wyvern, there's something not
right there. 'Wrong?' he suggested.

'Ring?' tried Marty.

'Spring?'

'Sting!'

'Yes! Sting!' Wyvern clasped his hands together.
'She'll sting.'

'Why would she do that?' asked Marty with a
frown.

'Because it's what the poem says.'

'Oh.' Marty lost interest and went back to his tap-
dancing. 'I can't decide,' he said, as much to himself
as to Wyvern, 'whether it should be a straightfor-
ward croon or something with a little more zing.'

'Zing?'

'Yeah. As in sting.'

'And,' said Wyvern, 'wing.'

'Yeah.'

Wyvern sighed. Marty simply wasn't getting it. 'Look, Marty. I'm really not sure about this Tallulah affair.'

'The affair, I assure you, was over a long time ago.' Half-way through a complicated routine, Marty suddenly stopped. 'Tallulah. I used to sing a song when...well, when Tallulah was around. It had a lot of zing. It had the punters screaming all over the place. Maybe...yeah, maybe I could resurrect it for my limbo concert.'

Wyvern was beginning to lose his patience. 'What I mean, Marty, is that you should listen to what the poem says.'

'What poem?'

'*Concentration*, Marty. How many times do I have to tell you? That's the key to everything. The poem,' he finished wearily, 'that I've just recited.'

Marty stopped dancing and turned to the other man. 'You think Tallulah isn't what she seems? You reckon that she might not have changed after all?'

'It's perfectly possible.' Wyvern looked pointedly at Marty. 'People are very resistant to change.'

'Nah.' Marty waved a dismissive arm. 'Not Tallulah. She was a real chameleon; she could adapt to any situation. Doesn't surprise me that she's part of the Angels outfit. From what Jeff says, it's above board and highly profitable.' Marty wagged a finger at Wyvern. '*That*, matey, is what Tallulah was all about. She wanted money and a good life. She was never happy with the bad boys.'

'Given that she vanished into thin air after you got her out of the clutches of those "bad boys", you seem remarkably forgiving.'

'Yeah.' Marty adopted an air of pious magnanimity. 'Well, water off a duck's back and all that.'

'Under the bridge.'

'What?'

'The water,' explained Wyvern, 'is under the bridge.'

Marty looked keenly at Wyvern. He seemed normal – well, as normal as an elderly white-haired supernatural being with a penchant for eccentric white suits and scarves had a right to look – but sometimes he wondered about the man. He knew he was there to help lost souls like himself, but now that Marty had found himself and his true vocation, he wondered if he hadn't outgrown Wyvern. He could be a little too schoolmasterly, a little too pedantic.

Wyvern knew exactly what Marty was thinking. He knew that when Marty was on a high, he threw caution to the wind and felt himself invincible. Unlike Wyvern himself, Marty simply refused to address the possibility of trouble lying ahead.

He tried again. 'Marty, I think you should be aware of the possibility that Tallulah's up to no good. I think you should be careful.' He moved closer to the now pirouetting dancer-in-the-making. 'I can't force you to listen to my advice, but from experience – and I do have a lot of experience – people on earth who adopt heavenly names are invariably up to no good.'

'Oh, come *on*, Wyvern! You're not trying to tell me that Tallulah is a heavenly name?'

Wyvern rolled his eyes. 'Not Tallulah. Angels. People have no right to call themselves angels unless they're divine messengers.'

Marty shrugged. 'It's a free world.'

Wyvern gave up. When Marty was like this, there

was no getting through to him. The only way would
be to confiscate his pass to limbo, but Wyvern
couldn't face what he knew would be the consequences of that act. He'd have to deal with a
renewed bout of petulance, which would be almost
worse than the current spate of euphoria.

'Well,' he counselled, in a last-ditch attempt at
caution, 'be careful. I don't like the sound of Tallulah
– or of this Terrapin Club.'

'Wyvern thinks I shouldn't be going to the Terrapin.'
   'Oh? Why?'
   'Well, I've been thinking about that. You see, Jeff,
I think he's jealous.'
   'Of you?' Jeff nearly lost control of the car.
   Thankfully, Marty didn't notice. 'Yeah. You see,
I've thought it all out. There he is, day in and day
out, stuck in that room, tending to lost souls. He
doesn't get out enough, Jeff. And he's jealous 'cos I've
got the chance to develop a new career. Makes sense,
doesn't it?'
   Marty turned to his partner for confirmation of
his theory. It wasn't forthcoming.
   'Marty. We're not going to the club to develop your
new career. We're going to try to find out about Dave
Day, remember? We're detectives. We've been hired
to find a man and we're going to find him, right?'
   'Wrong.' Marty nodded to the road ahead. 'We're
not going to find anyone at this rate. We're going to
end up splattered across the tarmac if you continue
to drive this fast.'
   'I'm driving,' protested Jeff through gritted teeth,
'at thirty-five miles an hour.'
   'Like I said. Too fast.'
   Jeff resisted the temptation to press his foot

harder on the accelerator. He also quelled the urge to look round at Marty, because he knew perfectly well that his partner would be wearing the supercilious expression of the driver who knows best. Instead, he stayed mute and concentrated on the road.

For years they had shared a running joke about Jeff inheriting the car in the event of Marty's death. 'Over my dead body,' Marty had quipped on numerous occasions. The very idea had been an assault on his sensibilities. He knew that Jeff would litter the car's pristine interior with empty crisp packets, turn it into a mobile rubbish tip and then, because he was a dreadful driver, write off the vehicle.

For his part, Jeff had derived amusement from imagining how Marty would react to his treatment of the car after he had inherited it. Understandably, he hadn't entertained the notion that he might inherit Marty as well.

The joke, then, had turned rather sour.

'On that subject,' said Marty, seemingly reading Jeff's mind, 'when did you last clean this? It's filthy, Jeff. Disgusting. It's an insult to my memory.'

Jeff sighed. 'The only part of your memory I'm interested in is the part relating to the Terrapin Club.'

Marty looked peeved. 'I've told you all I can remember.'

'What about all these powers you're supposed to have? Why don't they include total recall?'

'Dunno. Wyvern didn't tell me.'

'Well, what about when you died? Didn't your whole life flash through your head? They say that's what supposed to happen.'

Marty looked loftily at the smaller man. 'And who exactly is *they*? All the dead people you know? You're out of your league, there, buddy boy.' He held up a hand and pressed thumb against forefinger. 'You know *nothing* about dying. Zip. Diddly squat. Don't try to tell me what I felt, Jeff. It was a painful and traumatic experience, and if you don't mind I'd like to keep it to myself.'

Jeff shrugged. 'Oh, all right then. It was just a suggestion.'

'Not a very good one.' Marty stared straight ahead, trying to look wounded but in reality desperately searching his memory for what it had recorded on the day he had died. To his horror, his mind was a blank.

'Hey!' interrupted Jeff after a moment. 'I think we're nearly there. Don't you recognize this?'

Marty looked up. He had been too busy monitoring the speedometer to take in their surroundings but now, looking to either side, he felt a faint stirring of familiarity. The road they had turned into was long and neon-lit and wore a hangdog air of having seen it all before. There were no pedestrians; just the odd car coming or going but not staying. This wasn't a place to hang around. You came here to do your business and then you got the hell out. Only losers lived here.

As he peered through the windscreen, something else began to stir in Marty. In the core of his being a power was welling. Not one mastered since his demise, but something more fundamental. The power of a private detective.

As they cruised down the strip, Marty's eagle eye missed nothing. This was the familiar playground of racketeers, pimps and their playthings. A sad street for the lost souls of the mortal world. The bright mile or so of tawdry neon boasted nightclubs with famous names and equally famous gambling rooms. Occasionally they slid past a joint that was new to Marty, but most of the names were the same. And if he opened the window to let in the cool night air he knew it would bring with it the musky aroma of desperation tinged with fear.

'Yeah,' he drawled to Jeff. 'Hope Street. Hasn't changed much, has it?' As he spoke, he allowed himself a wistful smile. There, to the left, was Stingy Lulu's, its sad sign still offering cut-price morality under the guise of cheap food. Two doors down, the Dancers was still holding out to be the world's most popular nightclub and, on the opposite side of the street, Ray Malone's had withstood the test of time. And, thought Marty, the endless stream of nighthawks who fell through its doors because they had no place else to go and no one to go there with. He remembered it all as if it had been yesterday, not ten years, since his last visit. Another minute and they would be pulling up outside the Terrapin Club.

'Here we are,' said Jeff, neatly pulling up and reversing into a parking space.

'What?'

Jeff gestured behind him. 'The Terrapin. We've just passed it.'

Marty frowned. Had his memory been affected by dying? He made a mental note to ask Wyvern about the possibilities of total recall. His frown deepened when Jeff got out of the car, locked the door and began to walk in the direction of the club.

'Jeff! Hey! You can't do that!'

'Can't do what?'

Marty appeared at Jeff's side and gestured to his beloved Mercedes. 'Well, just leave it there.'

'Why not?'

Marty was horrified. 'Gangs. Thugs. Thieves. For God's sake, Jeff! The car won't last a minute.'

Jeff looked up and down the street. 'Er, Marty. How many gangs and thugs and thieves can you see?'

Marty looked. The street was completely deserted. 'Well,' he said, sounding peeved, 'they'll be lurking. Waiting to pounce. I'd better stay here to guard it.'

'Marty! You can't! I need you. I've never met Dave Day. I don't know what he looks like. You have to come with me in case he's there.'

Marty looked mutinous but after a long, loving look at his prized possession, he reluctantly accompanied Jeff towards the club.

'What's our story?' he asked Jeff as they reached the Terrapin. Like the other clubs on the strip, it hadn't changed a bit. The neon-lit reptile over the door beckoned invitingly, exactly as it had done ten years previously.

'Why do you mean?'

'We have to have a plan. Have to explain why we're here.'

Jeff looked puzzled. 'Why? It's a nightclub. We've come to go clubbing at night. Or rather, *I've* come to go clubbing at night. You're invisible, remember.'

As he opened the door he failed to notice the expression on Marty's face. His friend was looking mutinous again. Invisible he may be, but he had other ways of making his presence felt. And it was clear he was going to make use of them.

They passed into the foyer and were greeted by a surly doorman, who looked Jeff up and down, snorted at the innocuous polo-neck and battered leather jacket and barked a sneering 'Whaddya want?'

'To…er…to come into the club.'

'And why would I want to let you do that?'

Before Jeff could reply, he felt a sudden jolt, followed by a great internal heaving, and realized to his horror that Marty had possessed him. And it was Marty's voice, infused with a light American twang, that came out of his mouth.

'I'm a licensed private investigator and have been for quite a while,' he drawled. 'I'm a lone wolf, unmarried, getting middle-aged and not rich. I don't do divorce cases and I like liquor and women and crisps and a few other things. The cops don't like me too much, but I know a couple I get along with. Both my parents are dead, I have no brothers or sisters, and when I get knocked off in a dark alley some time, if it happens, as it could to anyone in my business, and to plenty of people in any business, or no business at all these days, nobody will feel that the bottom has dropped out of his or her life.'

The doorman greeted this salvo with another appraising look. Then he gestured to the door behind him. 'OK,' he said. 'In you pop.'

Jeff battled to retain his equilibrium as he brushed past and into the club. His insides were heaving once again as Marty left his body.

'Why,' he whispered as Marty materialized at his side, 'did you do that?'

'Because there's no way he'd have let you in if you'd said, "I'm Jeff Randall and I've come to go clubbing at night".' Marty was feeling, and looking, distinctly superior. 'You said you needed me, Jeff. You just didn't know how badly.' With that, he stalked towards the balustrade in front of him and peered into the smoke-filled den below.

Jeff followed him. 'Wow,' he breathed after a

moment. 'It's exactly the same. It's like stepping back in time.'

Marty nodded. It was. Beneath them and to the left, the long bar, stacked with every drink known to man, stretched out towards the dance floor at the far end. Opposite it, the ranks of wooden-backed booths gave privacy to groups of customers with business to discuss. And directly below them the expanse of floor, empty during the day, was beginning to fill up with the same sorts of people who had populated the space ten years previously. The roving flotsam and jetsam of society.

Jeff looked with amazement at the figures below. For a moment he followed the progress of a girl in a white sharkskin suit as she wobbled her bottom over to a small table in front of the booths and sat down beside a man in dark glasses and an even darker tan. Then he looked to one of the booths where four men were talking on telephones: three on mobiles and one on the phone attached to the table. They appeared to be selling something – but their currency was arm gestures and not money. Over at the bar the depleted remains of something once called a man was talking at the bartender. And the bartender was polishing a glass and listening with that plastic smile people wear when they're trying not to scream.

Jeff had been in the club only twice before, but it and its customers had looked identical.

Marty's reaction was even stronger. Ten years ago he had worked in this place; now it was as if those years had not passed. He felt distinctly peculiar. And he didn't need to ask Wyvern about total recall. It had all come back with a vengeance. To his intense surprise, he felt rather moist around the eye department.

Trying to quell the emotion, he turned to Jeff and announced, in a strangely gruff voice, that it was time to get a drink. 'And,' he counselled, as they headed down the stairs, 'you're drinking Bourbon, not beer.'

'I am?'

'You are. It's what they expect private investigators to drink in a place like this.'

'Which reminds me,' said Jeff. 'Why did you say I was a private investigator? There's nothing like having your cover blown at the very beginning.'

'Exactly,' said Marty. 'If people know who you are, it's just a matter of time before they start telling you things.'

'What things?'

'Ah!' Marty's smile was cryptic. 'Exactly. What things?'

Jeff shrugged and walked down another few steps. 'I am *not*,' he said, 'middle-aged.'

'Did I say that?'

'You did. You also said my parents are dead and I have no brothers or sisters. That's not true either.'

'Ah. Well, you see, I was talking about me...apart from the middle-aged bit, of course. And the bit about the crisps.'

Jeff sighed and followed Marty towards the bar. Catching the bartender's eye, he smiled and asked for a Bourbon.

'You shouldn't smile,' said an irritated Marty. 'And less of the "can I have" and "please". You just say "Bourbon".'

As he spoke, the bartender filled a shot glass and, without a word, sent it sliding down the bar towards Jeff. The movement was so quick that Jeff failed to stop the glass and it went shooting past him. It was

Marty, with a monumental effort of will, who sprang forward and stopped the glass before it fell off the edge of the bar.

The bartender watched the glass seemingly stop of its own free will. 'Cool.' He said. 'That's a new one on me.' He looked admiringly at Jeff and reached for the bottle again. 'Have another one. On the house.'

Jeff smiled uncertainly. He didn't even like Bourbon and the last thing he wanted to do was to get drunk. A sinking feeling in his stomach told him this evening wasn't going to go exactly as planned. That thought reminded him of another night when a similar fear had visited him, and of events that had taken place at that time.

Beside him, Marty was also thinking of the past. And this time his memory came up trumps. It allowed him complete recall of what happened on that fateful night...

Marty Hopkirk finished his act with a flourish and a theatrical bow. His final number was always fast, frenetic and furious, and this one had been no exception. Breathing deeply, heart thundering in his chest, he drew himself to his full height, lifted his arms into the air and bestowed a dazzling smile on his raucous audience.

Even the optimistic Marty had to admit that the raucousness wasn't really directed at him and that the word 'audience' was something of a misnomer. Half of the Terrapin's clientele were oblivious to his presence and those who had watched his routine had done so with expressions of such vacuity that their mental presence had to be doubted. The most vacant among them – men and women alike – wore heavy make-up and haunted expressions, staring at the world through ghoulish, unseeing eyes. One of them, a creature of indeterminate sex, shouted something in Marty's direction. Marty brightened and, gold suit shimmering, twirled niftily in response to the plea to 'Get them off!' It didn't occur to him that the strange creature had actually shouted, 'Get off!'

But Marty did get off the stage. He looked discreetly at his watch and weaved his purposeful way through the assembled throng. He had business to do – and very little time to do it.

As he weaved, the music began again. This time it was a slow, rhythmic yet slightly eerie throb that had an electrifying effect on the people on the floor. They began to move as one, but with no indication that they were together or even that they were enjoying themselves. Vacant and unblinking, holding glasses of fluorescent cocktails and not moving their feet, they bent their knees and, without moving their heads, bobbed up and down.

Marty felt a stab of irritation as he left the dance floor. What was wrong, he wondered, with proper dancing? Why couldn't they continue to enjoy *his* sort of music and celebrate the Bob Fosse moves that he had rehearsed with such gusto? People nowadays had no taste.

Marty didn't dare admit to himself that they had different tastes. Or that, at the grand age of twenty-eight, he was too old for them.

Beyond the dance floor, things were much more to his taste. The timeless quality that was the true hallmark of the Terrapin reigned among the booths and around the bar. For a moment he followed the progress of a girl in a white sharkskin suit as she wobbled her bottom over to a small table in front of the booths and sat down beside a man in dark glasses and an even darker tan. Then he looked to one of the booths where four men were talking. One was on the telephone attached to the table while the others were barking instructions at him and arguing with each other. All of them appeared to be selling something – but their currency was arm gestures and not money. Marty pressed on towards the bar, where the depleted remains of something once called a man was talking at the bartender. The bartender was polishing a glass and listening with that plastic smile people wear when they're trying not to scream. Marty tried, and failed, to catch his eye. As discreetly as he could, he raised a gold-clad arm in the air, but still the bartender failed to notice. Marty bit his lip. It was crucial that he attract Dave Day's attention in the next few minutes. Because from now on, every second counted. Every tiny ticking of the clock meant the passing of a vital moment.

While Dave continued to feign interest in the sad life of the no-hoper who dashed his dreams against every bar he could find, Marty looked around for Jeff Randall. He was glad to see that, unlike Dave, his solicitor friend was doing exactly what he had been rehearsed to do: engaging Don Carlos in a deep conversation about how he, Jeff Randall, could provide Don Carlos with the only thing he lacked – a bona fide lawyer with contacts in both the highest and the lowest places. Like others of his ilk, Don Carlos was monstrously vain, and Marty had known it would flatter his vanity to be actively courted by one of the city's leading law firms. The fact that Jeff was about to resign from that firm was, of course, irrelevant.

Marty was too far away to hear even snatches of their conversation, but Jeff's demeanour was enough to tell him that it was going according to plan. Jeff appeared enraptured by Don Carlos, nodding frequently, smiling continuously – and uttering hardly a word. Don Carlos needed little prompting to talk about his own importance. Marty sent a silent prayer of thanks to the Almighty for Jeff's involvement. Jeff was the perfect partner in this set-up: quiet, self-effacing and far happier talking about others than about himself. And he wasn't the only one listening to Don Carlos. At the neighbouring table, three of his minders were huddled together. Their conversation was desultory and sporadic; all three had their antennae strained for any strange move on Jeff's part and for any unsolicited approach by anyone even vaguely suspicious.

Marty looked at his watch again. Ten minutes to go. Dave *had* to get away from behind the bar. Again Marty approached him – and his heart leapt into his mouth. Dave was now serving another platoon of Don Carlos's minders, and that meant countless cocktails, shots and beers. There was no way he could leave the bar within the next few minutes. Worse, one suspicious move and the minions would be whipping out their semi-automatics. And if that happened Don Carlos would be out of the Terrapin like a bat out of hell. The big game would escape; the entire, intricate plan would be ruined.

He sidled as close as he dared to the bar. As he did so, Dave glimpsed him out of the corner of his eye. They exchanged a knowing, desperate look over Dave's cocktail shaker. 'I can't get away!' mouthed Dave. Marty looked bleakly back at his friend. Both men knew the consequences of that one. If Dave was caught with the rest of them, his elaborate computer scam would be uncovered in the ensuing inquiry.

Marty stood racking his brains for a solution, but it was Dave who found it. He leaned forward and, shielding his arm with his left shoulder, deftly extracted his keys and threw them at Marty. No words were exchanged. There was no need. Marty knew what he had to do.

He stole a quick glance at the beefy minders. Their collective stance assured him that they'd seen nothing. He slunk unobtrusively into the throng. There were two urgent tasks ahead of him. One was to wipe the computer program. The other was to find Tallulah Joplin and spirit her away before all hell let loose.

He found her at the other end of the bar. And the moment he saw her he stopped in his tracks and stared. He knew he was wasting precious time, but he couldn't help it. Tallulah was the sort of person you had to stop and stare at. No matter that he had seen her barely an hour previously, he still gawped. Tallulah wore that casually studied look that was all her own. One hand toyed with a glass of Bourbon. With the other she twirled a lock of hair in a gesture that was at once suggestive and innocent. The customer who occupied her attention was interested in the suggestion and not the innocence.

But Marty knew the suggestion was no more than that. It was a teasing indication of the fire that lay beneath the sultry exterior of the languid brunette. And the only person who could ignite that fire was Marty Hopkirk. The reptilian Don Carlos claimed ownership, but his rights were disputed. And not just by Marty. Tallulah had sworn that once tonight was over she would be with him for ever.

As if in affirmation of that fact, she suddenly looked up and locked eyes with Marty. Her expression gave nothing away, but the way her painted fingernails drummed against the bar was enough. She was primed and ready. Marty held up his right hand with all five fingers displayed.

Nothing in Tallulah's demeanour indicated that the sign had been a signal. She stared back in a vacant, unseeing way and then laughed at something her companion said. Seemingly in response, she pulled her scrap of mink over her bare shoulders, leaned towards the salivating man and whispered something in his ear. The rosebud lips touched his lobes. Then she giggled, put a talon-like finger to his mouth and slid elegantly off her barstool. Her companion responded with a leer that pretended to be a smile and took another slug of his drink. Tallulah had promised action and he had no reason to doubt her words.

But the action was not of the nature that he had anticipated. Precisely three minutes after Tallulah left him, the foyer doors burst open and riot police, guns and shields to the fore, stormed into the premises.

One of them stopped at the balustrade overlooking the club and yelled to the assembly below. 'Police!' he began rather unnecessarily. 'Hold your fire! We have you covered! Please put down your weapons!'

The words were the trigger for pandemonium Women began to scream, people stampeded to the back of the club, and Jeff Randall sprang from his seat and hurled himself behind the bar. That had been his instruction and he had rehearsed it to perfection. He had to. The consequences of failing to find cover would probably have led to his death.

A split second after the policeman screamed his warning, one of the minders at the bar lifted his pistol and shot him in the mouth. He screamed and toppled down into the scrum that was developing below. At the same time, the police flooding down the stairs opened fire on the group of minders and, where there had once been music in the air, there was now the deafening rattle of machine-gun fire. And where the atmosphere had been thick with cigarette smoke, it was now leaden and pungent with clouds of cordite.

The minders surrounding Don Carlos joined the fray, all the while protecting their boss and moving him back towards the rear of the club. Outnumbered by the police, they were aided by the mass of people trying desperately to escape with them and preventing the police from getting a clean shot.

They themselves weren't so concerned about sparing the lives of the Terrapin's clientele. They fired indiscriminately, aiming at the police in particular and at the room in general. The more bodies they could place between themselves and the police, the better their chances of escape.

The realization that they were being shot at increased the panic among the crowd. Several of them hurled themselves at the police in a desperate bid for protection; others flew up the stairs, hampering the descent of more of the riot squad.

But the minders at the bar caused the greatest mayhem. As soon as the policemen entered, they leapt on to the bar itself and, with the advantage of height, two of them began to pick out the policemen already on the floor. The other two turned to the sweeping staircase and fired repeatedly at the screaming mass of humanity. Policemen and punters alike tumbled over the banisters and added to the bleeding, writhing pile of bodies below.

Still more policemen kept coming. One scored a direct hit and a minder shooting from the bar screamed as a salvo of bullets ripped right through him. In the throes of death, he arched backwards – his hands still locked on the trigger of his weapon. As it swung up, the bullets kept pumping out, peppering the walls and the roof of the club. And the giant chandelier that hung above. Great shards of glass came raining down, spearing the screaming people below. And then, foreshadowed by an ominous lurch, the chandelier itself plunged thirty feet to the floor, flattening those beneath it. Pinned to the ground, several were killed instantly, while the rest were condemned to flounder in a bloodbath until the breath left their bodies.

Behind the bar, Jeff Randall and Dave Day found shelter under the shelves. Splinters of glass came their way as stray bullets smashed into the optics. Blood from first one dead minder and then another pumped and seeped its way down on to them, but neither man moved a muscle. Of all the places to be amid the carnage, this was the safest.

As planned, Marty and Tallulah missed the main part of the action. When the police stormed into the Terrapin, they were poised at the door that led to the offices and private rooms of the club. Poised because they had no intention of breaching the threshold until the posse of Don Carlos's minders in the quarters beyond were called out into the club itself.

They pressed themselves against the wall, Marty sheltering Tallulah's head in the crook of his shoulder. 'Any minute now,' he whispered. 'Any minute now and the rest of those goons will be called and we'll...Shit!'

The expletive coincided with the door beside them being kicked open with astonishing force and the emergence of Don Carlos's remaining body-guards. Like their peers, they wore dinner jackets that were bursting at the seams and dark glasses, and they carried sub-machine guns. With the exception of the last one to rush through the door. He was weighed down with a bazooka. All of them hit the room shooting and none of them noticed Marty and Tallulah cowering beside the door.

'C'mon!' urged Marty as soon as they'd passed. 'We haven't much time.'

Grabbing Tallulah's arm, he darted into the corridor and ran hell for leather along it and up the staircase at the end, Tallulah's six-inch stilettos clattering behind him.

At the top of the stairs they fell against the wall for a moment, gulping in great lungfuls of air. Marty was used to exertion from his dancing, but the added element of fear wasn't doing much for his heart-rate. And while Tallulah had made a career out of panting breathily, it wasn't usually from this sort of activity.

'If bloody Don Carlos,' heaved Marty, 'hadn't started posting guards all over the place, Dave could have sorted out the computer long ago. Why'd he do it anyway?'

'I don't know.' Tallulah rearranged her snippet of mink and her impossibly small black dress. 'Maybe he was suspicious or something.'

'He's always suspicious.' Marty shrugged, dismissed all thoughts of Don Carlos and his guards, and reached for Tallulah's hand again. 'Come on. Five minutes and it should all be over.'

'I'll be *so* happy when it's all over.'

'I know, love,' said Marty with a squeeze of her

hand. 'And then we can be together for ever, eh?'

They were running again, and Marty couldn't see the look on Tallulah's face. It suggested that she had other plans. Plans that didn't involve Marty.

They stopped at the door at the end of the corridor. 'Just hope they didn't have time to lock it,' said Marty as he turned the handle.

They hadn't had time. The door swung open.

'OK…computer.' Marty looked around the room that Don Carlos called his counting house. It was a veritable treasury, but the treasure was firmly locked in a bank of safes along one wall. Marty was looking for something that might have been valuable to a petty thief but small fry for Don – a laptop computer.

Tallulah found it. 'Here,' she gasped, still struggling for breath and pointing at the small machine on the desk at the far end of the room.

'Keys…keys,' mumbled Marty as he extracted them from his pocket.

Crossing the room, he chose the smallest one and inserted it into a lock beside the disk drive. A bright yellow disk popped out.

'Aha!' exclaimed a triumphant Marty. 'Eureka!' Then he sat down at the computer.

Tallulah frowned. 'What are you doing? Why don't you just take the disk?'

'The program's on the hard drive as well,' explained Marty as he tapped. 'Encrypted. But there's *just* a possibility someone might find it. I couldn't do that to Dave.' He smiled up at Tallulah as she undulated towards him, stood behind his chair and draped her arms around his neck.

'You *are* sweet,' she purred. 'A truly honourable man. Not many people would do that. Especially when they're in…danger.'

'But I couldn't let Dave down.' Marty sounded quite shocked at the very idea. 'The police will take everything, every bloody *paper clip*, and it wouldn't take them long to trace all these records back to Dave. He's been so good to us. This is the least I can do. I won't be a minute,' he added, tapping furiously.

Nor will I, thought Tallulah, eyeing the yellow disk beside him.

Then Marty did something that made Tallulah's blood run cold. Before she could even react, he switched off the computer, reached for the disk and snapped it in two. As the colour drained out of Tallulah's face, he snapped the halves into quarters, dropped them into the bin and turned his smiling face back to her.

'There...All evidence destroyed. Hey!' Noting her sudden pallor, he reached out to her. 'Are you all right?'

'Yes...Yes, I'm fine.' Tallulah steadied herself on the back of the chair as the bottom fell out of her world. 'Just...well, I guess I overdid it. All that running,' she added with a weak attempt at a smile.

But Marty was doubly concerned now. He stared at the door with a worried frown. 'Look...the police are going to...Well, I don't want to push you, but can you make one last effort? For me?'

Tallulah smiled again. 'Of course.' She stroked Marty's cheek with a long, pale hand. 'I'd do anything for you, Marty. Why,' she added in what she hoped was a nonchalant way, 'did you destroy the disk? I thought...I would have thought that Dave would want to keep it.'

'Oh, no,' said Marty. 'Doesn't need it. He's got another copy at home.' Then he started patting his suit pockets in a distracted fashion. 'Keys. What did

I do with his keys?'

A glint came into Tallulah's eyes. Dave's keys. Dave's house keys. She looked down at the desk. 'Here,' she said, picking them up.

'Ta.' Marty took them and slipped them into his jacket pocket. 'Now come on! We're outta here!'

Tallulah followed Marty to the door. As she caught up with him she slipped a nimble hand into the pocket, cupped her fist round the keys and extracted them. Still behind Marty's back, she then dropped them into her cleavage.

A minute later they were running down the lower corridor towards the back exit of the club when a violent crash came from behind, followed by the stentorian tones of the riot police. 'Stop or we'll shoot! Hands above the head and turn round. Slowly. But do it NOW!'

Marty did as he was told. Almost in slow motion, he raised his hands and swung round to face five policemen pointing guns at him. One of them, the tall man who had barked the orders, was bleeding profusely from a wound on his chin.

But it wasn't the wound, the orders or the armed officers who caused Marty to catch his breath. It was the absence of Tallulah Joplin. She had vanished.

He never saw her again.

'Marty? Mar-ty?'

'Oh…yeah…hi.' Marty blinked and looked at Jeff through unfocused eyes. Then he blinked again. Several times.

'You were miles away.'

'Was I? Oh…well, I guess I was. Well, I *am*. I'm dead.'

'Yes,' said Jeff, 'but you looked like you were having a dream. I didn't know dead people had dreams.'

'No…yes…well, I didn't know either.'

'Funny really,' mused Jeff. 'I was having a sort of dream as well. I was remembering that night, sheltering behind the bar while all hell was being played out. Christ knows how I got out of that alive.'

'Jeff?'

'Mmm?'

'I think I'm fading.'

'Are you?' Jeff peered at his friend. 'Yes…you do look a bit…vague.'

'I've run out of energy. I'm going to have to leave you.'

Jeff seemed unconcerned. The inquiries he had made thus far had led nowhere. No one he had talked to remembered Dave Day. He started to walk away from the bar and towards the sweeping stairway of the Terrapin.

'Never mind. We can come back another night. We'll probably have to come back a few times. Can't really expect to strike lucky with Dave Day on our first visit.'

'But we have struck lucky, Jeff.'

'Eh?'

'In my…dream. I remembered something. When Tallulah vanished, she stole something from me.'

'Oh? What?'

'Dave Day's keys.'

Jeff frowned. Then he shook his head. 'Nah. I know Jeannie said she's mad, but that can't be why she wants to find him.'

'You've lost me.'

'She's hardly going to move heaven and earth –

and pay us a lot of money – just so she can find him and give him his keys back. Anyway, he wants to kill her. Jeannie said so.'

But Marty was deep in thought. 'He has reason to want to kill her,' he said carefully. 'She stole the keys to Dave's house. Dave had a copy of his computer program in the house. That program was worth a fortune. Dave was going to develop it. He had this daft plan that one day he could tap into other financial institutions and take over the world.'

'And you didn't think to tell the police?'

Marty spread his arms before him: a metaphor for his innocence. 'Well, Dave went to prison...The police raided his house...I never even thought twice about the keys. I assumed,' he finished in a small voice, 'that the police had taken the program and destroyed it.'

'But Tallulah got there first?'

Marty flickered before Jeff's eyes. His ectoplasm was rapidly disintegrating. Struggling to stay with Jeff for a moment longer, he managed to utter an oblique answer. 'Beware,' he whispered, 'the Angel with the Broken Wing...'

Then he was gone.

chapter nine

The tall man was seething. 'We were *this* far away,' he said, extending thumb and forefinger. '*This* far.'

Tallulah looked at the monitor; at the brutal message that had appeared, yet again, on the screen: 'Access Denied'.

She sighed. 'And there's *nothing* you can do? Nothing?'

'No. I've tried everything.' Then he swivelled round in his chair and fixed Tallulah with a steely glare. 'I can't believe you could have been so stupid.'

Two livid red spots appeared on Tallulah's cheeks. 'How dare you?' she spat. 'How *dare* you blame me?'

'Because,' he said simply, 'it's your fault.'

Tallulah sprang up and began to pace the room, her stilettos snapping furiously against the steel floor. 'It is *not* my bloody fault! *You're* supposed to be the computer expert. *You're* supposed to be the genius.' She jabbed a talon-like finger in his direction. 'Why didn't you build in some sort of...well, anti-hacking thing?'

'Because,' answered her companion in a flat,

chilling tone, 'you told me there was no other program like this in existence. No other language like this. No way that anyone else could find out what we were doing. Well, there is.' He pointed at the screen. Below the 'Access Denied' statement there was now a polite and encouraging 'Try Again?'

'Aaaargh!' spat the tall man. He leaned forwards and switched off the computer. Then he took a deep breath and turned back to the furious Tallulah. 'Look, we're just going over the same ground again. We know it's Dave Day. We know,' he added, unable to resist another jibe at Tallulah, 'that he must have had another copy you didn't know about.'

'Wrong! There was only one disk. I searched everywhere.'

'Oh, yes. So you did. A proper little sleuth, aren't you, my dear?'

Tallulah ignored him. Instead, she started to pace the room again. Then she held up a hand, fending off a further flood of criticism. 'The only mistake I've made – the *only* mistake over the last ten years – was not knowing that Marty Hopkirk had died.'

The tall man looked intently at her. 'That really bugs you, doesn't it? It really, really, really needles you...'

'Stop it!'

'And why does it bother you so much, my sweet?' The tall man's voice was barely a whisper.

Tallulah whirled round. 'You know why! I wanted to kill him myself! I wanted Marty to know that *I* organized it all. That *I* knew all about Dave Day's program. That *I* – and nobody else – was going to rule the world!' Then she reached into her sleeve for a handkerchief and blew her nose. 'I wanted to show him that I wasn't just a sultry vamp.'

'Exactly.'

'Or,' sniffed Tallulah, 'a silly angel.'

'With Broken Wings.'

Tallulah shot a nasty look in his direction. Then she swallowed and held her head high. 'If Dave Day hadn't reappeared and ruined it all, I wouldn't even have thought of Marty again. I'd quite forgotten about him.' She uttered the last words as if trying them out for size. She decided they fitted. 'Yes. I'd forgotten about him.'

'And now,' said the tall man, 'instead of Marty, we've got this little Randall person and...what's her name?'

'Jeannie.'

'Yes. *Suspicious* Jeannie.'

Tallulah placed her handkerchief back in her sleeve. 'She's not suspicious any more. She...well, I think she thinks I'm mad.'

'Mmm.' The tall man lost himself in his thoughts for a moment. 'You know,' he said at length, 'the Randall and Jeannie thing isn't such a problem after all. We'll just have to kill them instead of Marty.'

'But how on earth are they going to be able to find Dave if they don't know what he looks like?'

'Are you sure about that?'

'Pretty sure.' Tallulah too remained pensive for a moment. 'I just don't think that Jeff Randall ever met Dave Day. There was something in his expression when I told him about Dave. At the time I thought...well, I thought he'd been transported back ten years. The more I think about it, the more certain I am that he didn't have a clue who I was talking about.'

'Then why would he have accepted the job?'

'Well, he can't be completely stupid. He knew who

I was. It wouldn't have taken much to realize I wasn't there just to bury some ghosts from the past. Anyway, I offered them vast amounts of money. They obviously needed it. You should,' she finished, in the superior way of one who owns an underground palace with all mod cons as well as a country house, 'have seen their office. Shabby was not the word.'

But the tall man wasn't interested in shabbiness. 'OK. But they're bona fide private detectives, aren't they? There's no reason why they shouldn't find Dave. When they do, we can send Lucifer or Gabriel or someone to bump him off.'

Tallulah, however, wasn't pleased with that one. She didn't want Archangels muscling in on her business. 'No! I want Dave here! I want to punish him for rewriting his program. And,' she added with a visible frisson of excitement, 'I want him to know that *I* was the mastermind all along!'

The tall man looked at her under his lashes. Tallulah had always had a high opinion of herself. But now she seemed to be teetering on the brink of egomania. And that really wouldn't do. He didn't want her trespassing on his territory.

'Fine,' he said. 'But in the meantime there's the rather more pressing matter of what we're going to do about this.' He gestured towards the computer.

'Ye-es,' conceded Tallulah. 'We do have a little problem. When are the delegates coming back?'

The question was rhetorical. Tallulah knew as well as he did when they were arriving. The tall man raised an eyebrow. 'Tomorrow.'

'Yes. Tomorrow. Well, we'll have to have something to show them.'

'If,' said the tall man, 'we can convince them that we're ready to be up and running, then they'll release the last payments.'

'And how are we going to do that? By showing them that we're "Access Denied" to the entire network? They'll love that.'

The tall man stood up and gesticulated wildly around him. 'Artifice, Tallulah! That's what this place is all about! Pretence. I mean, what use is it? It's nothing but a giant sham to impress them.'

'So?'

'So we create another giant sham. We've got print-outs; we've got access numbers; we can show them the balance of every major financial institution in the world. And,' he finished with a triumphant gleam, 'we can show them the money disappearing from those institutions.'

'No we can't,' said an exasperated Tallulah. 'We can't get *access*.'

'Indeed. So we just create a completely artificial program. It's as easy as falling off a log. I can do it in a matter of hours. And tomorrow,' he continued with a wild gesture towards the domed meeting room, 'when they're sitting there, they'll be salivating over a giant screen that shows money being siphoned into their accounts. Billions of pounds!' he shouted. 'Trillions! Great whacking heaving zillions of pounds pouring into their accounts!'

'And what happens when they find out it's all a great whacking heaving fraud?'

The tall man didn't reply. Instead, with the faintest hint of a suggestion, he looked straight at Tallulah.

It didn't take long for comprehension to dawn. A slow smile spread across Tallulah's face. 'Ah,' she said, turning on her spiky heels. 'I'll go and alert the girls.'

When she had left the room, the tall man turned back to the computer, rebooted and started accessing the files already saved. A few minutes were all he needed to confirm that he had enough information for his purposes. And the names and figures flickering in front of him would make for an impressive presentation. With a satisfied sigh, he applied all his energies to his task. As he worked, various financial institutions, together with details of their entire reserves, appeared on his screen. Among them were the Bank of Britain, the Federal Bank of the Federation, the Heavenly Dollar Depository of Guangzhou and the Rostov-Pereslavsky Bank of the New Rich. Those four institutions alone contained more money than he could even imagine.

But soon, of course, he wouldn't have to imagine.

Tallulah reverted to Angelic mode while she was in the lift. Sometimes she cursed the dual life she was obliged to lead, but on other occasions – like today – she sent up a prayer of thanks to the genius who had masterminded the Angels set-up.

That genius was none other than Tallulah Joplin. She was prepared to credit the tall man for organizing a few little details, like the construction of the underground palace and his international contacts but it was she, Tallulah, who had founded Angels with Broken Wings.

And what a success it had been, she reflected, as she exited the lift, strode along the corridor and peered through the tiny hole that corresponded, in the room beyond, to one of St Peter's chain links. The little camera hidden therein informed her that the library was empty. Satisfied, she pressed the button beside her. St Peter's arm slid back and Tallulah stepped into the peaceful, rarefied – and successful – world of the Angels.

The key, she thought, was gullibility. Women, and now men, were perpetually on the hunt for some sort of inner enlightenment, an elusive peace that, once found, would remain with them for ever. They seemed to have missed the point. There was no such thing as peace and enlightenment. There was only money.

Tallulah graciously conceded that the people who came to Angels were at least appreciative enough of money to have made, inherited or married vast amounts of it – and to give considerable amounts to her. And it wasn't as if they didn't see a return on it, mused Tallulah, as she left the library and padded (the stilettos had been replaced by white moccasins) into the marble hall. They had a nice rest in a beautiful house and, more important, a respite from their ghastly spouses.

As she headed for the staircase, two women came out of the drawing room. One of them was Emma, the housekeeper. The other was a stranger to Tallulah.

'Ah, Tallulah,' said the former in her matter-of-fact way. 'Meet Jemima.' Smiling, she turned to the other woman. 'Jemima, Tallulah – one of our founder members.'

Jemima was thrilled. Like her husband, she had little truck with people who weren't important. And founder members were nothing if not important. She felt an invitation to join a committee – or perhaps a garden fête – coming on. 'Oh, how delightful,' she trilled. 'You must be so thrilled to have made such a success of this. And this building!' Jemima looked around her with the air of one who was impressed but not overawed. It wouldn't do to give the impression that one wasn't *au fait* with country houses. 'This sort of house is so conducive to rest, isn't it?'

Tallulah correctly surmised that Jemima was in need of a nice break in a beautiful house and a respite from her ghastly spouse. 'Thank you,' she said. 'And are we going to have the pleasure of your company for a while?'

'I...well—'

'Oh, you must,' interrupted Emma. She looked rather rudely at Jemima's complexion. 'Looking a bit peaky, I'd say. A spell here will do you the power of good.'

Jemima offered a weak smile in return. True, she was desperate for a respite from Henry, but she was also quite keen to impress her friends as soon as was humanly possible with her intimate knowledge of the Angels set-up. A brief visit, as far as she was concerned, counted as intimate knowledge.

'Well...I have to sort out a few things before I make any firm decisions. I only came for a quick look around. I can't check in now. My family,' she finished with a laugh, 'would think I'd disappeared off the face of the earth!'

'Well, it's up to you...Whenever you want, just let us know.' Then Tallulah turned to the other woman. 'Emma, when you've finished showing Jemima round, could we have a word? I'll be upstairs.' Flashing a last smile at Jemima, she left them and headed for the stairs.

In the residents' wing, she headed straight for Patience's room. With any luck, she thought, Patience would be having a good day. If so, she might have something worth reporting.

Patience, however, was having a bad day. Tallulah found her slumped over her tarot cards in floods of tears.

'What on earth's the matter?' asked Tallulah with a notable lack of sympathy.

'My gift,' moaned the weeping woman.

'Oh, God.' This was familiar ground. 'You've lost it again?'

'Yes,' sniffed Patience. 'There was some sort of interference. I turned over the Jack of Pentacles and there it was.'

'There what was?'

'Death,' wailed Patience. 'And the Fool. And the Magician! Three of the Major Arcana. It shouldn't happen like that. And then…and then it just went.'

'Oh.' Rather than offering reassurance, Tallulah stayed where she was and glared at Patience. Where once the woman had been invaluable for her gift of second sight, now she was rather a nuisance. Age, admittedly, had something to do with it. Patience had made no bones about the fact that once she reached fifty her second sight was likely to fade. But she hadn't warned anyone about her incipient hysteria. 'Look,' said Tallulah, 'it'll probably come back. It usually does.'

'No! No, it won't. It's gone for ever!'

But then Patience always said that.

'Well, if that's really the case,' snapped Tallulah, 'you'll just have to pretend.'

'Pretend?' For the first time since Tallulah had entered the room, Patience turned to face her. Her mascara was coursing down her cheeks and her hair, normally neatly bundled into a chignon, was in wild disarray. She stared at Tallulah in wide-eyed horror. 'I can't pretend! It's…it's the ultimate sacrilege.

Pretence,' she finished in a fearful whisper, 'is the Sword and the Tower in the Tarrochi of Mantegna.'

As usual, Tallulah hadn't a clue what Patience was on about. 'I'm afraid I don't really care. You know the rules, Patience. You've always known them. When the time comes, you'll be required to act.'

'And the time has come?'

'Tomorrow.' Tallulah was tempted to add that if Patience hadn't mislaid her gift they might have had a prior warning. But that would just open the floodgates. Instead, she issued Patience with her instructions. 'You will be required,' she said, 'to deal with the delegate from Carpathia.'

'Carpathia?'

'Yes. He's superstitious. Spin him some yarn or other and he'll swallow it. But make it good. And keep him occupied until you get the signal.' Without giving her the chance to reply, Tallulah promptly left the room.

At the table, Patience sniffed and tentatively reached for a card. It was the Fool. She gulped back a sob and reached for the card beside it. The Magician. She burst into tears.

Tallulah stalked past the next-door apartment. As usual, the thin, reedy voice of the elderly woman wafted through the closed door and into the corridor. Tallulah frowned as she passed by. If Patience was next to useless, Shirley had lost it completely. Once famed for her booming voice and powers of seduction, she was now a mere shadow of her formal self. It was a pity, reflected Tallulah, that the time to act had come rather too late for some of the Angels.

Tatiana and Tiffany, on the other hand, were still very much on the ball. Tallulah visited their apartments next and issued them with their instructions. Rather than resist or demur, they listened intently and nodded enthusiastic agreement. Tiffany even licked her lips.

On the floor below, Sapphire and Xenia reacted in a similar fashion. So, further along the corridor, did Fatima, Kitty and Serenity Blush. Things were looking up. The delegates were going to get far more than they'd bargained for when they paid their next visit to Angels. Their last visit.

Tallulah's last port of call was to Rosa. But just as she raised a fist to slam it against the door and make herself heard, she caught a glimpse of her watch. Now wasn't the time. Smiling to herself, she headed for her own room to prepare for the meeting with Emma. Dear old Rosa, she thought. Despite her age and increasing decrepitude, she could still teach the younger girls a thing or two. Not, of course, about seduction. That had never really been her thing. But she was a fighter. And she was always at her best after her afternoon nap. Tallulah made a mental note to visit her later.

chapter
ten

Jeannie nearly dropped the armful of files she was carrying. 'Oh! I didn't see you there,' she said, startled. 'Er...can I help you?'

'I doubt it,' said the fat man who all but had her pinned against the office door. 'But you can relay a message for me.'

Struggling with the files, Jeannie threw him a tentative smile. 'And what's that?'

'You can tell Marty Hopkirk he's a dead man.'

One of the files slipped out of Jeannie's arms, sending its contents cascading all over the floor. She made no attempt to retrieve it, but hugged the others to her chest and looked at the man with a quizzical expression.

'No, actually,' she said at length. 'I can't.'

'And why's that?' sneered her visitor. 'Scared, eh?'

'No, I'm not remotely scared. I'm just being realistic.'

This time it was the man who looked puzzled. 'Eh?'

'You can't,' sighed Jeannie, 'tell a dead man he's dead. It doesn't work that way, you see.'

'What doesn't work that way?' The bluff confidence had gone and the man was beginning to look uneasy.

'The world,' said a world-weary Jeannie. 'You can't talk to dead people.'

The man's uneasiness gave way to unsteadiness. He leaned on the doorframe for support. 'You mean...Marty *is* dead?'

'Yup.' By way of illustration, Jeannie moved away from the door, revealing the glass pane inscribed with the legend 'Randall & Hopkirk (Deceased). Security Services'.

'Deceased,' explained Jeannie helpfully, 'means dead.' Then she saw the expression on the man's face and took pity on him. 'I think you'd better come in...Mr Day?' she said with a gracious smile.

'How...how do you know who I am?'

'How about,' replied Jeannie as she placed the files on the table in the outer office, 'if I say it's a long story? One that started ten years ago?'

'I was wearing a gold lamé suit, said Marty. 'With sequins.'

'Oh dear.' Wyvern wrinkled his nose. 'Well, we all make mistakes.'

'Actually,' said Marty with sartorial superiority, 'it was rather fetching. It was quite the thing ten years ago.'

'White,' said Wyvern, 'suits you better.' He wasn't having Marty getting all uppity about clothes. A white suit had been chosen for Marty and that, as far as Wyvern was concerned, was that. For ever. 'Anyway,' he added, 'white is *de rigueur* in limbo.'

But Marty knew better than that. 'The barman wears a pink suit.'

'No, he doesn't.'

'He does! I've seen him!'

Wyvern's patience was beginning to wear thin.

'No, Marty, you *imagine* he wears a pink suit. For some reason – I couldn't possibly hazard a guess as to why – you want the barman to stand out from everyone else. He is, in fact, wearing a white suit.'

'He is?'

'Yes.'

Marty thought about that one for a moment. He supposed it made sense. The booze in limbo was imaginary – that's why so many people were teetotal. What, a few bored souls had told him, was the point of drinking if you couldn't get drunk? In fact, lots of things in limbo were imaginary. Marty's subconscious had obviously invented the pink suit to add a bit of colour, a touch of spice. Just wait, he thought, until I give my concert.

'Does that mean,' he asked Wyvern, 'that I can imagine I'm wearing a gold lamé suit with sequins when I'm performing?'

'You can imagine whatever you want.'

Marty looked suspiciously at the other man. He detected a lack of interest, boredom even. Then he remembered what it was. As he had announced to Jeff, it was jealousy. Wyvern was destined to spend eternity here in this room, comforting lost souls, while he, Marty Hopkirk, was about to launch a new career and sing his way to stardom. Poor Wyvern.

Then poor Wyvern took the wind out of his sails. 'You can't, of course, give your concert in limbo while you're working on a case with Jeff.'

'What?'

'Oh, no.' Wyvern waved a finger in front of Marty's nose. 'That's definitely against the rules.'

Marty was horrified. 'But…but I've been to limbo before when I've been on a case.'

'Not in the capacity of an artiste.'

'Eh? I don't see...I mean, what's the problem?'

'Oh, Marty, you've still got so much to learn.' Sighing, Wyvern stood up and, bard-like, began to declaim:

Limbo forbids the performance at night
Of misguided souls who dare to moonlight.
First earthly cases must be solved,
Only then can the artiste be absolved.

Good, isn't it?' he said, finishing with a theatrical flourish.

'But I don't have any earthly troubles! Well, not beyond the usual ones, anyway.'

'I didn't say troubles, Marty. I said cases – and you have a case.'

'Oh.'

'Sorry, but those are the rules.'

Marty was beginning to panic. 'Daytime, then. Can't I perform during the day? A matinée. People love matinées.'

But Wyvern was at his most schoolmasterly. Resolute and intractable, he folded his arms across his chest and looked down at his sulking protégé. 'No. No, you can't perform during the day. And do you know why, Marty? You should – I've told you several times.'

Marty hung his head. 'No, I don't know.' He left the words 'And I don't care' hanging in the air.

'Because,' explained Wyvern, 'it's always night in limbo.'

'You never told me that.'

Wyvern rolled his eyes. 'I did, actually. Many times. Think of it, Marty. What would be the point of having days in limbo? Mythology would have to be rewritten and, goodness, that would be time-consuming. Oh, no.' Shuddering at the thought, he then sat down again beside Marty. 'It's always,' he repeated, 'night in limbo.'

'But...'

'And if you think you've been there in daylight then you've been imagining things.' For once Wyvern sounded quite cross.

'Oh.' Then Marty brightened somewhat. 'Oh, well, I suppose there's one good thing about it always being night. The bar,' he finished with a wicked grin, 'will always be open.'

'Oh, Marty. Booze and, well, girls and that sort of thing. You've left them all behind. Think of the broader picture.'

'What broader picture? All I see is an empty canvas stretching out before me.' Gloom descended with a vengeance. 'All I see are empty days—'

'And nights.'

'Stretching before me.'

Wyvern made a pyramid of his hands and looked piously at his companion. 'So why don't you go and help Jeff then?'

'Jeff doesn't need me. It's an open and shut case. Tallulah's the villain – not Dave Day. All Jeff has to do is tell the police...'

'And that,' finished Jeff, 'is the story so far.' He leaned back in his chair, looked at Dave Day and then flashed a smile at Jeannie, who was perched on the edge of his desk.

Jeannie was looking with concern at Dave. He must, she reflected, have been very good-looking when he was younger, before the black hair had turned grey and the weight had piled on. He would have been quite a catch. But not now. Not with the prison-issue moustache and the hangdog expression. Especially not now that he was slumped in his chair with his mouth wide open, his eyes signalling stunned disbelief.

'Tallulah Joplin,' he said, eventually breaking the silence. 'I can't believe it. She was just...well, she was a ...'

'A vamp?'

Dave looked up at Jeannie. 'Yeah. A sultry vamp. She was all fishnets and raven hair and stilettos and...well, she didn't have a brain in her head.'

'Wrong. She had – and has – a very good brain. There's a lot more to Tallulah than meets the eye.'

'Especially now,' added Jeff.

'You mean the Angels thing?' Dave's mind was still reeling.

'Yeah. Angels,' corrected Jeff, 'with Broken Wings.'

'But I can't believe she's smart enough to have opened the program and developed it to the extent she has.' Dave gestured to the laptop he had earlier placed on Jeff's desk. 'It takes a near-genius to crack into the likes of the Heavenly Dollar Depository of Guangzhou and the Rostov-Pereslavsky Bank of the New Rich. She was,' he said in awe, '*this* close to siphoning off most of their reserves.'

'Until you came out of prison and managed to stop her,' said an impressed Jeannie. 'You must have a fantastic memory to have been able to reconstruct the program in...What is it? Three weeks?'

'Oh, no,' said Dave. 'I rewrote most of it in prison. I did a computer course as part of my rehabilitation. It was just a question of waiting till I got out to set it all up.' He turned back to Jeff. 'But I still refuse to believe that Tallulah Joplin could have developed the program all by herself.'

'Oh, I don't think there's any question of that,' said Jeannie. She cast her mind back to her visit to Angels. 'If there's more to Tallulah than meets the eye, I think we can be pretty sure the same goes for Angels with Broken Wings.'

'But they're completely above board,' objected Jeff. 'You said so yourself.' He turned to Dave. 'They're even listed on the Stock Exchange. They're a really attractive investment. A philanthropic organization that makes money for its shareholders. Couldn't be better.'

'Precisely,' said Jeannie. 'It couldn't be a better front for hiding something illegal.'

'Like trying to take over the world with my computer program?' mused Dave. 'God, and to think I thought it was Marty.' He looked suddenly sad. 'Marty, my old mate Marty. Can't believe he's dead. And I never *really* believed it could be him.' He looked imploringly from Jeff to Jeannie. 'I didn't, you know. Marty would never have stolen from me. He wasn't a criminal. And he wouldn't have wanted to take over the world…Would he?'

Neither Jeff nor Jeannie responded. True, Marty hadn't been a criminal. But they both had a sneaking suspicion that he wouldn't have been entirely averse to ruling the world. It was the sort of thing that would have amused him – until, of course, he realized it was a full-time job.

'Well…' said Jeff.

But Dave's mind had gone back, yet again, to Tallulah. 'Now *her*…It doesn't surprise me one little bit that she was up to something dodgy. She was a right slippery thing. Finger in every pie, that one.'

'Oh?' Jeff was surprised. 'Marty told me you didn't know Tallulah very well.'

Jeannie looked curiously at Jeff. Odd, she thought. His memory seemed to be recovering at an alarming rate.

Dave snorted in derision. 'Oh, I knew enough about her...we all did. She played them all off against each other. Don Carlos...Marty...she even had the chief of police in her clutches at one stage. A right little minx she was. Always had her eye on the main chance.'

Had Jeannie been the sort of girl to indulge in bouts of feeling smug, she would have indulged herself to the hilt. She had been right. There were plenty of reasons to feel suspicious about Tallulah. And Marty, she thought. Poor, naïve, enthusiastic Marty. Look what he had unwittingly got himself into all those years ago. Blindly blundering in where angels fear to tread.

Jeff, however, had his mind on the present – and on one particularly pertinent part of it. 'Er...Dave?'

'Yeah?'

'We're in something of a fix here.' He scratched his head and looked at the spider plant on the filing cabinet. 'When I was a solicitor it would have been called "professional embarrassment".'

'Eh?'

'Well...Tallulah is our client, right? She hired us to find you because she claimed you'd been sending her threatening notes.'

'But I never! Why would I have been sending her threatening notes?'

It was a pensive – and accurate – Jeannie who responded. 'I suspect you had every reason to send her threatening notes.' She bent closer to Dave. 'Why did you go to prison, Dave?'

The newly released convict looked suddenly furious. 'Because of some trumped-up charges of possessing heroin. Some bastard stitched me up. Somebody...Oh!' Horrified comprehension was beginning to dawn. 'Oh, God.' Dave put his head in his hands. 'It was Tallulah, wasn't it? She was the one who planted the drugs in my locker before the raid.'

'It *must* have been her.' Jeannie cast her mind back to her visit to Angels. 'Tallulah told me that you'd tried to lay the blame on her during your trial. I thought that was a bit odd at the time. She wasn't at your trial, was she? She'd already disappeared.'

'Yep. Vanished into thin air. I did try to lay the blame on someone – Don Carlos. I was sure it was him. But he was dead, see. They wanted a scapegoat and the stuff *was* among my belongings, so...well, so there you have it.' Dave looked balefully at Jeff. 'Ten years of my life in the slammer. Ten years being branded a criminal when I'd done nothing wrong.'

Jeff was now beginning to look distinctly uncomfortable. 'Well...um, that's just what I was coming to. Tallulah is our client and, from what we've discovered today, she's been lying to us.' A fact corroborated, although he wisely didn't say so, by the memories evoked during his and Marty's visit to the Terrapin.

'So?'

'So we can't act for her any more. Because we suspect she's a criminal. Just as...well, just as you are.'

'I'm not a criminal!'

Solicitor-like, Jeff spread his hands on the desk and looked Dave in the eye. 'The credit card scam, that was criminal. And so is the little matter of you resurrecting your program and trying to take over the world's financial institutions.'

'Oh, come on!' snorted Dave. 'What do you think I spent most of the last ten years in prison doing?'

Eating by the looks of it, thought Jeannie uncharitably.

'Beyond rewriting your computer program,' replied Jeff, 'I don't know. Which is why,' he added, 'I called the police.'

'You did *what*?'

Jeff stood up. 'I called the police.' He gestured towards the outer office. 'When I went out to make coffee. They should be here any minute.'

'But…but, well, *hang on*,' spluttered Dave. 'Why?'

Jeannie, while remaining perfectly still, was wearing an expression that indicated she, too, would like to know why Jeff had called the police. The image of a large cheque from Tallulah fluttered before her eyes before vanishing into the ether. At least Jeff could have waited until they'd conveyed the success of their mission to Tallulah. They had, after all, found the man she had been looking for. Or rather, he had found them.

But where Jeannie's primary consideration was money, Jeff's was memory. Specifically, the memory of that fateful night ten years ago in the Terrapin Club when youthful enthusiasm, derring-do and, he now realized, sheer foolhardiness had impelled him and Marty to take enormous and catastrophic risks. He was older now, and wiser too. And his sense of mortality had been heightened since those far-off days. Marty, the man who had breezed through life with barely a care in the world, was now dead. Or sort of dead. That fact, combined with the memories reawakened on the previous night's visit to the Terrapin, served to convince Jeff that certain risks were not worth taking. Especially if they involved the likes of Tallulah Joplin and Dave Day.

Sensing Jeannie's unspoken objection, Jeff ignored Dave and turned to her. 'Look,' he said with a slightly embarrassed shrug, 'I just think we're getting out of our depth here. Tallulah's been lying to us, there's obviously something really fishy about the Angels and...well, we're now in the presence of an ex-convict who wants to take over the world. I think it's time we handed the case over to the police.'

Dave Day shot to his feet with such alacrity that his chair overbalanced and went crashing to the floor. 'Look, you,' he said, wagging a fleshy finger at Jeff, 'I'm not here out of selfish motives! I'm doing this for the greater good of mankind! And if you're not going to help me...if you're just going to hold your hands in the air and hand me over to the police, then I'm outta here!' With that, Dave reached for his laptop, snapped it shut, glared at Jeff and Jeannie and then stormed into the outer office.

And that was as far as he got. In the ten minutes since Jeff's phone call, the long arm of the law had flexed its mighty muscles and extended its sinewy grip as far as the front door of Randall & Hopkirk (Deceased). In the formidable form of Inspector Large and Sergeant Liddel, it was barring Dave's exit route.

'That,' boomed the former, 'is as far as you're going to get, my man.' To illustrate his point, he held out a hand in the confident way he had perfected after years of stopping traffic. It stuck out rather too far from his beige mackintosh, looking more like a prop than a hand. But its message was clear, as was the steely glint from behind the horn-rimmed spectacles. 'Police,' he said.

Beside him, Sergeant Liddel's mackintosh appeared to inflate with importance. 'Plain-clothes police,' announced its occupant.

'So?'

Dave's pugnacious tone did little to endear him to Large. 'Your pugnacious tone,' he said, 'is doing little to endear you to me. I am,' he finished, 'Inspector Large.'

'Yeah. Well, I'm Dave Day and if you don't get out of my way I'm going to…going to…'

'Call the police?' Inspector Large allowed himself a smile. 'I think not. I think you'd be best advised to rejoin Mr Randall and Miss, er…Miss Hurst, or else I shall arrest you.'

'For what? I've done nothing wrong.'

'For conspiring to conspire to obstruct the course of justice.'

Jeff, who had been hovering at the door of his office, sensed an impasse in the offing. He coughed loudly and then addressed the senior policeman. 'Look, I'm sure if we all sit down we can sort this out in an amicable way. Mr Day hasn't, in fact, done anything wrong.'

'Oh? I thought you said he was an escaped convict.'

Jeff sighed. 'An *ex*-convict.'

Sergeant Liddel, however, was having none of that. 'Once a criminal, always a criminal, that's what I say,' he announced in his own liberal way. 'They get a taste for it, you know. Prison.'

'Yes, but he hasn't *escaped* from prison. He's been let out.'

'Always a mistake,' said Large. 'Shades of the prison yard.'

'What?' asked everyone else in unison.

'It's a quote.'

Jeff ushered them into the room and gestured to the various chairs. 'Look, let's just sit down and...er, sort it out. This isn't about escaped convicts. It's about a fairly serious attempt to...um...to take over the world.'

'Are you sure that the police will believe Jeff?'

'Why shouldn't they? He's a pretty straight-forward bloke.'

Wyvern stroked his chin. 'Ye-es. But I can't help thinking this whole thing sounds rather...far-fetched.'

'Nah.' Marty returned to the task in hand – honing his skills with psychic wind.

'A plot to take over the world via computer?' continued Wyvern. 'An ex-convict sending death threats to a mad Angel with a Broken Wing? If I were a policeman I'm not sure if I'd have much time for a story like that.'

'Well, it's just as well you're a supernatural being, isn't it?' said Marty over his shoulder. 'Damn, why isn't this thing moving?' He straightened and, frowning, looked at the bowl on the table in front of him. He had been blowing like mad, but the wretched object had refused to budge. And that, he thought, was just ridiculous. He'd all but created typhoons before now. Bowl-blowing, really, was for beginners.

Still in his armchair behind Marty's back, Wyvern offered a suggestion. 'Perhaps there's too much hot air coming out of your mouth?' Too late, he remembered that Marty wasn't very good at sarcasm.

'Oh? D'you reckon? I'll try the other way round then.' Marty turned, bent forward and expelled a blast of psychic air from his nether regions. The bowl shot off the table and smashed to the ground. He was delighted. 'Hey! Not bad, eh?'

Wyvern was less enamoured of this display of skill. He held a hand to his nose and, looking balefully at his protégé, offered a suggestion that would oblige Marty to depart. 'Why,' he asked, 'don't you practise a spot of power-merging? You never know, it might help Jeff as well.'

'Do you really expect me to believe this?' asked the incredulous inspector. 'A plot to take over the world via computer? An ex-convict making death threats to a mad Angel with a Broken Wing. A ludicrous—'

'I did *not*,' protested Dave Day, 'send her death threats!'

'A ludicrous story harking back ten years to a man who might, just *might*, have some answers but who unfortunately can't share them with us because he's currently six feet under, fertilizing the daisies?'

Then Inspector Large remembered Jeannie and her loss. 'Oh…I'm sorry, Miss Hurst. That was tactless.'

Jeannie acknowledged the apology with a little bow of her head. But still she didn't speak – mainly because the only person she wanted to talk to was Jeff, and her words would not have been kind ones. This was one of the very few occasions when she was thoroughly annoyed with Jeff. First for calling the police, and then for regaling them with a story that, even to her, sounded preposterous.

Inspector Large took a few seconds to collect his thoughts and, in more measured tones, addressed

Jeff again. 'The thing is, Mr Randall, I really can't commit to wasting precious police time on a story about someone who may or may not have stolen a computer disk a decade ago. Furthermore, as you can't substantiate your accusations against this Angel with a Broken Wing, I don't see what grounds I could have for investigating her. It's very serious,' he finished in a reverential tone, 'to level such accusations against an Angel. They're...well, they're hallowed. Saintly.'

'God-fearing,' added Sergeant Liddel with authority.

Large turned to Dave Day. 'However, I'm prepared to concede that this gentleman is up to no good.'

'Oh, great. That's just great, isn't it!' shouted Dave. 'I'm the dodgy one – just because I've spent the last ten years in prison!'

A short silence greeted his outburst. Too late, even Dave realized his turn of phrase had not, perhaps, been terribly fortunate.

'Once a criminal,' reiterated Sergeant Liddel, 'always a criminal.'

Dave sighed and turned to the two policemen. 'What, in your opinion, is the purpose of sending people to prison?'

'To keep them as far away from civilized society for as long as possible so that they can't continue to pervert humanity or commit acts of lewdness that would result in the spawning of evil progeny,' replied Large without hesitation. Then he saw Dave's stunned expression. 'Er...sorry. Went too far there. Um...no. Prison is about punishing people.'

'No, it isn't,' countered Dave.

Large bristled. 'I beg your pardon?'

'It's about rehabilitating people.' Dave stood up. 'I admit,' he confessed, 'that I have committed crimes in the past. Not the crimes of which I was accused, but crimes none the less. The crime of credit card fraud and the crime of harbouring the intention of tapping into the world's financial institutions in order to take over the world. But I tell you, gentlemen – and Miss Hurst – that my decade in prison has rehabilitated me. I am a reformed character. I will never commit a crime again. I swear by almighty God that the evidence I shall give...um...no. The truth. That's what I wanted to say. I am only interested in the truth and the way and...Sorry.' He sat down.

Both policemen stared, open-mouthed, at the ex-convict. 'You mean,' they said in unison, 'that you've reformed?'

'Yes.'

Large and Liddle exchanged worried glances.

'In *prison*?' asked the former.

'Yes.'

'Surrounded,' said a disbelieving Liddel, 'by *criminals*?'

'Yes.'

Again the policemen looked at each other. They appeared more baffled than worried.

'Well,' sighed Large after a short silence, 'this really is *most* irregular. This is quite out of the ordinary...It puts us in a very difficult position. To be perfectly honest, I'm not entirely sure of the proper procedure in a situation like this.' He trailed off into silence and began to rummage furtively in his mackintosh pocket for the rule-book he carried to help him in the event of unprecedented occurrences such as this.

The level-headed Jeannie, however, had a far more appropriate response to Dave's outburst. 'If you have reformed,' she asked, 'why did you re-create your computer program? Surely its only purpose is to penetrate the world's financial institutions.'

'Or,' replied Dave, 'to put a stop to those...er, penetrations.'

Jeff's ears went pink at the tips. Determinedly not looking at Jeannie, he leaned towards Dave. 'You mean you re-created it because you wanted to *stop* people hacking into institutions?'

'Yeah. See, on the night of the raid at the Terrapin, I didn't expect to get nicked.' He looked at the assembled company. 'Why should I have? I didn't know someone had planted illicit substances in my possessions, did I? All I had to worry about was destroying the disk at the Terrapin – and Marty did that for me. Or at least,' he added through pursed lips, 'I *thought* he had. And I didn't worry about the copy I had at home 'cos I thought I was *going* home, didn't I? And when I didn't go home, I knew I'd been set up. By someone,' he added darkly, 'who knew I had a copy at home. By Marty.'

'Or,' said Jeff and Jeannie in unison, 'by Tallulah.'

'Yeah,' said Dave. 'I knew, in jail, that someone else had got their hands on the program. I knew they'd try to use it and expand it the way I'd intended to. And when I realized the error of my ways, I decided to re-create it to find out who else was using it. And to stop them.'

'Tallulah,' said Jeannie. Then she turned to Inspector Large. 'You see, Inspector, it *does* make sense.'

'Not in my book.' Large had, in fact, forgotten his

rule-book, but even without it he could see flaws in the argument. 'Nothing about this makes any sense at all,' he announced. 'Mainly because of this...this program thing.' He turned to Dave. 'If you can give me even the *slightest* indication that there's a conspiracy afoot to defraud the world's financial institutions, then I might, just *might*, take this seriously.'

The tall man was delighted with his creation. In every way, it replicated the program that he had spent so many years developing and honing to perfection. It looked like the original, the data corresponded to the original and the links related fluidly and enticingly to the original. Even better, he had built in a database that surpassed the original in its details of how, when and where the enormous amounts of money pledged by the delegates had been spent. It was, he thought, exceptionally brilliant. But then, he really wouldn't have expected anything else from its creator.

For several minutes he experimented with his program. A query posed by the delegate from Lapland? No problem. The tall man tapped at the keyboard and, within seconds, the screen displayed details of the institutions that delegate had nominated. With it came a breakdown of the companies in which they invested, a record of the amount of money placed in those companies by the delegate and a summary of how that money had affected share prices of those and other companies. The tall man rubbed his hands in glee. How the delegates would love it; how they would preen about their ability to affect – nay, lead – the progress of global financial institutions. And how thankful he was that he had chosen his delegates with such care. Wealth had of course been one of his criteria. But the absolute and fundamental code by which he operated was that his chosen ones must be stupid. Very stupid. Too stupid to know that in the normal world, ordinary people – and indeed middlingly stupid ones – were paid vast salaries to manipulate the world's financial markets under the guise of 'trading'. Too stupid to realize that every penny they had pledged had gone straight into the bank accounts of Tallulah and the tall man.

Tallulah. The tall man had plans for Tallulah as well. The price she had exacted for finding the disk had been a high one. Too high. True, he was prepared to credit her for founding Angels with Broken Wings and providing a cover for the global operation, but did she really possess the godlike qualities that he had in abundance? Was she worthy of striding to the top of Mount Olympus? Was her place at its summit justified?

No. At the end of the day, Tallulah Joplin was a pensioned-off tart. And she would end her days as she had begun them: grovelling among the detritus of mankind.

Satisfied with his creation, aware that when it was projected on to the giant screen in the domed room it would look sensational, the tall man turned to the laptop beside the bigger machine. He eyed it with trepidation. Would it reveal its secrets today? Or was the spectre of the unmentionable Dave Day still hovering over it? With his heart in his mouth, he booted the computer and watched the screen flicker and bleep its way into life.

A moment later his pounding heart was evicted from his mouth by the wave of bile that rose from his vented spleen.

'I recognize that!' shouted an excited Sergeant Liddel at the screen. 'God, must be at least ten years old! If not twenty. Galactican Griffins. Christ, that really takes me back!' Feeling inordinately pleased with himself, he looked around him for confirmation.

It was not forthcoming. A thin-lipped Inspector Large looked at the screen, at his watch – and then at Dave Day.

Jeannie and Jeff exchanged furtive glances that withered on the vine of dashed expectations and turned, inexorably, to anguish.

And Dave Day broke out in to a cold sweat. 'No!' he screamed. 'This can't be right! I know I can access the program! I can get there! I can't make transactions, but I can do everything else!' In desperation, he began to punch the keyboard. 'I can show you! I really can. I can show you...'

'Little griffin-things buzzing round and trying to zap you,' drawled Inspector Large. 'Very droll. Very interesting.' Sarcasm dripping from every syllable, he rounded on Dave Day. 'And a *very* severe threat to global financial institutions. No wonder there's a world-wide panic.'

Dave stabbed at the keyboard again. 'No, really, it's just a little glitch. It's just...Oh!' As he spoke, and as the others watched, the screen turned completely, utterly and devastatingly blank. Dave moaned, slumped forwards and buried his head in his hands.

The others reacted with, variously, disappointment, glee and sympathy. Except Jeff. His reaction was one of unbridled horror. For while the others were staring at blackness, he was staring straight into the face of Marty Hopkirk.

'Psst!' said Marty. 'Jeff?'

As unobtrusively as he could, Jeff slowly shook

his head and mouthed the words 'Go away!'

Marty winked. 'Look,' he whispered, 'I know you've got company, but I thought I might be able to help. Sorry about the griffins – that was my fault. But you see, Wyvern said—'

'For God's sake! I'm not interested in Wyvern's...Oh!' Remembering where he was, Jeff bit his lip and tried to pretend the last sentence hadn't happened.

But it had.

'Wyverns?' asked Jeannie. 'What are Wyverns?'

'Fictitious monsters,' said Sergeant Liddel. 'They have wings and two legs. The same genus,' he went on, nodding at the screen, 'as griffins. And dragons.'

For the first time, Jeff found himself warming to Liddel. He threw him a grateful look and then glanced back at the screen. Marty was still there. 'Jeff, I'm your man, don't you see? I'm a real whiz in cyberspace. Computer programs? Pah! Internet browsers? Easy. Marty can motor through the ether as quick as—'

'This,' thundered Inspector Large as he looked at the still blank screen, 'is an outrage.' He stood up and looked from Jeff to Dave and back again. 'I've a good mind to arrest you for wasting police time, but something tells me that would only lead to more wasted time.' He tapped Liddel on the shoulder. 'Come on, Sergeant. We have business to attend to.' He glared at Jeff again. 'Real business. Good day, Miss Hurst,' he said, nodding at Jeannie. Then, stomping angrily in his thick-soled shoes, he turned and left the office. A puffed-up Liddel trickled along in his wake.

They left a very miserable-looking trio huddled around the computer. Dave Day was still slumped in front of the machine, moaning softly to himself. Beside him, Jeannie looked tense and slightly angry. 'Why on earth,' she asked Jeff, 'did you call the police? I could have told you this would happen.'

'I...um...'

'My program!' wailed Dave. 'Ruined! Gone for ever. Wiped by some bloody Galactican Griffins!' He looked up at Jeff with murder in his eyes. 'I'll kill that woman. I swear it. I'll kill that Tallulah Joplin.'

'Maybe,' said Jeff, 'it was just a glitch. You know...something in the ether. These things happen with computers, don't they?'

He looked again at the screen. Marty was still there, looming up at him. Jeff waved a dismissive hand. His deceased partner did not take the hint.

'I'm sorry, Jeannie,' said Jeff. 'It *was* a mistake. I just thought...Well, it doesn't matter what I thought.' He looked bleakly across the desk. 'We're on our own with this one.' Then he clapped Dave on the shoulder. 'But,' he added, 'I don't think you should give up hope, Dave. I'm sure it was just a glitch.' He glared at the screen. 'A virusy thing...a temporary bug.'

'I am not,' protested Marty, 'a bug!'

'So stick around and help us.'

'Oh, I will,' said Dave, suddenly resolute. 'I'm not giving up that easily.'

'You said yourself that you're a whiz in cyber-space.'

'And so I am,' smirked Marty.

'Did I?' said Dave. 'Yes, I did, didn't I?' He stood up. 'Yes, I am! I'm a genius. And I'm not letting that wretched woman get the better of me!' In a gesture that spoke volumes about his feelings for Tallulah Joplin, he leaned forward and bashed at the keyboard. 'I am going to gain access if it kills me!'

'Ouch!' said Marty, before disappearing into the ether.

A highly relieved Jeff turned to Jeannie. 'We'll stop her yet.'

'Ye-es. But, Jeff, we can't prove she's done anything wrong.'

'Can't we?'

'No. But we might be able to.' Jeannie reached for the phone. 'Especially after we tell her we've found Dave Day.'

chapter eleven

'Oh, how marvellous,' trilled Tallulah. 'Where is he?'

Jeannie looked across the desk at the man in question. Now recovered from his bout of near-suicidal despair, he was once again tapping away at the computer keyboard. Confidence oozed from his every pore. Whatever unfortunate event – Tallulah's interference, a virusy thing or a temporary bug – had given him Galactican Griffins and then a blank screen, he was determined to solve the problem.

'I don't know where he is at the moment,' lied Jeannie, 'but we've been trailing him. Getting to know his haunts, that sort of thing.'

'Really?' purred Tallulah down the line. 'But you don't know where he lives?'

'Not at the moment, no. I thought you'd want to know that we're making progress, that's all. Wouldn't want you to think,' Jeannie said with a laugh, 'that we're wasting your money. Which reminds me. We...er ...we haven't actually received the down payment yet.'

'Haven't you?' Tallulah made an utterly convincing stab at sounding horrified. 'My dear, how awful.

I sent you a cheque several days ago.'

'Did you?'

'Yes. Perhaps it's lost in the post. Never mind. I'll send you another one, shall I? And if the first one arrives, you can just tear it up, all right?'

'Very kind of you.'

It wasn't, of course, at all kind. Tallulah hadn't sent the first cheque and had absolutely no intention of sending a second one. But something in Jeannie's tone bothered her: the other woman's 'very kind' had a distinct air of *froideur* about it. She had a sneaking suspicion that Jeannie, in turn, was entertaining her own little sneaking suspicion. There was a possibility she could confirm that.

'So,' said Tallulah, 'his haunts. What's he up to? What's he been doing since his release? Apart, of course, from sending me death threats.'

'As we suspected,' replied Jeannie, 'he's been sniffing around at the Terrapin. He's been asking questions about you...and he's made a few attempts to recruit some of the seedier clientele. He's been talking about...about some sort of deal. A business proposition.'

I'll bet he has, thought Tallulah. But not at the Terrapin. The Archangels would have told her. Jeannie was lying. Jeannie had made a fatal mistake. And Jeannie would pay dearly for it. So would that little man Randall. So would Dave Day. So would—

'Tallulah? Are you still there?'

'What? Yes, yes, I'm still here. I was just...thinking about what to do next.' Tallulah was indeed thinking. Very fast. She considered and dismissed several options in the space of a few seconds. To her consternation, she realized there was only one viable

course for her to take. She would have to stall
Jeannie. 'Look,' she said eventually, 'I'm afraid
you've caught me at rather a bad time. I've...er, got
to fly. You don't think,' she added for safe measure,
'I'm in any immediate danger from him, do you?'

Jeannie looked over at the fat man beside the
computer. 'No. No. Absolutely not. Jeff would have
let me know. He's...keeping tabs on him.'

Which indeed he was. Jeff was watching Dave,
fervently hoping that Marty wasn't planning to
stage an imminent comeback and interfere with the
ether.

'Good. Well, congratulations, Jeannie. Keep
watching and I'll get back to you as soon as I can.
Bye!'

In the offices of Randall & Hopkirk (Deceased),
Jeannie slowly replaced the receiver and turned to
Jeff. 'I don't know why, but I think something I said
made her suspicious.'

'Oh? Why? What did she say?'

Jeannie frowned. 'She said she was in a hurry
and would call me back. Isn't that rather a peculiar
response? I mean, I've just told her we've found the
person who's been sending her death threats.'

'I have *not*,' said Dave, 'been sending her death
threats.'

'The person she *claims* has been sending her
death threats,' corrected Jeannie. Still quizzical, she
looked back to Jeff. 'Strange to greet the news so
casually, don't you think?'

'Mmm.' Jeff began to pace the floor. 'If,' he said,
'just *if* she's suspicious, it must be because she
thinks we've done more than see Dave. She thinks
we've spoken to him, right?'

'Presumably.'

'And so she thinks we know the truth?'

'Yes.'

Jeff stopped pacing and locked eyes with Jeannie. 'So she's stalling for time, right?'

'Right.' And it was Jeannie who articulated the question that was hovering on Jeff's lips. 'So...what's she going to do?'

Tallulah made a beeline for the tall man's office.

'They've found him,' she announced as she strode through the door.

The tall man didn't look round from his screen. The Galactican Griffins – caused, no doubt, by a glitch or a temporary bug – had disappeared. The computer was working normally. Or as normally as was possible when access to the vital program was still denied. 'Who,' he said to the screen, 'has found whom?'

'That little Randall man,' sighed his exasperated accomplice, 'has found Dave Day.'

The tall man swivelled round in his chair. Always careful to compose his expressions, he looked at Tallulah with an air of cautious optimism. 'Ah.' He rested his chin on his fingertips, the pose adding to his gauntness and somehow emphasizing the scar on his right cheek. 'So where is he?'

'Well, this is the irritating thing,' said Tallulah. 'That Jeannie person said that they were "keeping tabs" on him. I think they've been doing more than that. I think they've been talking to him.'

'Oh? What makes you so sure?'

'Because I asked where he'd been hanging out.' Tallulah's glance was heavy with meaning as she looked at the tall man. 'And that's where Little Miss Perfect made a mistake. She said he'd been in the Terrapin.'

'Ah.'

'Gabriel and Lucifer miss nothing,' continued Tallulah. 'There's no way he's been there.'

'No.'

Tallulah threw herself into the steel chair beside the main computer. 'I wish,' she snapped, 'you'd be a little more forthcoming. "Ah" and "No" aren't really going to get us anywhere.'

'No.'

Tallulah glared at her companion.

'What,' he asked quietly, 'did you say when she told you?'

'What? About the Terrapin? Well, I wasn't going to let on that we'd posted Archangels there, was I? Give me a little credit.' Tallulah crossed her legs and began to drum her fingers on her raised knee. 'I had to stall for time. I told her she'd caught me in the middle of something and that I'd call her back.'

The tall man raised his eyebrows. 'A slightly strange response, don't you think? This is a man who's been issuing death threats, a man you live in fear of.'

'I told you,' hissed Tallulah. 'I was stalling for time. I didn't have a chance to *think*. To plan.'

'Well, now you do.'

'Yes.' Still furiously drumming her fingers, Tallulah appeared to reach a decision. 'If they really have been talking to Dave Day, then the cat's out of the bag.'

'Not necessarily.'

'What?'

The tall man studied his fingers. 'If they've been talking to Dave Day, they're in something of a predicament. He would have called *you* into question – but what do they think of *him*? Why would they be so sure that he's telling the truth?'

Tallulah mulled over that one in silence. He had a point. It was Dave's word against hers. And she had far more credibility than he did. She was an Angel. A slow smile spread across her face. 'You know,' she said, 'I'm beginning to think it's a positive advantage that Marty Hopkirk's dead. The last thing we want is for him to start going over the events of ten years ago. He might figure out that I stole the key. He might be able to back up whatever story Dave's been telling them.'

'Yes. The true story.'

Tallulah uncrossed her legs and leapt to her feet. 'OK, so they're in a predicament – they don't know who to believe. But who would you believe? A criminal or an Angel?'

'An Angel,' corrected the tall man, 'with a Broken Wing.'

Tallulah waved an impatient hand. 'Whatever. The important thing is that they don't *know*. They need more information.' She gestured at the computer. 'They might swallow Dave's story about the computer program, but there's absolutely no way anyone can prove who's using his program. Or where. Is there?'

Her last words carried an element of doubt. She looked at the tall man for reassurance.

'No,' he said. 'They can't find out. Not unless they've got a tame gremlin who can invade cyber-space *and* talk to them in English. And that,' he finished with the smirk of the supremely confident, 'would be a physical impossibility.'

'Precisely. So they need more information. And where are they going to try to find it?'

'I couldn't possibly think.'

'Quite.' Tallulah was now as confident as her companion. 'They're going to come nosing around here. And they're not going to find anything.'

The tall man looked upwards. He was envisaging the quiet country house fifty feet above them, the peaceful Angels going about their philanthropic business, the efficient Emma ensuring that everything ran smoothly – and the bare forearm of St Peter that provided the only bridge between that world and the secret, subterranean universe over which he ruled.

'No,' he whispered, 'they're not going to find anything. Unless—'

'Unless what?'

'Well, the entrance the delegates use? Supposing they find that?'

'That,' said Tallulah with vehemence, 'is impossible. It's about as likely as their finding a tame gremlin who can invade cyberspace and talk to them in English.' There was a glint of pure triumph as she looked at the tall man. 'It's perfect,' she said. 'Perfect. There's no need to send Archangels to get them. No need for messy murders in public places. No need,' she continued, her voice rising as she wallowed in her wonderfulness, 'to steal the computer program! No need to do anything except sit and wait for them to come here!' Whipping round to face her companion, she lowered her voice to a dramatic whisper. 'To come to Angels with Broken Wings and to end up in the Pit of Oblivion!'

'Hello? Ah...Tallulah.' Jeannie nodded in Jeff's direction and raised her eyebrows. This was it.

She listened with interest to Tallulah's next words – and stiffened as she realised what was being asked of her. 'I'm really not sure,' she replied, 'if we could persuade him to do that. Remember, we haven't even talked to him yet. And...Oh! Oh, I see...' Jeannie cradled the receiver under her chin and grimaced at her companions. 'Ye-es,' she said after a moment. 'Yes, I can see why he might do that. Yes, I suppose anyone who'd spent the last ten years in jail might be interested...'

Beside her, Dave strained to hear what Tallulah was saying. But the only sound that drifted over to him from the other end of the line was an unintelligible squawk.

'Well,' said Jeannie after another tirade from Tallulah, 'I'll certainly put it to him. I can't *guarantee* anything, but I agree it's probably the best shot. Fine. Yes. I'll phone you back when I've got something concrete.' Then she laughed. 'No, I agree! I won't mention it. Don't want him to think he's being lured into the lion's den...OK, bye!'

'Well?' said both men the second Jeannie replaced the receiver. 'What,' added Dave, 'is that witch up to?'

Jeannie's face was inscrutable as she looked at him. Was he *really* a reformed character? *Was* he trustworthy? Suddenly she felt less sure. There was something nagging in the back of her mind; a little voice casting doubt on Dave, on Tallulah and on the wisdom of this entire operation. Panic gripped her momentarily and she had a horrible suspicion that it was she and Jeff, not Dave, who were being lured into the lion's den. She felt Jeff had been sensible in calling the police. And then she remembered why the police had treated them with such derision.

'Tallulah,' she sighed, 'wants us to persuade Dave to go and see someone from his past. Someone who must remain nameless. Someone who can give him something that will be to his advantage.' She was careful to focus on Dave as she spoke. She wanted to monitor his reaction and see if it would confirm or allay her suspicions.

It did the latter.

'Ha!' snorted the fat man. 'She wants to do a deal. She's banking on the fact I haven't told you about the program. She thinks I'm still interested in ruling the world. Silly cow.'

'Yes,' said Jeannie. 'That thought had occurred to me.'

Dave, however, was really quite put out. 'She must think I'm really stupid. Do a deal with Tallulah Joplin? Not in a million years. Anyway,' he added with an ominous frown, 'Tallulah doesn't do deals. She never did deals. Anything she ever did was entirely for her own benefit.'

'Yes,' said Jeff. 'I think you're probably right. But the question is, do we go for it?'

'We don't really have very much choice,' replied Jeannie. 'We're damned if we don't and...' She finished the sentence with a wary look at the two men.

'Yes,' concurred Jeff, 'and we're probably damned if we do.'

'Ah,' added Dave. 'But if we do, damned or not we've got a chance of destroying Tallulah's plans to take over the world. Once and for all.'

chapter twelve

As always, the delegates arrived separately. This had been the tall man's idea – ostensibly for security purposes but in reality because he and Tallulah had skimped on limousines. If twenty delegates were to be collected from the airport at the same time, they would have needed ten limousines, because, as the tall man well knew, the very rich took a dim view of being cramped. Two to a limo was quite enough.

So, throughout the morning, the two large black cars in which Tallulah and the tall man had invested ferried ten pairs of delegates at various times from the airport to the underground palace.

While overt displays of excitement (like being cramped) were not in the canon of the behaviour of the very rich, the delegates always experienced a frisson of delight at the ingenious route to the palace. Even after all these years. It was, they all felt, so devastatingly simple, so delightfully unexpected.

The delegate from Carpathia arrived with his counterpart from Ushuia. Again, this was the result of careful planning on the part of Tallulah and the tall man. It wouldn't do, they felt, to place people from neighbouring countries, or even neighbouring continents in the same vehicle. That sort of tactlessness invariably led to the reopening of old wounds, the rehashing of old wars and, ultimately, dissent. It was imperative to nurture friendships between the delegates. Alternatively – as with the candidates from Carpathia and Ushuia – one could make sure peace was kept by the simple expedient of pairing two men who had difficulty with each other's languages. It meant not just peace, but silence. And the tall man's knowledge of human behaviour informed him that the very rich enjoyed travelling in total silence, because it made them feel more important.

As the car purred through the leafy country lanes, the delegate from Ushuia looked to his left and caught the eye of his companion. Again. This was the umpteenth time they had unwittingly courted embarrassment by admiring the scenery at the same time but in different directions. Both men nodded and turned back to look out of their own windows, silently regretting their lack of linguistic dexterity. In Ushuia they spoke only Spanish and Welsh; in Carpathia Magyar still fought bravely against the increasingly ascendant German – but none of those languages could smooth the way to dialogue between the delegates. And while the Carpathian also spoke perfect English, the delegate from Ushuia's command of that language was quite simply not up to conversation.

The delegates were heartily glad when the familiar turning in the road loomed ahead. The uniformed chauffeur (nationality: Filipino; language: Tagalog) silently indicated to the left and slowed down. A minute later the huge car pulled into the turning and drove 100 yards up the smaller road. Then he turned left again and eased the limousine into a driveway. A moment later they gilded to a halt outside a plain wooden garage and the chauffeur alighted. His passengers, however, remained where they were. The delegate from Ushuia looked without any great interest to his left, at the unassuming house to which the garage belonged. It was much like the other houses that peppered the English countryside. Neither large nor small, neither beautiful nor ugly, it was just there, its very anonymity providing it with cover against anybody who snooped too close. A cursory glance through the windows was enough to tell anyone that the contents were as unremarkable as the house.

And the garage. The small building backed on to the hill that rose steeply towards the rear of the house. In winter it was probably damp. In summer, as now, it was half-covered in foliage and purple flowers that cascaded over its roof. It looked as if it were blushing, apologizing for being there, desiring only to sink back further into the hill.

The delegate from Carpathia watched the chauffeur go about his familiar routine of opening the double doors, getting back into the car, inching forwards into the garage and alighting once more to close the doors behind him. Then he got back into the car again and closed his door.

For a moment the three men sat in the near-darkness, looking at the rough stone of the steep hill that formed the rear wall of the garage. Then, in response to the press of a button on the dashboard, the wall began to move sideways, revealing a tunnel beyond and sending a frisson of excitement through both delegates. This was their favourite bit: leaving behind the verdant pastures of rural England and entering a hidden world open only to people like themselves. People with enough money to buy those verdant pastures, but whose playground of choice was in the depths of the underworld.

The car crept forward and, as soon as it had cleared the confines of the garage, the wall slid silently back into place.

The tunnel the chauffeur accelerated into was no meandering grotto created by the forces of nature. It was a monument to the power of man (and of one lofty man in particular) and a record of nature's easy capitulation in the face of several tons of dynamite. Floodlit and paved, it ran straight into the bowels of the hill and beyond, and terminated a mile after it began. Anyone duplicating its course by following a road would have had to travel five miles. For that was the distance between the house with the wooden garage and Angels with Broken Wings.

The car drew to a halt in front of the enormous pillared entrance to the underground palace. In designing it, the tall man had had in mind a modern version of the Treasury at Petra, and all the delegates had been hugely impressed – apart, that is, from the Jordanian delegate, who had been rather miffed because the tall man's creation was possibly even more impressive than its original. And, for the tall man, there was a delicious irony about the façade, as it closely resembled the neo-classical portico of the building directly above – the building that none of the delegates knew existed.

But neither of the delegates in the car had time to admire the glorious edifice in front of them. As soon as the car stopped, a woman leapt forward and opened the near-side passenger door. Clad in a skin-tight leather catsuit, her brown hair neatly bobbed, her make-up applied with precision and to stunning effect, she looked two decades younger than her fifty years.

'Welcome, gentlemen,' said Emma. Beaming broadly at the two men as they alighted from the vehicle, she gestured grandiloquently towards the great door of the underground palace. 'The girls,' she said as the door opened, 'will show you to your rooms.'

Now it was the two men who were beaming. Standing coquettishly in the doorway were two of the most beautiful women they had ever seen. Girls they were not, but they were, none the less, magnificent specimens. The one with her hair in a smooth chignon wore a kaftan with a strange yet intriguing pattern. The other had long blonde hair which fell in perfect curves on to the shoulders of her bright-red suit. And as they stepped forward, both looked straight into the eyes of their respective delegates, sending another, rather different thrill shuddering through their hearts.

It had been a long time since Serenity Blush and Patience Trump had been called upon to practise their skills, but true experts never forget their craft.

Inside the palace, Tallulah and the tall man were making last-minute preparations for the afternoon's presentation. The giant screen on the far wall of the meeting room was still blank, but soon it would display a dazzling array of figures, a map of the world and a giant demonstration of how money would start pouring out of the world's leading financial institutions and into the delegates' bank accounts. The tall man had been so enamoured of his creation that he had excelled himself with his graphics. He had created dummy newspaper headlines that would flash up before the delegates to show them the devastating magnitude of the project. In all probability, the headlines merely anticipated what would transpire after the real computer program was activated. *If* the real computer program could be activated.

'Isn't there any way,' snapped Tallulah as she surveyed the room, 'to shut off those bloody wind chimes?'

'No. They're supposed to have a calming effect.'

'Well, they're getting on my nerves.'

'Too bad, Tallulah. I'm not interested in your nerves, or in the bloody wind chimes. I'm interested in when – indeed if – we're going to get our hands on Dave Day and his program. I'm quite happy about showing the delegates all this,' he continued, gesturing at the screen. 'They'll never know it's a fake. But we need the real thing. We need to get rid of whatever bug he's put into the system.'

'I know, I know, so you keep saying.' An increasingly irritated Tallulah glared at the tall man. 'Let's just get through today first, shall we?'

'Supposing they come today?'

'They won't.'

'What makes you so sure?'

Tallulah angrily swept her raven hair off her forehead and, eyes blazing, started shouting. 'Look, you moron. It doesn't matter either way, does it? They *won't* come today. Principally because it's highly unlikely they'll get Dave Day to cooperate so soon, and secondly because I told them not to. And even if they *do* come, so what? We're still prepared, aren't we?'

The tall man pointed upwards. 'We're under-staffed on top.'

'Big bloody deal. We can still cope.'

The tall man looked searchingly at Tallulah. 'Why did you tell them not to come today? Isn't that just a red rag to a bull?'

Tallulah shrugged. 'I said we were having an Angelic Host and that we couldn't be disturbed. You seem to forget, my dear, that *up there*' – Tallulah jabbed a livid red fingernail at the ceiling – 'every-thing is above board. Kosher. Legal. Profitable. Listed, for Christ's sake, on the Stock Exchange. There's no way a couple of two-bit private detectives are going to waltz in and find anything suspicious.'

'Supposing they decide to call the police?'

'Oh. The police. Yes, they're going to take that very seriously, aren't they? "Oh, by the way, Chief Superintendent. An ex-convict told us that Angels with Broken Wings is a front for a secret organiza-tion that plans to take over the world."' Tallulah's imitation of Jeannie's clipped tones wasn't very convincing, but the import of her words most emphatically was. The police would laugh in their faces. They might even arrest them for wasting police time.

Dimly aware that she was becoming increasingly excitable, Tallulah took a few deep breaths to steady herself. 'The main issue,' she said, slightly calmer now, 'is to get through today.'

'We'll be fine.'

'Twenty delegates is rather a lot all in one go.'

'Well, we were always going to do it, weren't we? It's just happened a bit sooner than anticipated, that's all.'

Tallulah bit her lip. 'I'm worried about some of

the girls. I'm just not sure they're...fresh enough.'

If Tallulah had been aware of the activities taking place in the palace's bedroom suites, she might have been less concerned. Kitty, Tatiana, Fatima and Sapphire were being very fresh. And the delegates were loving it. Several of them, snuggled up with their respective partners, were already at the champagne and caviare stage. The delegate from Ushuia was murmuring sweet nothings in Welsh into the velvet ear of Serenity Blush. The French delegate, admittedly, was having problems, but those were not the fault of the understanding Tiffany. And the man from Carpathia had fallen asleep beside the gentle Patience, blissfully unaware that she couldn't share his somnolent state. She couldn't. She was fretting about what she had read in the cards.

chapter thirteen

'Well,' asked Jeff. 'Anything?'

'Thing is,' said Marty, 'there's some sort of interference.'

'I thought *you* were the interference.' Jeff plucked another crisp out of the bag and looked at his screen. It was odd, he thought. However much he had got used to the idea of being haunted by Marty, he still had problems with the computer aspect. He wondered if he'd ever feel comfortable with Marty's face looming up at him.

For his part, Marty wondered if Jeff would ever stop insulting him.

'Oh, no,' he pouted. 'I'm more than just interference. I'm a glitch, remember? A temporary bug. Do you have any idea what it's like to be stuck in a computer while you lot make fun of me?'

Jeff rolled his eyes. 'Oh, God, let's not go through all that again, Marty. We were *not* making fun of you. Anyway, there's only me here now, so we can have a proper conversation.'

But not yet. 'Where's Jeannie?' barked a suspicious Marty.

'She's gone to Wendy's. Apparently some friend of

hers knows something about Angels, so she's gone to investigate.'

Marty swelled with pride. 'Good old Jeannie. That's what the best private investigators do. They *investigate*, Jeff. They don't sit around eating crisps and looking at...what are you looking at anyway?'

'If you'd come out of there you'd be able to see.'

Marty sighed and, concentrating hard for a moment, exited the screen into the office and appeared at Jeff's shoulder.

'A map? Why are you looking at a map?'

Jeff scratched his head. 'To be honest, Marty, I don't really know. I just thought if I could get a picture of where Angels was, something might spring to mind.'

Marty cast a withering, downward glance at his partner. 'Like what?'

'Well, I'm not really sure. But we're going to have to go there, so I thought it might be an idea to do some sort of recce beforehand.'

'Now that, my little man,' commented Marty, 'is the first sensible thing you've said.'

Jeff recognized that tone. He looked up and, sure enough, there was a knowing and – because this was Marty – superior look in the other man's eye. 'You've found something, haven't you? C'mon, spill the beans.'

'Well,' said a suddenly serious Marty, 'I found the duplicate program. It's exactly the same as Dave's; exactly the same configuration, so there's no doubt it's the one we're looking for. And,' he added, 'it's got the virus Dave put in. Just like he told you. Every time Tallulah tries to enter it she just gets a message saying "Access Denied". But then clever little Tallulah established a retro-virus that bounces back to Dave again. Stalemate, you see.'

'Yeah, we know that. But anything else?'

Marty wrinkled his nose. 'Well, I can't destroy it, I'm afraid. Anyway, even if I could that wouldn't help you lot. As far as she's concerned, it might already be useless. It's Dave and the new one she wants. Or rather, *they* want. There's no way Tallulah's doing this on her own.'

'Yeah. I know that. But is there anything else? Anything *new*?'

While Marty was largely oblivious to sarcasm when it came from Wyvern, he was hypersensitive to the same treatment from Jeff. 'My, my,' he said. 'Touchy, aren't we?'

'Look, Marty. We're dealing with people who stand a very good chance of stealing money from every major financial institution in the world. If they succeed, the entire *planet* will be affected.'

'Except you.'

'Me?'

'Yes. You've never had any money, so it won't make any difference to you.'

'I used to have money, Marty. Remember? When I was a solicitor; before I got into this lark with you. Anyway,' he added, hitting home, 'it'll affect Jeannie.'

'Yes, yes, I know.' Serious now, Marty sat down. 'And I know how damaging this could be. I'm the one who can surf through cyberspace. I know, *first hand*, how easily all the money in the world could disappear into a computer. Which is why,' he finished, 'I think it's a good idea you're looking at a map. Especially an Ordnance Survey map.'

'Eh?'

Marty tapped the creased expanse of paper in question. 'The energy fields round their computer are different.'

Jeff looked blankly at Marty's hand. 'I can't see what that's got to do with a map. Anyway, how d'you mean "different"?'

'Well, I had a discussion about this with Wyvern. The energy fields around the computer that Tallulah – or whoever she's in league with – uses are different from those around other people's. And,' added Marty, stabbing the map at Angels with Broken Wings, 'the computer used *here* is normal. Like other people's. Even,' he said graciously, 'like yours.'

'Thanks. But I'm still lost.' Jeff scratched his head again. 'What does a difference in energy fields mean?'

'It means,' said Marty, 'the computer in which they've installed the program is in a different place. A place with a different gravitational pull. A place with greater magnetic wotsit.' Aware that he was about to embark on unfamiliar ground, Marty lapsed into silence and beamed confidently at Jeff.

'Marty, I haven't a clue what you're talking about.'

'Well, it's what Wyvern suggested. Something to do with rock and density and all that.' Skipping further explanation, Marty pointed to the map again. 'The point is, the computer is underground.'

'Underground?'

'Yes.'

'Under Angels with Broken Wings?'

Marty stroked his chin. 'Well, no. Not exactly. I'm a bit vague on this one. I mean, fair's fair, Jeff. I haven't been dead for all that long. I've had a lot to learn and…'

'I'm not about to criticize you, Marty! Just tell me what Wyvern said.'

'He thought – and even he was a bit vague about

this one – that it was underground, *near* to Angels, but even nearer a hill.'

'Wow.' Jeff leaned forwards over the map. 'That would explain a lot, Marty. It makes sense, doesn't it? Not to have their operation in the same building as Angels. After all, they have all those pop stars and people going there, all those bigwigs who invest in them. It would be far too risky to have anything dodgy happening on the premises.'

Marty's furrowed brow indicated he wasn't entirely convinced. 'Yes, but why would they need a whole different building. I mean, as Dave said, the whole thing can be done with a laptop. You don't need a separate building just to house a laptop.'

'Maybe not. But what if Tallulah's in league with a whole bunch of people? People, say, who stumped up money to found Angels or something. They've got to have somewhere to live, haven't they?'

'Yes. But...*underground*?' Marty wrinkled his nose.

'Don't see why not. After all, you live in a grave.'

'I do not! I do *not* live in a grave! Yuck! That's a really horrible thought, Jeff.'

'But you're dead! Where else do dead people go?'

'Well...heaven.' Marty fixed Jeff with a distinctly unfriendly look. 'Unless, of course, they're trapped. Fated,' he added in a theatrically morose voice, 'to haunt the earth until their chosen one shuffles off his mortal coil!'

Jeff looked back at the map. 'Well, I didn't ask you to nominate me as your chosen one. Anyway, you don't spend all your time haunting. You've got Wyvern, you've got limbo, you've –'

'Got a concert to do in limbo that's been cancelled until I solve this case. So let's get on with it.'

Sorely tempted though he was to smack Marty round the head, Jeff refrained from doing so – largely because, depending on Marty's level of concentration, his hand might or might not go straight through Marty, but also because he, too, wanted to get on with it.

'OK,' he said as they pored over the map. 'What we're looking for is a hill somewhere near Angels, right?'

'Right.'

'How near?'

'Dunno. Wyvern didn't really say. There can't be many hills in that part of the country anyway.' Marty looked more closely at the map. 'These squiggly circular things indicate hills, don't they?'

'Mmm.'

'Oh. Oh dear.'

Marty and Jeff looked at each other. 'That's a lot of hills,' said the latter. Then, after a long, disappointed silence, he began to fold up the map. Being Jeff, this meant scrunching it together, because, no matter how hard he tried, somehow the original folds just didn't work any more. Maps always did that to Jeff

'No need to rip it up just because it's got a lot of hills,' said Marty.

'I'm not ripping it up. I'm taking it with me.'

'With you? Where?'

'On the recce. Might as well go for a drive and see if I can find anything that looks likely.'

'But what about Jeannie? What about Dave? There's no point in going without them. Where is Dave anyway?'

'Working on the program at home. And Marty, I'm not going to *do* anything. I'm only going to look.'

Marty drew himself up to his full height. 'Less of the "I", please, Jeff. The word you're looking for is "we".'

For the second time in as many minutes, Jeff suppressed the desire to smack Marty round the head.

Jeannie's plan to spend an hour or so with Wendy pre-dated the information that Jemima had been to Angels and might have some news for her. Just as well, thought Jeannie, as she pulled up in front of the Old Rectory. She really didn't hold out much hope of a lead from the Jemima. Her – albeit limited – experience of the older woman had left her with the suspicion that any news she had to impart would be along the lines of her own superiority to the young private investigator.

Jeannie wasn't far wrong. Letting herself into the house, she strode unannounced into the kitchen to find Wendy and Jemima sitting at the table chatting over coffee. Wendy's vaguely strained manner, noticeable only to Jeannie, indicated that such an activity was not top of her list of priorities. And the uncomfortable way Jemima was perched on her chair, combined with her evident unfamiliarity with the object she held in her left hand – a mug – sent out the clear message that she was most definitely not a kitchen person.

'Jeannie! How lovely.' Wendy jumped up and kissed her sister on both cheeks. 'You remember Jemima, don't you?'

'Yes, of course. How nice to see you again.'

'And you,' responded Jemima with the casual ease of the insincere. 'When Wendy told me you were coming,' she said, dispensing with further preamble,

'I felt I just had to pop along and tell you about Angels with Broken Wings. I've been there, you see.'

'So Wendy told me,' said Jeannie, sitting down.

'Coffee?' asked Wendy.

'Mmm. Please.'

'And,' continued Jemima, 'I'm actually going to check in for a while.'

'Are you?' Wendy looked intensely surprised. 'You didn't tell me that.'

'No, I've only just decided.'

Jeannie surmised – correctly – that Jemima's decision wasn't entirely unrelated to her own visit.

'And I thought,' continued Jemima, 'that there might be something I could do for you while I'm there.'

'Well, I...Oh, thanks, Wendy.' Jeannie smiled up at her sister and cupped her hands round the mug she had just been handed. Then she turned back to Jemima. 'It's terribly kind of you, but I couldn't impose on you like that and—'

'Oh, it wouldn't be an imposition. It would be fun! I'm always being told how frightfully observant I am.' Jemima leaned further towards Jeannie. 'I'm sure I could do a spot of...sleuthing and report back.' The glint in her eyes confirmed two of Jeannie's theories about Jemima. First, that she was bored sick of her vacuous life, and second, that she had been head girl at school.

'Well, really, Jemima, it's kind of you to think of me, but the fact is we really don't need to do any...sleuthing at Angels. Our brief was to find a missing friend of one of the Angels – and we've found him.'

'Oh.' Jemima looked distinctly put out. 'So your case is closed?'

'Well, nearly.'

'Nearly?' The eyebrows suggested that 'nearly' didn't exist in Jemima's vocabulary.

'Yes.' Jeannie chose her next words carefully. 'The...er...friend wasn't very keen on being found. He...he doesn't want anything to do with the Angels.'

'Why?'

'He thinks there's something a little, well, strange about them.'

'Ah!' Jemima sat bolt upright. 'Well, there you are. That's where I could help. Of course,' she continued in her blisteringly tactless way, 'you don't really need to do any sleuthing to know what's strange about them.'

Beside her, Wendy stifled a giggle and looked at Jeannie over the rim of her mug.

Suppressing a grin, Jeannie looked across the table. 'Oh? What *is* strange then?'

'They skimp,' said Jemima crisply.

'Skimp?'

'Yes. On details. Naturally I *insisted* on being shown round the entire place, and while the overall effect is glorious, the detail isn't *quite* what one would expect.' Jemima's expression indicated that one expected rather a lot.

With a sinking feeling that this was even more of a waste of time than she had anticipated, Jeannie could only manage a polite 'Oh?' in response.

'Yes. The drawing room, for example. That boulle cabinet was definitely not *grand siècle*.'

Wendy exploded, and only just managed to transform her splutters into a coughing fit. Jeannie bit her lip and replied that she had thought the cabinet rather fine.

But that made Jemima even more cross.

'You've been there? You saw it?'

'Well, yes. Thanks to you, Jemima. After you told me that the woman who came to see me was an Angel, I went to see her.'

Jemima was only slightly mollified by the compliment. 'Oh. I see. Well, in that case you'll know what I'm talking about.'

Jeannie took a sip of her coffee. 'Not really,' she said with a smile. 'I don't know anything about fine art. I'm sure I couldn't tell a fake from the real thing.'

'Oh, you could. Any fool could tell that the Guercino was a copy.' Jemima wrinkled her nose. 'And a pretty appalling one too.'

Neither Wendy nor Jeannie had a clue what she was talking about. 'Guercino?' asked the former.

'Yes. That was his nickname, of course. He had a squint, so they called him Guercino.'

'Er...yes.' Jeannie looked at Wendy, who shook her head.

'He really was the *most* dramatic of artists,' continued Jemima. 'Such an instinct for bodily and psychic reactions. He would have been horrified by such a dreadful copy. The real one, of course, is in the Prado.'

'Oh.' Jeannie was beginning to experience the same surreal feeling of displacement that had overcome her at Wendy's dinner party. 'You...you seem to know a lot about painting.'

'And thank goodness I do. I'm sure that's why they didn't want to show me the library. That's what I mean about skimping.' Jemima looked from Jeannie to Wendy. 'They don't show you the room with those...those *apologies* for works of art until you've already signed up and it's too late. I think it's disgraceful.'

'Come to think of it,' mused Jeannie, 'they didn't show me the library.'

'Well, there you go then. They didn't want you to see *The Liberation*.'

'I beg your pardon?'

'*The Liberation of St Peter by an Angel*. That's the Guercino they copied. Although quite why they chose that instead of *The Dead Christ Mourned by Two Angels* I've no idea.' Now in full flood, Jemima was also becoming rather hot under the collar. 'The *Christ*, you see, is a far better painting. The light just floods in and, frankly, if you're going to cover an entire wall with a copy you'd be far better advised to use that one. *St Peter* is much darker – and it's much more static than the *Christ*. I think it's his arm, you see. To my mind it rather breaks up the piece, and *it's even worse* in the copy they've had done. You should see it; it's *far* too big. Even to the untrained eye. Even you, Wendy,' she said graciously, 'would be able to tell that there's something wrong with it. If they'd asked me,' she added, turning to Jeannie, 'I would have been able to put them right. Forget Guercino, I would have said. Go for landscapes. Much easier to copy. Now Derain, there's an artist who copies well. And Monet. A bit *ordinaire*, you might say, but frankly more modern and probably more in keeping with the ethos of the place...'

Jeannie sank deeper into her chair and began to feel highly envious of St Peter. He, at least, had been liberated. She held out little hope of ever escaping Jemima.

chapter fourteen

Even if he said it himself – and he did, repeatedly – the tall man felt that the presentation had gone swimmingly. It had, in fact, gone glowingly and gorgeously well. His powers of oration had never served him so spectacularly. His persuasive abilities had been at their zenith. The delegates had listened open-mouthed as his sensational words, had resounded throughout the room in their mellifluous magnificence. His fake program had utterly enthralled and completely convinced them. He was a towering and incomparable genius. A genius who could allow himself to wallow in superlatives.

So superlative had been his performance that none of the delegates had balked at signing the cheques for their final instalments. Even the delegate from the Ukraine, much given to moaning about his depleted oil reserves, had signed without complaint. And now they had all gone back to their rooms for a rest – or whatever – before the evening's entertainment.

Or so they thought.

'Well?' Tallulah interrupted the tall man's reverie. 'Ready?'

The tall man opened his eyes and looked up. Really, he thought, Tallulah was wearing remarkably well. The figure was still lithe and supple. The raven hair still silken. Her face, admittedly, spoke of more time than Tallulah cared to acknowledge, but the layers of make-up concealed that flaw. In the twelve years he had known her, she had changed very little. The years had been kind to her. But then so had he. He had put up with her tantrums and her escalating monomania. At one point he had actually loved her. It was such a shame that all good things had to come to an end. And soon.

He stretched his legs in front of him, raised his hands above his head and, yawning, flexed his fingers. 'Yes,' he said, slowly getting to his feet. 'I'm ready.'

Tallulah let him pass her and then followed him out of the room. As they walked together through the main gallery of the palace, she stole a sideways glance at him.

What was it, she tried to remember, that had initially attracted her to him? His power, she supposed. When she had first met him, he had been in a position of authority; he'd been a power to be reckoned with. People had respected him, and respect was something that Tallulah both admired and craved. Most of all, she craved it, and, with his assistance in the founding of Angels, the tall man had helped her get it. Yet Tallullah had to concede that the attraction had been physical as well. He was well built and good-looking in a slightly hawkish way. The scar, inflicted at an early stage of their relationship, had enhanced rather than detracted from his good looks. Tallulah used to enjoy running her fingers across it.

Not any more. Not since the tall man's ambitions
had reached dizzying heights and his acquaintance
with rational behaviour had become dangerously
fleeting. His outbursts she could cope with, but not
the near-insane egomania that was now his prime
motivator. And the fact that he had allowed Dave
Day to penetrate the system was the last straw.
Tallulah was positive that if she had been the
computer expert, none of this would have happened.
Yet, inevitably, it was she who had ended up with the
responsibility of ensnaring Dave and recovering the
program. Tallulah looked again at her companion
from under her lashes. It was a shame, she thought,
but things that had once been good were destined to
come to an end. And soon.

The tall man broke what used to pass for a
companionable silence between them. 'Who are we
going to first?' he asked as they turned into the wing
that housed the bedroom suites.

'Canton,' replied Tallulah.

'And who's with him?'

'Tara.'

'And she's got the equipment?'

Tallulah bit back her instinctive, angry response.
'Yes,' she sighed. 'Of course she's got the equipment.
They've all been well primed.' By me, she felt like
adding. While you were making pathetic attempts to
mend the system.

Tallulah's fractious tone angered the tall man.
What, he wondered, did she think he had been doing
while she was briefing a bunch of superannuated
trollops? He knew that Tallulah was no towering
intellect, but even she ought to have some notion of
the care needed to prepare such a glitteringly
successful presentation.

Tallulah had already bleeped Tara's ear-pager to warn her of their imminent arrival. No response was asked or required of Tara. She knew exactly what to do.

'Where are you going?' asked a peeved Mr Wu as Tara slithered off the bed. 'Not leaving me already?'

'Of course not,' purred Tara. 'I just thought you might like to play a game.'

'A game?' The Cantonese delegate's eyes lit up. 'What sort of game?'

Tara had her back to him as he asked the question. When she turned to face him, it was with a heavenly smile and a handful of black silk material. 'A game,' she said, 'of blind man's buff.'

'Of what?'

'You're in the buff,' teased Tara as she approached the bed, 'and I'm going to blindfold you.'

Not being *au fait* with esoteric Western customs, the delegate from Canton wasn't aware that Tara's interpretation of the game was a little odd. Her smile, however, was enough to break any cultural barrier, and the black silk looked promising.

Tara crawled on to the bed and began to unravel the material. 'First,' she whispered, 'I'm going to blindfold you...There. Then...like this...I take your arm and put it here...Now that's nice, isn't it?'

Her willing subject couldn't see what she was doing, but he could certainly feel it. And he had to admit that it did feel good to have the black silk against his wrist. And, a moment later, against the other wrist. 'Ah,' he said, nodding in approval. 'Tie up. Yes. Very nice.'

But if he could have seen exactly what Tara was up to, he wouldn't have thought it nice at all. The fact that he could move his arms relatively freely made him think she had bound his wrists extremely loosely. He was blissfully unaware of the fact that any sudden movement and, like seat-belts, his restraints would bind him into traction. It was only when Tara started on his feet that he began to feel uneasy.

'Tara?'

'Yes, my sweet?'

'I...I don't know if this is really a good idea.'

'Hush!'

'I don't think I like blind man's buff.'

'That's what they all say,' purred the temptress. 'But it's always worth it in the end.'

'No!' The delegate tried to wrench the blindfold off with his right hand – but to no avail. As he swung his arm, it snapped back and fell, as if manacled, to the mattress. 'Tara! Help! What is happening? Get this thing...OFF!'

As he screamed, he tried an identical manoeuvre with his left arm. The same thing happened. In a blind – literally – panic, he kicked out with both feet. Snap! They, too, ended up bound on the mattress.

'Tara!' he yelled in desperation. 'Tara! What are you doing? This is no joke. This is well beyond a joke! Tara!'

His shouts met with total silence.

'Tara!'

Again, silence.

'Tara?'

His panic now tempered with doubt, he lowered his voice. 'Tara?'

'Tara,' whispered a voice close to his ear, 'has gone.'

The delegate started in surprise, causing his bindings to tighten. Rigid with fear, he lay helpless on the bed. 'Who?...What?...Who are you?'

In response, the tall man leaned over the other man and pulled off the blindfold. 'I've come to give you your reward,' he whispered.

Confused, the little Cantonese blinked rapidly. The face leering above him was familiar, but the situation was most decidedly strange. 'You? What...Where's Tara?' Then confusion and panic gave way to deep embarrassment. He was lying naked and bound in front of the man in whose venture he had invested millions. This was the ultimate indignity; a catastrophic and complete loss of face. Totally lost for words, he stared in horror at the tall man.

'I wouldn't worry about being embarrassed.' The tall man smiled again. 'It won't last long.'

'I...I don't understand.'

'No, I don't suppose you do.'

The tall man disappeared from the delegate's view. He strained to see where he had gone, but was rewarded only with a glimpse of the woman standing by the door. She, too, was familiar. The woman in black who never spoke to the delegates but who strode around the palace in her high stilettos as if she owned the place. 'Help!' he croaked.

Tallulah didn't move a muscle.

Then the tall man came back, accompanied by a strange hissing noise. He bent down again to the delegate. 'What,' he asked, 'has China ever given the world?'

Desperately trying to save face, the Chinese delegate answered with alacrity. 'Lots of things. Porcelain...Bamboo...Pandas...'

'Wrong. Try again.'

'Terracotta armies?'

'No. I'll put you in my little red book if you don't

tell me,' teased the inquisitor.

'Chairman Mao?'

The tall man shook his head.

'Rickshaws?'

'No.' The hissing noise increased as the tall man moved his hand closer and held up its contents for the delegate to see. He was clutching a handful of lit sparklers.

'Bonfire night?' hazarded the desperate man.

'No, you idiot. We invented that.' He bent even closer over the bed. 'The only useful thing that China ever gave the world was gunpowder! Gunpowder! The ability to make great big bangs and weapons that kill people!'

More rapid blinking. 'If you say so...but I don't see what this has to do with...'

'With why you're here?'

Mr Wu nodded.

'Actually, it doesn't really have anything to do with why you're here. You were here to give me money, but you've done that now.'

'So I can go, yes?'

'Oh, yes. You can go with a bang.' The tall man roared with laughter and loosened the bindings on the delegate's arms. 'You can sit up now.'

He couldn't. Not really. All he could do was raise his head and his chest enough to give him a clear view of the room. What he saw puzzled him at first. Then, as realization dawned, he stared in open-mouthed horror at the array of objects spread out across the room. 'No,' he whimpered. 'No, this cannot be. This is not right. This is...'

'As you know,' said the tall man, 'I like to do my homework. Historians generally agree,' he continued in a chatty way, 'that the Mongols probably introduced

Chinese gunpowder and rockets into Europe in about 1241. So I've used that date to guide me.'

'To guide you?' The whites of Mr Wu's eyes were showing as he looked upwards.

'Yes. I think you'll find 1,241 fireworks here. Not, of course, that you'll have time to count them.'

'Look, perhaps we can reach a deal? I can give you more money, yes? Much more money...I have a lot of money. Yes?'

The tall man ignored him and held up the fizzing sparklers. 'These will burn down in about thirty seconds, giving my companion and myself enough time to leave the room. It's a shame you're rather tied up at the moment, but if you crane your head to the left you'll see that if I place them here, they will burn out and ignite this little trail of sulphur leading to the first firework, which, in turn, connects to the others. Ingenious, don't you think?'

Despite himself, the delegate from Canton looked to the bedside table, where the tall man had placed the sparklers. Sure enough, a little trail of powder led to a small firecracker. He shuddered, moaned softly and made another futile attempt to free himself from his bonds.

'You'll find that some of the fireworks are placed close to your arms and wrists,' said the tall man. 'With any luck, they may burn your bindings and you will be freed. This,' he added kindly, 'will give you a sporting chance to escape. Or rather, it would if there was any way you could leave the room. Unfortunately, that is impossible. As you know, there is no window, the walls are coated in steel and we will lock the door behind us.' The tall man moved away. 'Tallulah, my dear, I think it's time we left, don't you?'

Without uttering a word, Tallulah moved towards
the door. The tall man followed her.

'No!' screamed Mr Wu. 'No! This is inhuman…
impossible! You can't do this! Please!'

'Oh, don't be so dramatic. If I were you,' advised
the tall man as he opened the door, 'I'd pray instead
of shouting. There's every chance that some of the
fireworks may be duds. Although I have to say I've
made contingency plans for that. The Catherine
Wheels are in perfect working order, you see. I made
them myself – out of magazines from an AK-47.'

'No!'

'Goodbye, Mr Wu.' The tall man followed Tallulah
out of the room and closed the door. Five seconds
later the explosions started.

'That,' said the tall man to Tallulah, 'went rather
well, don't you think? Who's next?'

Patience was so worried that she began to confide
her doubts to the delegate from Carpathia. 'It just
shouldn't happen,' she moaned. 'Three of the Major
Arcana.'

'Let me try,' said the delegate.

Patience looked dubiously at the man kneeling on
the bed beside her. A little voice in her head told her
that she shouldn't really be doing this. Yet another
voice told her that she had found a kindred spirit in
Count Bathory and that he was as worried as she
was about the continued appearance of Death, the
Fool and the Magician.

'Oh dear,' he said as he dealt and they appeared
yet again. 'Not good, is it?'

'It's terrible…terrible,' wailed Patience. 'And the
awful thing is, I don't really know what it signifies.'

'No, nor do I. Look, why don't I go and get my

tarot book? That might give us a clue.' Without waiting for Patience to respond, the Count crawled off the bed and walked over to his briefcase in the corner of the room.

The little voice grew louder. It told Patience that she shouldn't be admitting weakness to a delegate and that by now she ought to have suggested that he wallow in the bath to give her a chance to prepare the room. It also informed her that her hair was escaping from its chignon again.

But Patience didn't care. She stayed where she was, kneeling on the bed and snivelling at the mocking cards. Death. It could, of course, be something to do with the fate she should be preparing for Count Bathory. But why was it always accompanied by the Fool and the Magician? It just didn't make sense. The sign of the Fool was weaker than that of the Magician, which meant, according to Patience's ailing powers, that the latter was in the ascendant; that a magician who enjoyed playing the fool was somehow linked to death. But she couldn't for the life of her work out what it had to do with Count Bathory. He had no magic powers and he wasn't a fool. In fact, Patience thought him very bright. And very kind.

As he crawled back on to the bed, she felt his gentle touch on her shoulder. A warm glow suffused her whole being and, as he sat cross-legged opposite her, she found their eyes locking in mutual admiration. Oh dear, she thought. This *really* shouldn't be happening.

'The book,' whispered the Count, 'doesn't give any suggestions.' He inched closer to her. 'Look, why don't we try to forget all about it and just...enjoy ourselves?'

Oh, yes, please, said the inner voice. The dissenting voice, however, told Patience that she should get cracking with the blindfold, stakes, fangs and the coffin. But she simply couldn't bring herself to do so. Instead, she reached over to the Count, placed both hands on his shoulders and looked once more into his eyes. 'Count...'

'Please, call me Vladimir.'

'Vladimir, then. There's something really quite important I have to tell you.'

'What has Brazil ever given the world?'

Still reeling from the shock of finding himself tightly bound and staring up into the face of the tall man, the Brazilian delegate tried desperately to concentrate. 'Well,' he began, 'Brazil's a huge place with an awful lot going for it, so it's hard to say exactly—'

'Shut up! Tell me! Tell me what Brazil has given the world?'

'Sugar.'

'No!'

'Yes! Brazil exports masses of sugar all over the world.'

'I don't want you to say sugar! I want you to say something else!' screamed the tall man. 'Tell me. What else?'

Belatedly, fear clamped its steely claws around the Brazilian's befuddled brain. A moment ago, he had been looking forward to playing more games with the frisky Kitty. Now he was bound, defenceless and at the mercy of the man in whom he had laid his trust. Not to mention a considerable slice of the fortune he had made from exporting sugar. He looked up, saw the manic expression on the other man's face and realized he would be wise to humour him.

'Rubber,' he said, nodding his head. 'Brazil has given the world rubber.'

'What else? What else?'

'Tin?'

'No!'

'G-strings?'

'No! Something different! Things that bite.'

'Er...footballers?'

'No! We invented those.'

Under normal circumstances the delegate would have taken issue with that. But these were not normal circumstances.

Suddenly the tall man moved away. 'You're a fool. You're stupid. An idiot. A sad, pathetic blithering idiot! I'll tell you what Brazil has given the world.'

Craning his neck, the Brazilian could just follow the tall man's progress as he moved to the far wall of the room. The first thing he noted was that the tall man, in a strange departure from his usual sartorial smartness, was wearing wellington boots. The second was that he stopped at the console controlling the lights and the temperature, extracted a small key from his pocket and inserted it into the hole on the panel. As he turned it, the sound of gushing water began to fill the room. Puzzled, the hapless delegate looked around to see where it was coming from. His eyes widened as he realized what was happening: it wasn't just the sound of running water filling the room, it was the actual liquid itself. Great tumbling torrents were cascading from what he had taken to be air-conditioning vents a few feet above the floor.

The tall man came back to the bed.

'What...what are you doing?' stammered the terrified delegate. He tried, and failed, to move his arms and legs. 'I'll drown.'

'Oh, no, you won't,' said the tall man. He smiled reassuringly at his victim. 'No chance of that.' Then he pulled a small knife from his pocket and poised it above the Brazilian's hairy chest.

'You're…you're going to stab me first?'

'Oh, pul-ease! Have faith! Why would I want to do that? No, no, all I'm going to do is nick you there.' As he spoke, he lowered the knife and made a small incision on the Brazilian's shoulder. 'There!' he said as a few spots of blood oozed out. 'That didn't even hurt, did it?'

'No, but…'

'But it *smells*, doesn't it? And it smells delicious to the creatures that Brazil gave to the world.' With a wild burst of laughter, the tall man gestured to the wall beside the bed: to the fish tank that the Brazilian had so admired. 'Piranhas,' he said with glee, 'love the smell of blood. And it's such a shame, don't you think, to keep them cooped up in such a small tank? Much better to let them have more space. A completely watertight room, perhaps? That would give them space.' He bent down, dabbed his finger in the trickle of blood and licked it with relish. 'Space to enjoy the pleasures of the flesh…'

'No! Please! No!' The Brazilian turned his pleading face to the tall man, but he was already retreating towards the door. He gave the fish tank a friendly little tap as he passed. The piranhas reacted with anger, opening their mouths and displaying sets of fine, white, deadly little teeth.

Patience had intended to tell Count Bathory only about the fate the tall man had in store for him. She hadn't planned to recount the entire story of Angels and the underground palace, yet she found herself spilling out the whole saga, sniffing and trying desperately to hold back the tears as she did so. She even told him about her own past, and the nasty time she'd had in Jamaica when she had unwittingly involved herself in voodoo. The only detail about the present situation she omitted was the preparatory part she should have played in the Count's demise. She knew now, as she stared into Vladimir's eyes, that she could never have bound him to the bed to await his death. She didn't want him to die. She wanted him to live. She wanted…

'Hush,' said Vladimir as the tears began to flow. 'It's not your fault, Patience. You're as much a victim as I am. A poor innocent caught up in the machinations of evil people.'

'Am I?' she snivelled.

'Yes. And so am I.' Vladimir reached out and held the sobbing woman in his arms. 'I wasn't doing this for me. I'm not a megalomaniac, Patience. I'm doing this for my country. All the money I gave, you see, was for the sake of Carpathia. My quota of the money that should have been siphoned out of the world's institutions wasn't going to *me*. It was going to the Carpathian Charitable Foundation.' With exquisite gentleness, he pushed Patience away from his shoulder, held her face in his hands and looked her in the eye. 'You do believe me, don't you? Tell me you believe me, Patience. It's important.'

'I believe you,' cried the half-laughing, half-tearful Patience. 'Oh, Vladimir, I really do believe you. I will always believe you!'

'Good.' The resolute delegate from Carpathia leapt off the bed. 'We have to get out of here. Tell me how, Patience. There must be a way.'

'Oh.' Patience's befuddled mind hadn't yet got

round to the thought of escape. 'Well,' she said after a moment, 'there are only two ways. There's the way you came in and the way the Angels descend.'

'Which is safer?'

Patience looked at her watch. 'If they're going according to the timetable, they should be with the delegate from Italy and...'

'And what?'

No, thought Patience. Vladimir didn't need to know that, as they spoke, the air-conditioning ducts in the Italian's room would be spewing forth mountains of pasta and that the hapless delegate would soon be smothered – or stuffed – to death with the glutinous export from his nation.

'And,' said Patience, 'that means we've got about ten minutes before they come into this room.' Trying to remember the configuration of the palace, she pondered which escape route was closer and quicker. Then she jumped off the bed and joined Vladimir. 'The way the Angels descend,' she said with conviction. 'That'll be safer. And quicker.'

But Patience had been thinking about only Tallulah and the tall man in her plan. In the excitement of the moment, she had forgotten about the army of Archangels patrolling the palace and the residence of the Angels with Broken Wings.

chapter fifteen

To their mutual surprise – and relief – Jeff and Marty weren't bickering. Instead, they were enjoying a companionable conversation, a leisurely drive and the joys of the unusually clement weather. They had almost forgotten they were on the lookout for the headquarters of the people who were trying to take over the world.

'The thing about these winding lanes,' Marty was saying, 'is that they discourage you from driving too fast.'

'True. You never know when you might meet a horse or something,' said Jeff, carefully negotiating the hedgerows hugging a blind corner. 'Different, the country, isn't it?'

'Yeah. Nice. Did you ever think of living in the country, Jeff?'

'Nah. Not really me, is it? I mean, you can't nip out for a pint of milk in the dead of night, can you?'

Marty chuckled. 'Oh…I don't know. A quick dash across a field, find a cow and just get on with it.'

'Yuck!' Jeff wrinkled his nose.

'Anyway, since when did you ever nip out for a pint of milk in the dead of night? There's never any milk in your flat. No food either.' He looked in wonder at his slight, slim companion. 'Don't know how you survive.'

'You're a fine one to talk. You *can't* eat.'

Marty rolled his eyes. 'Oh, please! Not that again. You know perfectly well I *want* to.'

'Still, it's quite convenient in a way,' mused Jeff after a short silence. 'Surviving on nothing but energy.'

Marty, however, wasn't keen on pursuing this line of conversation. He looked to his left for distraction – and almost immediately found a vital one. 'Slow down!' he shouted. 'Hill!'

Jeff looked in the mirror and, seeing nothing behind, immediately applied the brakes. Then he, too, looked out of Marty's window. 'That was a bit sudden. Wasn't it on the map?'

Marty looked at the crumpled expanse of paper in his lap. 'Well, yeah, it *is* on the map, but it's a bit difficult keeping track since you made such a mess of it. We're supposed to be looking for this grid reference' – he pointed vaguely –'which leads over there, see? But you folded it wrong.'

'All right, all right, sorry!' Jeff peered at the steep hill visible over the hedge. 'D'you think this one's worth investigating? How far are we from Angels?'

'About five miles. Bit far, don't you think?'

Jeff sighed. 'Maybe, but we haven't had any joy with the others. How many hills have we looked at. Ten? Fifteen?'

'Yeah. About that.'

'And they've all been crap. How about we look at this one and then call it a day?'

Marty shrugged. 'Fine. Suits me.'

Jeff looked around for somewhere to park.

Inching forward, he saw that there was a driveway leading to a house nestling in the lee of the hill. Best, he thought, not to park there. They'd already encountered one irate householder with objections to their parking in his driveway and scrutinizing his hill. Jeff looked in the mirror again and saw a gate that marked the entrance to a field on their right. He reckoned there was just enough room to tuck the Mercedes beside it and leave the road clear for passing traffic.

'Careful!' cautioned Marty as he began to reverse.

Jeff ignored him and, in one neat manoeuvre, slotted the car into the verge on the other side of the road.

Marty simply couldn't bring himself to congratulate Jeff on his handling of the car. Ignoring the loaded look from the driver's seat, he shimmered out and walked into the driveway.

Jeff locked the vehicle and followed him, stopping only to look at the weather-beaten signpost half covered in ivy. 'There's a name here,' he called to Marty, sweeping away the tendrils of creeper.

'Yeah,' said Marty over his shoulder. 'It's a thing they do in the country. They name their houses. Silly names, too. Houses in the middle of woods are always called Green Meadows or River View or something.'

But this house, as Jeff discovered by peering at the faded lettering, had an even sillier name. Shrugging, he left the ivy to its own devices and jogged up to Marty. 'Orpheus House,' he said. 'Mean anything to you?'

'*Orpheus?*' Marty was deeply scornful. 'Well, that's really daft. See, what did I tell you? Orpheus was one of those Greek blokes. God of sleep. I mean, what's that got to do with a little house beside a hill?'

'Christ, they had gods for everything, didn't they?' Then, as they approached the house, Jeff considered its situation. 'I don't know if it's *that* silly, Marty. I mean, look at it – tucked away, nestling beside a hill. It's sort of sleeping, isn't it?'

Marty's withering look was accompanied by an unspoken invitation for Jeff to consider the sadness of his life. Marty strode towards the nearest window of the house, shaded his eyes and looked inside. 'Now, if I were a burglar,' he said after a moment, 'I'd be sick as a parrot.'

'Why?'

'Well, look. There's nothing worth taking. Nothing!'

Jeff, too, peered into the uninspiring interior. 'Well, I'll grant you it doesn't look too promising, but you never know. Hadn't you better go inside and check?'

Marty shook his head. 'Waste of energy, Jeff. Anyway, my psychic powers tell me this isn't the place.'

'Since when did your psychic powers run to telepathy?'

'Since…since…Well, OK, they don't.' Marty turned to Jeff and clutched his stomach. 'I just have this feeling, *here*. A gut reaction. I used to have it when I was alive, remember?'

Jeff didn't remember. The only gut reactions he recalled Marty experiencing had invariably been to do with beer and spicy food. Wisely, he let that one pass. If he challenged Marty, he would no doubt be subjected to a treatise on psychic wind which, in anyone else's book, was known as farting. 'Well, then,' he said, turning away from the house. 'What about the garage? It's even closer to the hill. In fact,' he added as he walked towards it, 'it's almost part of the hill. Definitely worth checking out.'

'Nah,' said Marty. 'My gut tells me that a little wooden building isn't what we're looking for. Now, if it had been made of something a bit more sophisticated...hey! What's that noise?'

'What noise?'

'*That* noise.' Marty put a hand to his left ear. 'That sort of rumbling noise.'

Jeff shrugged and walked on. 'Can't hear anything. It must be your gut.'

'There *was* a noise, I tell you! See, Jeff, when you're dead, your senses become more acute. Your sensory things become more...well, sensitive.'

But Jeff wasn't listening. Now at the garage door, he reached out and pulled at the rickety wooden handle.

'There'll be nothing there, you know,' said Marty. 'Nothing but an old rusty wheelbarrow and maybe one of those old lawn-mowers you push and...Oh!'

Jeff had opened the door and, like Marty, found himself staring in some surprise at the large black limousine taking up most of the garage.

'Not exactly your rusty old wheelbarrow, is it?' said Jeff.

'Er ... no.' Marty went right up to the vehicle and tried to peer through the rear window. 'Tinted,' he mused. 'Odd.'

'P'rhaps not,' said Jeff. 'What do you bet this is where the chauffeur lives?'

'What? In the car?'

'No, you dork.' Jeff gestured towards the house. 'There. It's obviously some sort of lodge or something. Chauffeur's lodge – for the big house nearby.'

'Oh.' Marty had to concede – but not out loud – that it was a perfectly feasible explanation.

Except it wasn't the correct one. With neither wishing to admit that they wanted to beat the other in identifying the mysterious marque of the vehicle, the two men walked its length and stopped in front of the radiator. It was then that the rumbling sound began in earnest. Both turned in surprise to the wall behind them. Or rather, what had been the wall behind them. As they looked, it slid back to reveal a long, straight, floodlit tunnel leading into the depths of the hill.

'Christ!' said Marty.

'Bloody hell!' exclaimed Jeff.

'Shit!' cried the man who, seconds after the wall slid back, shot out of the tunnel.

He stopped in his tracks and glared in horror at Jeff.

An equally horrified Jeff stared back.

As did Marty who, in one of the very few occasions in his life (or death) found himself at a complete loss for words.

Count Vladimir Bathory, so far down the road to freedom, was now trapped again. The last thing on his mind had been the possibility of a guard stationed at the entrance of the tunnel.

The last thing on Jeff Randall's mind had been the possibility of actually finding the entrance to a secret, underground world and, worse, one of the inhabitants of that world.

Vladimir was the first to recover. The man in front of him, he reckoned, was unarmed. And he was short. Much shorter than the swarthy Carpathian. He lunged forward and grabbed Jeff by the lapels. The sudden movement took the detective completely by surprise.

'Hey! Gerroff! What d'you think ...?'

But Vladimir had the superhuman strength of the truly desperate. He slammed Jeff against the bonnet of the vehicle and repeatedly banged his head on the hard metal. 'Do something!' gasped Jeff. 'Please. Marty!'

The last word, however, prompted Vladimir into an excess of rage. He let out a great bellow and banged even harder.

'Marty!'

But the anguished Jeff had no idea that his cries to Marty only served to drive the other man to extremes of anger; no clue that *mārtý* was the Magyar equivalent of a comprehensive and damning indictment of every single member of someone's family – including those not yet born.

Marty himself, although equally ignorant as to the reason for the stranger's primal fury, was far from insensitive to Jeff's plight. The moment the other man had pinned Jeff against the vehicle, he stepped back from the car, took a few deep breaths and revved-up for a powerful burst of psychic wind. Whilst he could blow from both ends, he was well aware that wind from the mouth carried full lung capacity and was, therefore, infinitely more powerful that its equivalent in the rear-end.

Turning back to the car, he blew at the point where, seconds before, the Carpathian had been standing. Unfortunately, he had expelled all the air before he realized both Jeff and his attacker had moved. The wind which would have blown the Carpathian away from Jeff instead hit the limousine with full force, sending it straight into the tunnel. And with it the two men grappling against its bonnet.

The moment the limousine left the garage, the stone wall slid silently back, plunging the small building into darkness, separating Jeff and the Carpathian from the outside world and leaving a bemused Marty with the niggling sensation that he had done something very, very unfortunate.

Initially, both Jeff and Vladimir were so preoccupied with not being run over by the vast limousine that it took them a few seconds to realise what had happened. Only when the wall closed with an ominous thud did they appreciate the reality of the situation. Leaning against the wall of the tunnel, alone in a subterranean world, they looked warily at each other; Jeff fearful of a renewed attack, Vladimir suspicious that, despite his apparent helplessness of a moment before, Jeff had somehow orchestrated the movement of the wall.

Sensing that all was lost, Vladimir closed his eyes and slumped further against the wall. It was only a matter of time before the guard called reinforcements and he was dragged back to the underground palace. He had managed to avoid the guards in the palace, he had got so close to freedom, only to find himself face to face with a small man with no visible weapon. Now he was trapped and he had lost his only chance to find the other entrance to that palace and try to rescue his beloved Patience. His eyes filled with tears as he thought of her. 'Patience,' he moaned.

Jeff was completely flummoxed. First by his attacker's sudden *volte face*, secondly by the word he had uttered. 'Er…patience?' he asked the other man.

Vladimir opened his eyes. To his surprise the guard was still standing beside him, looking more than faintly uneasy. Then, slowly, it began to dawn on him. The guard had never been inside the tunnel. He was merely a sentry. Or possibly even a chauffeur. He didn't know what to do.

Vladimir's suspicions were confirmed when he stood up and took a tentative step towards the steel door that formed the reverse of the sliding brick wall. Rather than moving to stop him, Jeff backed away. He watched as the Carpathian approached the metal control panel at the side of the wall and pressed the door release button.

Nothing happened.

Vladimir tried again, this time with more force. Still the wall refused to slide back. Beads of sweat broke out on his forehead as he tried a third time. Then he began to pound the panel with his fist, shouting guttural obscenities as he did so. All the while, he ignored Jeff.

His behaviour confirmed the suspicions that had been forming in Jeff's mind. The person who had shot out of the tunnel wasn't one of Tallulah's henchmen. He was merely a lowly vassal who had somehow found himself trapped in the tunnel. He was, most likely, the chauffeur.

With that thought uppermost in his mind, Jeff tried to break the impasse. 'Look,' he began, 'I think there's been some sort of misunderstanding here.'

'Eh?' The Carpathian finally gave up trying to open the wall and turned round. Still suspicious, and still intent on escape, he looked warily at Jeff.

'I think,' repeated Jeff, 'there's been a misunderstanding.'

'I don't think so,' said Vladimir. 'I was trying to escape – you were trying to stop me.'

'Escape? Why were you trying to escape?'

This time Vladimir was flummoxed. 'I…I don't understand. I…who…?'

'That's why,' said Jeff, approaching the other man with increasing confidence, 'I told you there had been a misunderstanding. I, well, I thought you were the chauffeur.'

'I thought *you* were the chauffeur.' Vladimir looked Jeff up and down. 'Who *are* you, then?'

'Jeff. Jeff Randall. I'm a private investigator.'

'Good God!'

'And who are you, then?'

Vladimir stepped forward to shake hands. 'Vladimir. Vladimir Bathory. I'm a count.'

'I beg your pardon?'

'A count. I'm a Carpathian count.'

Jeff pointed to the tunnel behind them. 'And you were trapped down there?'

'Yes.'

'I think,' said Jeff, 'you should tell me all about it.'

'Not now.' Vladimir looked pointedly at the steel wall. 'When we're out of here. I don't know why the door mechanism isn't working, but we'll find a remote control for it in the car.'

But they didn't. There was nothing in the black limousine that would help them escape.

Jeff watched with a renewed sense of unease as Vladimir pushed and pressed every button he could find on the dashboard. The discovery that the other man was friend rather than foe was all very well, but he would have preferred to forge that friendship outside the confines of a tunnel that led, indubitably, to something nasty. Equally disturbing was that the only other person who could help them seemed disinclined to make an appearance. Either Marty had disappeared into the ether or, for some reason, he had found himself unable to pass through the wall.

Then Jeff remembered what Vladimir had said when he had been slumped against the wall. 'Why did you say "patience"?' he asked as the dejected count emerged from the vehicle. 'Is someone else on their way to rescue you?'

Vladimir scowled at Jeff. It was one thing to have discovered that he was friend not foe, but he wasn't having him using his beloved's name in vain. How could Patience rescue them? She, too, was a prisoner. The thought brought tears to his eyes. He would never forget how the great front door of the palace had slammed shut in her face, trapping her inside, leaving only Vladimir free to escape.

Vladimir stared at Jeff. How did he know about Patience? A niggling suspicion suggested to his subconscious that there was more to Jeff than met the eye. And then he remembered the word that Jeff had used when he was thumping his head against the bonnet of the car. Odd, he thought, that an English private investigator should be fluent in Magyar. Vladimir didn't quite like it. Ignoring Jeff's question, he asked one of his own.

'Why were you swearing at me?'

'Swearing?' Jeff was pole-axed. 'I wasn't swearing.'

'You were,' replied an indignant Vladimir. 'You said *márty*. That,' he added, bristling, 'is the worst insult anyone can use in my language.'

'Oh. I didn't know. What does it mean?'

Vladimir looked around. He had never uttered the words out loud and he certainly wasn't going to start now. Bending forward, he whispered the explanation in Jeff's ear.

Jeff recoiled in horror. 'That's *terrible*! That's really offensive.'

'Told you,' said Vladimir. Then he frowned. 'Why were you saying it anyway, if you don't know what it means?'

Jeff took a deep breath. Here he was, trapped in a tunnel that led he knew not where with a Magyar he knew not at all – heading for heaven knew what. Nothing, now, would surprise him. He hoped the same held true for Vladimir Bathory. 'What would you think,' he began, 'if I told you I'm being haunted by a ghost who only I can see and who might, just might, be able to get us out of this mess?'

Vladimir pondered that one for a few seconds. Then he pointed down the tunnel. 'And what would you think,' he replied, 'if I told you I'm trying to escape from a bunch of egomaniacs who live in an underground palace, have Angels as accomplices, specialize in particularly macabre methods of torture and are trying to take over the world?'

'I'd believe you,' said Jeff.

Vladimir smiled and held out a hand. 'I think, Mr Randall, we have an understanding.'

chapter sixteen

'So what exactly are...your friend's powers?'
Vladimir still couldn't bring himself to utter the
word.

'Well, there's psychic wind – that's the power to
blow things.' Jeff wrinkled his nose. 'From, uh, both
ends. Then there's telekinesis, which means he can
move things by sheer will-power. And he can also
possess people. Y'know, enter other people's bodies
and control them. That's it, really.'

'No, it isn't! No, it isn't!' An outraged Marty
leaned forwards to the passenger seat. 'You forgot
power merging! How could you forget that? Tell him,
Jeff. Tell him.'

'Oh, sorry.' Jeff turned again to Vladimir. 'He's
just reminded me that he can power merge – that's
entering cyberspace and, er, messing about.'

'Huh!' said Marty.

Vladimir grinned. 'Forgive me, Jeff, but I still
find it hard to believe that I'm in the presence of
a ghost.'

'Oh, don't worry. You'll get used to it.'

'It's a pity I can't see him. I thought I might be
able to. I used to have the gift, you see. Lots of us do.

We Carpathians are a deeply superstitious people.'

'Superstition,' said a deeply scathing Marty, 'isn't enough. I mean, anyone can be superstitious, for Christ's sake! Tell him he's arrogant, Jeff.'

'No, I will not.'

'What was that? What did he ask you?' inquired Vladimir.

'Oh, he just asked me to open the window.'

'Odd,' said the Carpathian. 'It's not as if he's going to get any fresh air in here. Probably a bit confused, eh? Apparently that's quite common. They do get a bit confused, poor wretched creatures. Wandering about going "woo, woo!"'

'Oh, no. Mar – er, my friend doesn't woo.'

Marty had missed Vladimir's remark, but he was on to Jeff in an instant. 'That's right,' he snapped. 'Rub it in, why don't you? Marty doesn't woo 'cos Marty can't woo, can he? Oh, no. So it's Jeff that does the wooing. "Would you like a cup of tea, Jeannie?"' he mimicked, '"Why don't we go out to dinner, Jeannie?" Oh, yes. A regular little Rudolph Valentine, aren't you?'

'Valentino,' corrected Jeff.

'How very observant,' said Vladimir, patting his trousers. 'My favourite designer. I prefer the cut to that of Versace. Used to go for Armani in a big way but, frankly, he's just a little too ubiquitous nowadays, don't you think?'

Jeff, whose wardrobe could fit into a Valentino sponge bag, hadn't the faintest idea what Vladimir was on about. He had, anyway, a rather more pressing agenda. The replica of the Treasury at Petra was looming ahead. He nudged Vladimir. 'We're here,' he said. 'Christ, it's huge!' he added in an awe-struck whisper. 'Bloody amazing.' Then, doubt creeping in, he added, 'Are you *sure* they're not going to be on the lookout?'

'Oh, no,' said Valdimir with airy confidence. 'Absolutely not. They're still torturing, you see.' He looked at his watch. 'They won't even have realized that Patience and I are missing yet. They're not due to visit me until at least...Oh, *poor* Patience! I hope she's all right. If that door hadn't closed...' Distraught at the memory, Vladimir fell silent.

'I'm sure,' said a reassuring Jeff, 'she'll be fine. She'll have made her way to the entrance to Angels and even as we speak she'll be on her way to...well, freedom.'

Privately, he wasn't so sure. Vladimir had told him everything he knew about Angels and the secret world beneath it. Likewise, Jeff had shared his own knowledge with the other man. Their combined intelligence suggested to Jeff that the operation would have been monitoring every movement in the palace. Especially any attempt at escape. Wasn't that why the sliding door at the top of the tunnel had refused to open? And wouldn't that have been the reason for the door slamming and locking in poor Patience's face?

Jeff was positive that was the case. Marty, however, when he had eventually joined them in the tunnel, had demurred. 'No,' he had said. 'I know a thing or two about gadgets, Jeff. Those doors would be programmed to be opened once to anyone who wanted to open them, but the second time you'd have to know the code.'

'Why?' Jeff had asked.

'Security.'

'Security,' Jeff had relayed to Vladimir.

'So ask him,' countered the Carpathian, 'why the

door slammed in Patience's face.'

Marty's reply had been deeply mysterious. 'Psychic wind,' he had said. 'Accidental psychic wind. There's a lot of it about in the underworld. Trolls and whatnot.'

Vladimir had accepted that explanation. But then he was, as Jeff reminded himself, from Carpathia. Jeff, however, knew Marty inside out and had recognized the expression on his face as he had pontificated about trolls. He had been desperate to regain his credibility after blowing the car into the tunnel and then taking ten minutes to materialize on their side of the sliding wall. 'The combination of rock and steel,' had been his rather grand explanation for the latter, 'is the natural enemy of ectoplasm.'

Jeff had agreed with Vladimir that the only course of action open to them was to get into the limousine and go to the underground palace. Yet as Vladimir parked the vehicle outside the grand portico, he felt a sense of vague discomfort, mingled with a gnawing fear. He had hoped to arrive by design, not as the result of an unfortunate accident. Yet it was mishap, not planning, that saw them pulling up outside the lion's den.

'I hope you realize,' said Marty as they alighted from the limousine, 'that my powers are going to fade soon.'

'*What?*'

'What did he say?' asked Vladimir, sensing Jeff's panic.

'He said his powers are going to fade soon.'

'Rubbish.' Vladimir couldn't see Marty, but he looked disparagingly at the space he reckoned he was inhabiting. 'What about adrenaline? Haven't you ever heard of that? That'll keep you going for a while.'

'Oh, pul-ease!' said Marty. 'How can I have adrenaline if I don't have a bloodstream? Tell him, Jeff. And you can tell him he's a twat while you're at it.'

'What did he say?' asked a suspicious Vladimir.

'You're a twat,' said Marty.

'I can sense by your silence, Jeff, that he's being rude about me. *Me!* Count Vladimir Bathory. I'm not remotely impressed by ghosts. We've had more ghosts in our family than you've had hot meals.'

'Oh, rub in it, why don't you?' jibed Marty. 'I can't eat, can I? Still, I wouldn't want what you lot eat. Dumplings and goulash and...and—'

'Oh, for Christ's sake!' snapped Jeff. 'This is serious! We're in trouble and all you two can do is bicker. Which, come to think of it, is pretty strange, since you can't even communicate with each other. Stop it, will you? Just stop it!'

Surprised by his outburst, yet recognizing its validity, Marty and Vladimir stopped arguing. Marty contented himself with sticking his tongue out at Vladimir. The Carpathian count, ashamed that someone as small as Jeff should have witnessed someone of his status trading insults with a spectre of uncertain ancestry, drew himself up to his full height and mounted the steps to the great front door.

'Right,' he said as he reached it. 'If you could ask your friend if he would very kindly open this door for us, I should be enormously grateful.'

'Can you do that, Marty?'

'S'pose so,' sulked his friend. 'It's a case of moving the lock, though. That requires a big burst of energy.'

'Well, have a go anyway.'

Marty screwed up his face, looked hard at the left side of the door, closed his eyes and concentrated. A moment later they all heard the sound of the lock snapping back.

'Bravo!' congratulated Vladimir. 'Well done, M—my man.'

'Patronizing git,' mumbled Marty.

Jeff ignored him, instead reaching forward to open the door. 'Wow,' he said as he crossed the threshold into the palace. 'This is really something. It's like in…I don't know, the *Arabian Nights* or one of those fairy things. It's—'

'Magnificent, is it not?'

'Eh?' Puzzled by the apparent change in Vladimir's voice, Jeff turned back to face him. As he did so, and as Vladimir stepped into the building behind him, the great front door slammed shut and, from behind the pillars flanking the entrance, two black-clad men with sub-machine guns materialized and grabbed both intruders in vice-like grips.

Oh dear, thought Marty.

'Hey!' yelled a struggling Jeff.

'Get off!' shouted Vladimir, flailing against the steely embrace.

But neither man was a match for the menacing, muscular Archangels.

'I wouldn't waste your energy,' said the still-unidentified voice. 'Struggling against Gabriel and Lucifer. They're crack troops, you know. Ex-riot police. Trained by the best in the business.' Then he called out to the duo, 'Search them, boys!'

The Archangels deftly rummaged in both men's pockets. Because he had left the building in such a hurry, Vladimir was carrying nothing more than a monogrammed handkerchief and a wallet. Jeff, on the other hand, had his usual eclectic collection of empty crisp packets, crumpled bills, long-forgotten notes on which he had written reminders to himself, coins of varying denominations – and his car keys. The Archangel in whose grip he was held looked with particular interest at the keys. 'I think,' he called out, 'these are what they used to get in.'

Beside him, Marty allowed himself a smug little grin. The disembodied voice, however, soon wiped that away. 'Well done,' it said. 'Bravo! Imagine being able to turn such a big lock with such a little key. But you really needn't have bothered, you know. The small door on the left was unlocked all along. We were, you see, waiting for you.'

The last few words were accompanied by the sound of footsteps on the stone floor and, seconds later, by the owner of the voice. His bearing matched his deep baritone: tall, well-built and carrying himself with supreme authority, the man moved out of the shadows behind the pillars and stood in front of Jeff and Vladimir. The harsh light emphasized the long scar on the right side of his face. Vladimir groaned and slumped in Gabriel's embrace.

'Not pleased to see me?' chided the tall man. 'After all I've done for you.'

'You've done nothing!' yelled the irate Carpathian. 'Nothing! All you've done is rob, maim and kill! You're evil! The spawn of the devil!'

'My, my, harsh words indeed,' mused the tall man. 'And from someone who really ought to know better, what with all that Carpathian baggage you carry. Still, we'll deal with you later.' His gimlet eyes moved from Vladimir to Jeff.

'What have you done with Patience!' the Count shouted.

'Who? Oh, *her*.' The tall man looked amused. 'Oh, we've designed an appropriate little fate for her. You'll see in a minute. Just have patience, my dear Count. We have. Now,' he said, still smiling from his little joke, 'Mr Randall...'

Jeff looked balefully at the imposing figure in front of him. This, then, was Tallulah's accomplice, the power behind the throne of the Angels, the mastermind behind the plot to rule the world. Everything Vladimir had told him fitted. He was confident, authoritative and, judging by the look in his eyes, slightly mad.

'We were hoping,' continued the tall man, 'that you'd all arrive together. Much...much less messy.' Stroking his scar, he looked Jeff up and down. Mild disapproval seemed to be his verdict. 'Still, this way has its advantages. I'm sure the divine Miss Hurst would be distraught to know that you've landed yourself in such an *uncomfortable* position. I'm sure she would do *anything* to secure your release, don't you think?'

'Yeah,' said Jeff. 'The moment she finds out she'll go to the police.'

'Oh? And what will she tell them?'

'That I'm in the hands of an egomaniac who has killed a whole bunch of international businessmen in his underground palace and has plans...'

'To take over the world? Yes.' The tall man stepped closer. 'Doesn't sound terribly believable, does it? I'm sure the police have other things on their mind, aren't you?'

Jeff's silence was, they both knew, tacit acknowledgement of how the police would react.

'Now,' said the tall man, 'it's really most inhospitable of me to keep you hanging around in the hallway. Perhaps we should retire to a more...a more *interesting* room. And then we can compose a little invitation to Miss Hurst and Mr Day. I don't know why, but I have this feeling they'd like to join us.' With that, he indicated to the Archangels to propel their prisoners further into the underground palace.

Secure that he was utterly in control of the situation, he had a glow about him as he marched forward, an air of inviolate supremacy. But he wasn't in control. Not really. He didn't know, for example, that a man in a white suit had fallen into step beside him, biding his time until the moment when he would wrest control from the hands of a madman.

chapter seventeen

'He really should be back by now.'

Dave looked at his watch. 'Well, yeah. He should.' He looked up at Jeannie. 'Not much point in doing a recce in the dark.'

'Mmm.' Frowning, Jeannie reached for the phone. 'I'll try his mobile again.'

But her attempt to contact her partner was, once again, in vain. The irritating female voice informed her for the umpteenth time that the number she had called was currently unobtainable. 'Jeff *never* switches off his mobile,' sighed Jeannie.

'He could be somewhere where you can't get a signal,' pointed out Dave.

'Yes, but *where*? I've never had problems in that part of the countryside.'

Dave shrugged. 'Dunno. I'm not much of an expert on mobiles. I've spent the last ten years in prison, remember?'

Jeannie started drumming her fingers on the desktop. 'I don't really understand why he went anyway.'

'I thought you talked to him?'

'I did. But that was ages ago.'

Jeannie cast her mind back to her last conversation with Jeff, after her return from her fruitless visit to Wendy's. Disgruntled that she had wasted so much time, she had been further annoyed that Jeff had taken it upon himself to do a recce in the vicinity of Angels, looking, as he had put it, 'for clues'. The image of Jemima and her 'sleuthing' had sprung to Jeannie's mind. They'd make a fine pair, she had thought. Then she had decided they wouldn't. Neither individual would have a clue how to relate to the other. Jeannie looked back to Dave. 'And he definitely didn't say anything more in his note?'

Dave rolled his eyes. 'No, I told you. All it said was, "Gone out – back soon".'

Jeannie realized she was clutching at straws. She had anyway believed Dave the first time. That sort of note was vintage Jeff. Short, elliptical and basically completely unhelpful. 'Look,' she said, 'I think I ought to go and look for him. He might be...in trouble.'

'Broken down, you mean?'

Jeannie refused to meet Dave's eye. 'That sort of thing, yes.'

Dave stood up. 'You don't really mean that sort of thing at all, do you?'

'No.'

'You think he's run into trouble with Tallulah's lot.'

'The thought had occurred to me.'

Dave switched off his laptop and snapped it shut. 'Well, you're not going without me.'

'Don't be ridiculous, Dave. I'm not going to be responsible for...Well, I just don't think it's fair on you.'

Dave eyed Jeannie with interest. 'OK, so you're

going to go to Angels, right?'

'Well, yes.'

'And how are you going to get in?'

Jeannie looked up in surprise. 'The same way as I did last time. Why?'

Dave scratched the stubble on his chin. 'Because, if I remember correctly, you told me that the drive-way is lined with hidden cameras.'

'Ye-es...'

'So your arrival won't be a secret?'

Jeannie had to admit he had a point. 'All right, I'll try to find a back entrance or something.'

'Which is exactly what Jeff was trying to do before he went...unobtainable.'

Jeannie sighed. 'So what do you suggest then?'

'I suggest that you go to Angels with someone who is an expert with all things electronic. Someone,' he continued as he delved into the ruck-sack beneath the table, 'who knows how to disable cameras.'

'Hidden cameras,' corrected Jeannie.

'Cameras,' declared a grinning Dave as he extracted a pair of goggles, 'whose infrared beams can be detected with night sights.'

Jeannie knew when she was beaten. 'Touché,' she said in reluctant admiration. Then she leaned across the desk and grabbed her car keys. 'C'mon then, let's go.' As she turned towards the door, she saw, out of the corner of her eye, that Dave was picking up his laptop. 'You're not bringing that, are you? It's valuable.'

Dave tried, and failed, to take the edge off his voice in his response. 'Yes,' he said. 'And it's also a valuable bargaining tool.'

Less than an hour later they were speeding past the pub called the Sign of the Angel and, minutes after that, Jeannie switched off her headlights and cruised to a halt at the top of the driveway of Angels.

For all his bulk, Dave proved to be a nimble as well as an instinctive accomplice. Without even exchanging a word with Jeannie, he leapt out of the car, donned his goggles and disappeared from her view.

Less than ten minutes later he was back in the passenger seat. 'Done,' he said succinctly.

'But won't they notice they're not working?'

'Ah!' Dave's gleeful expression told her he had thought of that. 'I haven't exactly disabled them. I've locked them.'

'Locked them?'

'Yeah. I've locked the circuit so that each camera shows a static image. The image they were displaying when I locked them. As in,' he continued, 'the image of an empty driveway with no yellow Triumph Stag anywhere in sight.'

'You,' said Jeannie as she started the car again, 'are a genius.'

With the headlights still off, they made fairly slow progress down the long, winding drive. 'In a way it's a shame you can't see this,' commented Jeannie. 'It's stunning. Really beautiful.'

'I've lived without stunning beauty for the last ten years,' mused Dave. 'I'm sure I can last another few hours or so.' Secretly, however, he was feeling rather chipper. A ride in a Triumph Stag with a beautiful, feisty girl at the wheel was, in his book, infinitely preferable to boring bits of countryside.

'Tallulah said,' remembered Jeannie after a few

minutes' silence, 'something about a Host today. Any idea what that means?'

'No. A choir practice maybe? An angelic meditation?' Then Dave snorted. 'Anyway, it's all a load of old cobblers as far as I'm concerned. They may have hoodwinked people with more money than sense, but, you mark my words, this whole thing is a front.'

But even he had to admit it was a pretty impressive front as the ponderous, majestic façade of the building rose out of the darkness in front of them. 'Shit!' he exclaimed. 'That's quite a building.'

'Mmm,' said Jeannie. 'And they haven't skimped on the interior either.' Another vision of thin-lipped, outraged Jemima floated in front of her. Jemima had thought they'd skimped in a heinous way. The library, remembered Jeannie, had made her apoplectic with rage.

Turning her thoughts to the task in hand, Jeannie slowed down and looked for a safe spot to leave the car, hopefully to hide it. She found what she was looking for in a copse to her right, just before the parkland gave way to the more formal landscape of the garden. She steered the vehicle off the drive and inched it slowly into the darkness of the trees. 'It's not perfect,' she said to Dave, 'but it's probably our best option. I don't want to leave it too close to the building.'

'No.'

Dave was wondering if Jeannie, like himself, was beginning to have doubts about the wisdom of their mission.

She wasn't. Fuelled by adrenaline, she leapt out of the car, closed the door with a little click and then went round to the boot, her high heels sinking a little into the soft ground as she walked. Too late (why, she wondered, was it always too late?), she remembered that she was inappropriately dressed for the occasion. High heels, a short black suit and her pink plastic mac were probably not best suited to her purposes.

Dave, now following her out of the car, looked more the part, with his black leather jacket, polo neck and straining black jeans. Shame about the rubber shoes, she thought. But then he *was* a computer genius and was therefore entitled to such an aberration.

And the proof of his trade was in his hand as he eased the door shut. Jeannie decided not to comment on the laptop. There was, after all, only one reason why he had chosen to bring it.

'Torch,' she said as she closed the boot.

'Good idea.'

'Ready?'

Jeannie's eyes, noted Dave, were bright and dancing with excitement. 'As ready as I'll ever be,' he replied without enthusiasm.

'Oh, come on.' Jeannie gave him a friendly pat on the shoulder as they made their stealthy way through the shadows towards the house. 'We'll make a private investigator of you yet.'

They remained silent for the next few minutes, concentrating on the ground in front of them, anxious not to have to use the torch to help them negotiate the uneven surface. As they approached the great sweep of gravel in front of the building, Jeannie prodded Dave. 'Do you think the cameras on the house are on the same circuit as the ones you disabled?' she whispered.

'Should be.'

'So,' said Jeannie more to herself than to Dave,

'it's people we have to be on the lookout for.'

Dave inched closer and pointed to the house. 'Doesn't look like there are many people around.'

'Not many guests,' replied Jeannie, looking at the blank windows of the main building and the wing nearest them. 'But the residents' wing is on the west side. Most of the Angels will be there. And if they've got Jeff, that's probably where he'll be.'

'What about the Host?' whispered Dave.

'Hostess,' replied Jeannie. 'They're all women.'

Dave stifled a giggle. 'No, the Angelic Host.'

'Oh, I see.' Jeannie shrugged. 'Your guess is as good as mine.' Then she paused, considering the best route to take. 'The service quarters,' she said. 'That's probably our best option.'

It was. A few minutes later, hugging the sprawling servants' wings at the rear of the building, just two more shadows in the night, they hit upon a half-open window.

'Are you sure about this?' asked Dave as Jeannie raised it further and, nimble as a mountain goat, leapt on to the edge.

'Trust me,' she whispered. 'I'm an expert in martial arts.' Then she lowered herself into the interior of the house and disappeared from view. Her voice, however, wafted over to him. 'The laptop,' she hissed. 'Pass it through and then follow.'

The passing-through element was achieved without difficulty. But the following was another matter, being accompanied by a series of grunts and, as Dave lowered his bulk on the other side, a little moan.

'Shhh!' said Jeannie.

Dave obliged and, once inside, remained mute, waiting for his eyes to adjust to the gloom. There was no moonlight to guide them here, no stars to illuminate the blackness.

Jeannie risked a quick flash of the torch. 'A pantry,' she said. 'Come on.'

Wordlessly, Dave followed her, amazed by her easy confidence – and somewhat bucked up by her revelation about martial arts.

The pantry led to a small, windowless lobby. Completely in the dark now, Jeannie was forced to use the torch again. Four small doors and a larger one led off the lobby. Without hesitation, she chose the larger one. It opened on to a long, dimly lit corridor with, at the far end, a green-baize door. Again, Jeannie made her confident way towards the door.

Puzzled by her seeming familiarity with the house, Dave followed on. As they reached the door, Jeannie turned to him and put a finger to her lips. 'We've got to be really careful now,' she said in an all but inaudible whisper. 'If there's anyone around, they'll be on the other side of the door.'

'How do you know?'

Jeannie touched the door. 'Green baize.'

'Oh. Right,' said Dave, completely mystified.

Jeannie opened the door a fraction – and immediately closed it again. Her glimpse of the marble hallway and its flickering lights had been enough to show her that she had been right: there was a black-clad, muscle-bound individual patrolling the room beyond. And Jeannie reckoned she knew enough about firearms to know an AK-47 when she saw one.

'Damn!' She turned round and whispered her intelligence to Dave.

His response, however, was pleasingly positive. 'If it's anything like prison,' he said, 'he'll have a timetable. Y'know, a minute to patrol one way; a minute in the next direction. That sort of thing. They always stick to routine, these people.'

'Thanks.' Jeannie pulled at the door again, this time opening it only enough to hear, not see, the activities in the hall. After thirty seconds she heard the sound of the guard's boots on the echoing marble. Like the ticking of a clock, they worked to a regular rhythm, becoming louder by the second. Then, after another thirty seconds, they began to recede, finally disappearing out of earshot. Jeannie waited with bated breath for them to come back. Another thirty seconds.

Still she waited, giving the guard time to repeat the manoeuvre not once but three times. Then, when she was certain that Dave had been right and his patrol was as regular as clockwork, she turned and whispered her plan to him.

Dave wasn't going to demur. As far as he was concerned, she was the boss.

Jeannie took off her shoes, held them in one hand by their straps and darted into the hallway. Dave followed her, secure in the knowledge that his rubber soles would make no noise.

But almost as soon as they entered the cavernous room, another noise greeted them. 'Shit!' Jeannie darted behind the cantilevered staircase. Dave needed no instructions to join her. Huddled together against the wall, they listened as the sound increased in volume. The noise – a sort of scratching followed by two soft thumps – was unfamiliar to both of them. As it grew ever louder and closer, Jeannie thought she detected a vague, guttural muttering accompanying it. She was still weighing up the chances of being spotted if she peered round the staircase when another, this time unmistakable noise reverberated throughout the room.

'Rosa! Rosa!' cried a man's voice. 'Where do you think you're going!'

The footsteps that Jeannie had identified as belonging to the guard quickened their pace and became louder. 'Rosa! Not in there, now. You know you're not up to it!'

But still the scratching and the thumping continued.

Jeannie knew it was now or never. She had to find out where the old woman was heading. She took a deep breath, smiled reassuringly at Dave and peered round the edge of the stairs.

And there, supporting herself on a zimmer, was Rosa. The elderly lady had her back to Jeannie as she pushed the walking frame forwards with a grating scratch and then laboriously and painfully dragged her creaking limbs after it. It was quite clear where she was heading – to the room directly opposite Jeannie's refuge. And the open door to the far left of that room indicated where Rosa had come from.

'Rosa!' Puffing slightly, the guard reached her and clamped one powerful arm on the zimmer. 'Rosa! I'm sorry, but I've got my orders. You're simply not fit enough…Ouch!'

The guard screamed and clutched his shin as Rosa, with a force that belied her frailty and minute stature, lashed out with one foot. A volley of irate Russian accompanied her kick.

'Rosa! You evil old bitch! You cunning, conniving…Christ that hurt!' Evidently in severe pain, the guard began hop up and down.

Rosa saw her chance. Lunging sideways, she made a bid for the AK-47. The guard, however, was far too quick for her. Forgetting his agony, he grabbed the tiny woman round the waist and scooped up her into the air. As he did so, her bright-red wig fell to the ground. Screaming like a stuck pig, terrifying in her baldness and feet flailing in all directions, Rosa was, nonetheless, helpless. The guard was twice her height. He rearranged the rifle round his shoulder, hoisted Rosa high above his head and marched off in the direction of the west wing. 'If I had my way, you old tart, I'd shoot you dead right now,' Jeannie heard him shouting as he disappeared from view.

Jeannie expelled a lungful of air and looked back to Dave. He, too, had poked his head round the staircase and had witnessed the astonishing performance. He raised his eyebrows. 'Quite a show,' he said. Then, incredulity writ large on his face, he added, 'Don't tell me *that* was an Angel?'

'I'm afraid it was, Dave. And while they're not all as old as she is, I've got a horrible feeling they're just as evil.' Then she gestured towards the door that the ailing, arthritic Rosa had been so desperate to open. 'Did you hear what he said?'

'Yeah,' whispered Dave. '"You're not up to it." Don't know about you, but I reckon whatever we're looking for is behind that door.'

'I told you,' replied Jeannie, 'that we'd make a detective of you yet. Come on,' she added as she stepped out into the hallway. 'Time's on our side. For the moment.'

As light and delicate as a gazelle, Jeannie ran across the hall. Dave lumbered after her.

'I thought I saw this room,' mused Jeannie as she looked through the keyhole, 'but maybe I was wrong. Maybe this is the library.' Then she turned to Dave.

'It's dark.'

'Fine.' Dave's confidence was growing by the minute. 'Not even a flicker of light?'

'No.'

'Then we can assume no one's there.'

Dave was right. Jeannie opened the door and, with Dave right behind her, darted into the room. This time there was no need to wait for their eyes to adjust to the darkness. For while there was no illumination within the room, the three enormous windows let in enough moonlight to enable them to see.

'The library,' said Jeannie after a moment's perusal of the room.

'Yup.' Even Dave could tell that. 'The library.' He turned to Jeannie. 'But why on earth would that old woman have been so desperate to get in here? Why would the guard have said she wasn't up to it?'

'I haven't the faintest idea,' replied Jeannie with a sinking heart. Supposing, she thought, Rosa had a penchant for visiting the library at night and trying to find a book that was too high for her to reach? She quite evidently wasn't "up to" clambering on the library steps. That could explain the guard's reaction. And Rosa was obviously near the end of the road to insanity. That, in turn, would explain why she was prepared to shoot the guard for thwarting her in her ambition.

Jeannie sighed and walked into the centre of the room and, unbidden, Jemima's shrill voice rang in her ears. 'I think it's his arm, you see. To my mind it rather breaks up the piece, and *it's even worse* in the copy they've had done. You should see it; it's *far* too big. Even to the untrained eye.'

St Peter. Of course. She was staring at the

painting of *The Liberation of St Peter by an Angel*.

'What are you looking at?' asked Dave, sidling up to her.

Jeannie nodded at the wall opposite them. 'That painting. Is there anything peculiar about it? Anything you find a bit odd?'

Again, Dave scratched the bristle on his chin. 'Well, I can't say I know anything about art, but from what I can see it looks a bit fake.'

'Really? Why do you say that?'

Dave didn't hesitate. 'The arm. At least I *think* it's an arm. Looks far too big. On the other hand, maybe it's the light.'

'Hmm.' Jeannie looked at the torch in her hand. Dare she risk it? She didn't know why, but a little voice was telling her that she should, that St Peter had something to tell her.

He did.

Jeannie flashed the torch at the painting, illuminating the central portion of the vast canvas. The arm, as Jemima and now Dave had suggested, was definitely out of proportion. But it wasn't the arm that caught Jeannie's eye: it was the little beam of light reflecting back at her. She studied it for a moment and then, frowning, looked at Dave.

'Do you see what I see?'

'I think so. There's a reflection from the torch. Funny, 'cos there's no glass on the painting...' As he spoke, Dave walked towards the giant canvas. 'Keep the torch on, Jeannie,' he said over his shoulder. 'If we're right, then there's a little window in one of those links. Or a lens.' Reaching the painting, he extended a finger and poked it into one of St Peter's chains, and made contact with a minuscule piece of glass. Heart pounding, he turned back to Jeannie.

'There's something here, Jeannie. And it's definitely a lens.'

Jeannie bounded forward. 'Why,' she mused, 'would there be a lens embedded in a painting?' But even as she asked the question, she arrived at the answer.

So had Dave. 'Because,' he said, 'there's something behind this painting.'

'And if there's something behind it...'

'There must be a way in.'

In perfect accord, Jeannie and Dave began to explore the painting with their fingers.

It was Dave who found it: a tiny hole on another of St Peter's chain links. He pressed the little button in the middle of the hole and, even before he had time to relay his discovery to Jeannie, St Peter's arm slid silently sideways.

'I think,' he said, 'we've found the secret behind Angels with Broken Wings.'

chapter eighteen

'The secret behind Angels with Broken Wings,' said the tall man, 'is simplicity. All is calm and orderly. Nothing is complicated. Everything may not,' he conceded, 'be exactly what it seems, but that again is for a simple reason. It is to keep things orderly. And calm.'

Mad, thought Jeff. Stark-raving mad.

'Doubt, Mr Randall, is written across your face. That is rather unfortunate. For I must ask you this: are you in a position to doubt me?'

No, conceded Jeff to himself. He wasn't. Not at all.

But Jeff wasn't in quite such an unfortunate position as Vladimir and Patience. The latter in particular was having a truly unpleasant time and, from the look of her, had been suffering long before they had entered the 'interesting' room. Dishevelled and distraught, mascara running in thick black lines down her face and hair now a stranger to her chignon, she was tightly bound to a pole in the corner of the room. And while nobody was visibly inflicting pain on her, every few minutes she appeared to suffer from a minor seizure. Jeff had yet to work out that they were caused by the woman standing close to her in the tight black catsuit sticking pins in a miniature Patience doll.

Marty had.

He had noticed Patience the minute they had entered the interesting room. And Patience, despite her pain, had noticed him. 'You!' she had said.

Vladimir had bowed his head. 'Yes. You didn't think I'd leave without you, did you?'

'Death.'

Vladimir understandably thought Patience had lost her mind. His own mind, however, did not have time to dwell on his beloved. Lucifer, his guardian Archangel, dragged him across the room where the fate for which Patience should earlier have prepared him was belatedly awaiting him. This time there would be no escape from the fangs, the coffin and the stake. But no blindfold. Vladimir Bathory had sinned and for that he would witness the excruciating countdown to his own demise.

It was slowly dawning on Marty that Patience might, perhaps, have the sight, that she could be talking to him.

'Death,' she repeated again. 'And the Fool. And the Magician.'

Still armed with her pins and the miniature of Patience, Emma decided to give the woman a break. The tall man had instructed her to make Patience's death slow and painful – and appearances suggested she was already delirious. Best, thought the housekeeper, to leave off for a while.

'I knew you would come,' said Patience. 'I knew I hadn't lost my gift. I still have the sight!'

'Me?' Marty prodded his own chest. 'You can see me?'

'Oh, yes. Quite clearly. You were written in the cards. Death, the Fool and the Magician.'

'Look, hang on! I admit I'm dead and something of a magician, but less of the fool, eh?' Marty looked closely at Patience and then over to the woman in the catsuit. 'That doll, it's a miniature of you, isn't it? She's doing…What's it called?'

'Voodoo.'

Marty made a sympathetic moue. 'Look, don't worry, love. I'll soon have us out of here.'

'How?'

Marty rather wished she hadn't asked. He hadn't quite worked that one out. 'Er…well, any hints?'

'The Magician,' said Patience. 'The Magician is the one with the power.'

'Will you shut up, you stupid cow!' yelled the tall man. 'You're disturbing my train of thought.'

Marty and Patience exchanged a look and nodded in mutual understanding.

'Count Bathory,' continued the orator, 'will shortly meet the fate assigned to him.' As he spoke, the Archangel pushed Vladimir into the coffin and slammed the lid. 'But you, Mr Randall, will be with us for some time. You have not served your purpose yet. And do you know what that purpose is?'

Jeff had a vague inkling that it had something to do with computers and Dave Day. 'The computer program?' he ventured.

The tall man didn't reply immediately. Instead he watched as Gabriel secured the knots behind Jeff's back. He wanted to make sure the little man was firmly tied to the chair before he approached him.

'Aha! The computer program! I must congratulate you, Mr Randall. It seems that you do, after all, have some vague notion of what being a private detective is all about.' He walked up to Jeff and leered at him. 'And do you have the program?'

'No.'

'Do you know who has?'

Jeff didn't reply. He correctly surmised that the tall man was going to answer his own question.

'Dave Day,' he said, still looking down at Jeff, 'has the computer program. Do you know,' he continued, indicating the room at large, 'that in all the years of our magnificent endeavour, we have made only one mistake? Or rather,' he added with a vicious little grimace, 'Tallulah made a mistake. She thought the culprit was that blustering fool Hopkirk.'

'Hey!' said Marty. 'Steady on! That's the second time I've been called a fool.'

'Or perhaps,' corrected the tall man, 'he wasn't such a fool after all?'

'That's better,' breathed Marty.

'He was clever enough to get himself killed, wasn't he?'

In the corner beside Patience, the dead detective looked wounded — and increasingly pensive. The more the tall man talked, the more Marty felt there was *something* about him. Something familiar…

'Which means,' continued the tall man, 'that he will be spared the fate assigned to you.'

'Er…what's that?' Jeff's quizzical expression had its roots in more than the question. He was looking at Marty.

And Marty was gesticulating wildly at the tall man. Then he walked over to Jeff and whispered in his ear. 'Jeff! Jeff! Haven't we seen him somewhere before?'

'I don't know.'

'I know you don't know,' said the tall man. '*I'm* the

one who knows what your fate will be. But you will have to wait. You will have to wait until we have what we want. Dave Day.'

'I've *definitely* seen him before,' said Marty.

'I've never clapped eyes on him in my life.'

'Oh, come *on*, Mr Randall! We know you've seen him. Your little Miss Hurst phoned to tell us. And,' he added, 'do you know what little Miss Hurst is doing as we speak?'

'No.'

'She's on her way here with Mr Day. To rescue you, Mr Randall. Or so she thinks. Tallulah has phoned her and—'

And then the door burst open and Tallulah Joplin stormed into the interesting room.

'Bloody hell!' said Marty.

'Bloody woman!' screamed Tallulah. 'You'd think a bloody private detective would have a mobile phone, wouldn't you? And has she replied to the messages I've left at the office? No!' Then Tallulah noticed Jeff. 'Ah! You've got him! Good.'

Tallulah's demeanour changed completely as she sauntered over to Jeff. 'Recognize me, Mr Randall?' she purred. 'I look different, don't I?' She put her hands on her hips and licked her lips. 'No longer the Angel with a Broken Wing but' – Tallulah leaned down and brushed her mane of hair against Jeff's face – 'the sultry vamp.'

Not exactly, thought Jeff, recoiling in disgust.

Jesus! Thought Marty. Tallulah Joplin. Same voice, same clothes, same swagger. Different face. Tallulah, he reckoned, had not aged well.

'Where does she live?'

'What?' asked Jeff.

'Jeannie Hurst, you idiot! Where does she live?

242

We've got to get her here. Now! I want her now!'

Tallulah, reflected Marty. Always all want.

'My dear,' said the tall man. 'We don't need her *now*. We have all the time in the world.' He gestured to Jeff. 'We have Mr Randall. We will, therefore, get Miss Hurst.'

'But I want her *now*! I want her to see all this before it's over!'

'All what?' The tall man's voice was dangerously low.

Tallulah gestured to Patience and then to the coffin in which the hapless Vladimir was still trapped. 'She must see what I'm capable of! She must see what I've done! She must see the power I have. I can't get Marty Hopkirk to see it, so I'll have *her*.' Tallulah glared at Jeff. 'Oh, I *know*. I could tell by the look in her eye. She loved Marty, didn't she? She...'

'Tallulah!' The tall man marched over to the ex-vamp and grabbed her none too gently by the arm. 'Look, you stupid bitch,' he seethed. 'This has nothing to do with Marty Hopkirk. Or him,' he added, looking at Jeff. 'Or Jeannie Hurst. You seem to have forgotten what this is all about.'

'So what is it all about?'

'*Me!*' screamed the tall man. '*Me!* Taking over the world. The realization of a vision. Ten years I've waited! Ten years.' He turned and glared at Tallulah. 'So don't you bloody dare jeopardize it for the sake of—'

'The Queen of Cups,' said Patience loudly.

'What?' said everyone else.

'The Queen of Cups,' she repeated. 'That was the last card I saw. She's coming.'

'Oh, stick a pin in her!' snapped Tallulah.

Emma duly pierced the Patience doll.

'Ow!' winced Patience the woman.

Marty rushed over to her. 'S'all right, love. Just hang on in there. I'll...I'll...' I'd better act, he thought. And soon. 'Who,' he added, 'is the Queen of Cups?'

'Her,' whispered Patience. 'The one she's talking about. It makes sense now. She's on her way.'

Shit! thought Marty. That's all we need. Jeannie trapped as well. He turned back to the woman on the pole. 'Look, I've got to do something,' he said in desperation. 'I can blow things, I can possess, I can power merge, I can—'

'Fire and Water,' said Patience. 'Fire and Water.' But this time she forgot to whisper and her voice carried right across the room.

'Pin!' yelled Tallulah.

'Ouch!'

'And while we're at it,' said Tallulah, 'it's time we dealt with him. Open the coffin!' she barked to Lucifer.

Lucifer prised off the lid and pulled the pale and trembling Vladimir from the box.

'The coffin,' said Tallulah, 'was just a joke really. A sort of teaser.'

'I...I didn't find it very funny.'

'No, but we did.'

For once Tallulah and the tall man seemed to be in accord. Putting paid to the last surviving delegate was on top of the latter's agenda and, equally important, it seemed to be keeping Tallulah from doing anything too rash.

'Fire and Water,' repeated Patience again, this time in the softest of whispers.

She seemed to Marty to be floating on the brink

of unconsciousness. But from the look of things, Marty wasn't going to have time to research either of those elements. He was beginning to feel rather bad about Vladimir. True, he had called him a twat and an arrogant git, but there was no way he was going to stand back and watch Tallulah drive a stake through his heart. And judging by the looks of things, that was what she was about to do.

'Marty!' urged Jeff. 'Can't you do something? You can't just stand by and watch him die!'

'Who're you talking to?' barked Gabriel.

'Er…no one.'

'Well, shut up then.'

Marty watched in increasing horror as the tall man took a small knife from his pocket, leaned down to the coffin and picked up something from behind it. A stake.

'This knife,' he mused, 'is probably sharp enough. After all, Mr Randall, it nicked a man's body and sealed his fate not one hour ago. Still, best to make sure, eh? We like our stakes to be sharp.'

'Lucifer,' said Tallulah, 'put the coffin upright against the wall, will you?'

'What?'

'Against the wall.' Tallulah stood back, contemplating the tableau that she was creating. 'I want everyone to see this…especially,' she added with a smirk, 'little Jeff over there. Maybe the shock will prompt him into divulging the whereabouts of Miss Hurst.'

But Tallulah was about to experience a nasty shock of her own.

Lucifer had to leave Vladimir for a moment in order to rearrange the position of the coffin. But even though his hands and feet were bound,

Vladimir reckoned he still had a chance. Granted it was slim, but it was still worth taking. Especially as Lucifer had to replace his rifle in his shoulder sling in order to move the coffin.

It only took a few seconds, but to Jeff, watching from the other side of the room, it appeared to happen in slow motion. The Carpathian narrowed his eyes, measuring the distance, and then, with every ounce of his energy, hurled himself towards Tallulah.

His aim was far more deadly accurate than he had dared to hope. He hit her with such force that she spun round, let out a piercing yell and, with nothing to grasp that would break her fall, toppled backwards into the coffin. The coffin shot backwards and knocked the crouching Lucifer to the ground. His head hit the steel floor with a resounding smack.

For a moment there was a stunned silence, then it was broken by the incongruous sound of laughter.

'Oh, Count Bathory,' gasped the tall man, shoulders heaving. 'What a splendid effort! And what a sweet, delicious irony! Tallulah in a coffin!'

'You...you *bastard*!' screamed Tallulah from her box. Then her hands appeared, the red talons flapping at the sides as she grappled to get out. 'Help me out of here!'

Gabriel immediately moved away from his post beside Jeff.

'Stay where you are!' barked the tall man. 'We don't want another one playing the hero. I'll help her.'

But the furious Tallulah didn't really need help. Even as the tall man laid down his stake, she had already levered her torso out of the coffin. She made a perfect target.

Like Vladimir before him, Marty narrowed his eyes, concentrated all his energy – and looked at the stake. It flew up from the ground and, in a perfect arc, shot straight towards the coffin.

Tallulah didn't even see it coming. And by the time she had registered what was happening she was back in the coffin. But this time she would never get out. The still-quivering stake had pierced her straight through the heart.

Again silence reigned in the now very interesting room. This time it was broken by a faint scratching sound as Tallulah's fingers clawed once again at the sides of the coffin. But there was only a glimpse of the now enfeebled talons before they fell back into their final resting place.

The tall man wasn't laughing now. Unable to believe his eyes, he looked down at the coffin. Then he looked at Vladimir. Slowly, he turned round and looked at Jeff. It was only when he registered Emma's hysterical screams that he found his own voice.

'Who...What? I...I don't understand...'

'The Magician!' shouted Patience. 'The Magician! And now is the time for the Fire and the Water!'

Emma stopped screaming and cast a terrified look at Patience. Suddenly the pins and the doll seemed to be burning holes in her hands. 'It's her!' she shouted, throwing them to the ground. 'She's a witch! She's mad. I always knew there was something about her!' Then Emma turned on her heel and fled the room.

That, at least, was her intention. As she raced to the door, it burst open, hit her full in the face and sent her sprawling and unconscious to the ground.

Jeannie had arrived.

The first person she saw was Jeff. Gabriel, aiming his gun at her forehead, was the second. But in her progress through the palace, Jeannie had already dispatched two Archangels and she wasn't going to stop now. She leapt into the air and aimed both feet at Gabriel's head.

He never knew what had hit him.

'Jeff! Jeff! Are you all right?' she asked as she landed at his side.

'Jeannie!' Jeff had never been so delighted to see her. 'Yeah, yeah...I'm fine, but...'

'But,' said the tall man as he aimed Lucifer's gun at both of them, 'you soon won't be.'

'Who...'

'Miss Hurst, I believe.' Ever polite, the tall man inclined his head towards her. 'And Mr Day? That's you behind the door, isn't it, Mr Day. Come along, Mr Day. Don't be shy now.'

With a heavy sigh, Dave slunk out from behind the door and looked apologetically at Jeannie and Jeff. Acrobatics and heroics, his expression indicated, were not really his thing. Then he turned round, saw the body in the coffin and let out a little yelp.

'Careful, Mr Day. You wouldn't want to drop your computer, now would you?'

Dave looked down at his laptop. So did Jeff and Jeannie. Vladimir, trussed up on the floor, stared balefully at the innocuous-looking machine. So this, he thought, is what all the fuss has been about. This is the reason for the palace, for Angels. And for Patience. He looked over at Patience. Oddly, she was smiling and seemed to be looking straight through the wall.

Patience, he remembered, had the sight. Then he remembered about Marty.

Marty had never seen anything like it. One room was awash with oil. Another seemed to be heaving with worms. One was flooded. Great mounds of earth littered the room next door, while, on the other side of the corridor, a dead body lay under one of the little Japanese vehicles dominating the room. But it wasn't until he had done a full circuit of the palace that he found what he was looking for.

'Shame about Tallulah,' said the tall man. Then he shrugged. 'Not, of course, that it's a tragedy. I had plans for her anyway. It's just that I'm a bit hacked off that you pipped me to the post.'

His audience stayed mute.

'A glum little trio, aren't you? I can't presume to know about you, Miss Hurst, but I've seen your companions being a little more...well, chatty.'

'Eh?' It was Dave who answered. 'You've never seen us before.'

'Oh, but I have, Mr Day. Let me see, it must have been about...what, ten years ago?' The tall man began to stroke his scar. 'On rather a dramatic night, actually. A night at a certain club...Oh, yes,' he continued as he saw realization dawn. 'The Terrapin Club. Such a...seedy joint, don't you think?'

'You never went there,' said Dave. 'Never saw you there.'

'Oh, you did. Perhaps you only got a glimpse, though. I made a rather dramatic entrance.' The tall man's lip curled with pleasure as he remembered. Then he fingered the scar again and winced with pain.

'Christ!' A stunned Jeff looked up at him. 'I know who you were! Bloody hell. The policeman!'

'*Please!* The chief of police. The chief of the riot

police, in fact.'

'But...' Myriad questions swarmed into Jeff's mind, and with them the vision of the uniformed policemen storming the Terrapin. 'But how did you...Why...' And suddenly Jeff realized he knew the answer. He looked towards the coffin.

Still with his weapon trained on them, the tall man followed his gaze. 'Yes,' he sighed. 'Tallulah. She was a clever girl, you know. She played everyone at their own game – and beat them. Don Carlos, Marty Hopkirk, Dave Day...oh, the list goes on. I was fond of her once, you know. We had the perfect partnership. She had the ear of gangsters...I was above suspicion. Oh, yes, it worked like a dream. Until, that is, she became too ambitious.' The tall man paused for reflection, looked again at the coffin and then, voice rising, turned back to Jeff, Jeannie and Dave. 'She thought she could rule the world. And she thought she could beat me! *Me!* Nobody beats me at my own game. I am the only one with the intelligence and the ambition to succeed where others have failed! I was *never* going to be thwarted. And I was always...'

Behind him, Patience was smiling again. Vladimir couldn't understand it. But Vladimir didn't have the sight; he didn't know that Marty had found what he was looking for. He had found the fire.

'*Always*,' repeated the tall man. 'I was always destined to be the one who would...'

But he never finished his sentence. In the room behind him, Marty had found the last Catherine Wheel in Mr Wu's room. Mr Wu himself was no more, but the substance his country had given the world was, as the Catherine Wheel spluttered into life, destined to save the world. With every remaining ounce of his dwindling powers, Marty blew at the revolving wheel.

It tore through the steel wall and, bang on target, emptied its entire cargo of bullets into the tall man's back.

The tall man bent forward, as if in supplication. He tried to speak, but no words came from his mouth. Instead, a trickle of blood emerged and ran gently down the length of his scar. Then he fell to the ground and, destined never to rule the world, he died.

That was when the water started flowing.

'Jeff?' said Marty.

'Mmm?'

'I'm fading fast. Don't say anything. Just listen. I've only got a few seconds.' Shimmering in and out of focus, Marty had to made a huge effort to stay with Jeff. He nodded towards Patience. 'She knows,' he said. 'She helped me. She told me to how to direct the water into the air conditioning units. Soon, the water...'

'Soon,' cried Patience, 'the water will flow. The flood will come. We must leave. Now!'

Jeannie turned to Jeff. 'What's she talking about?'

Jeff had to think quickly. 'This place,' he said. 'I think she's put some sort of curse on it.' As he spoke, the first jet of water spouted from the air conditioning unit. Quick!' he shouted, hurrying towards Patience and the still-bound Vladimir. 'We've got to untie them...we've got to get out of here!'

'Jeff...?' whispered Marty, oscillating between this world and the next.

But Jeff didn't hear him.

'Quick!' repeated Jeff, untying the knots that secured Patience. Jeannie did the same for Vladimir. Neither noticed Dave Day's thoughtful expression as he looked at the body of the tall man. Nor did they see him stepping forward, stooping down and placing something in the man's lifeless hand. 'Yours,' he said. 'For ever.' Then he stepped back and watched as the first wave of water covered the hand and the laptop that, at last, was within its grasp.

Seconds later the five survivors were making a desperate dash towards freedom. And this time, as he rushed out the door, Jeff did hear Marty.

'Jeff...?' The voice was disembodied now – and even fainter. 'Jeff...do something for me...please ...look after Jeannie...I'll always love her...

Then he was gone, fading into a firmament untainted by Angels with Broken Wings.

epilogue

Marty Hopkirk finished his act with a flourish and a theatrical bow. His final number was always fast, frenetic and furious, and this one had been no exception. Breathing deeply, heart pounding in his chest, he drew himself to his full height, lifted his arms into the air and bestowed a dazzling smile on his raucous audience.

That, at least, was how he remembered it. Had not thunderous applause erupted as soon as he took the first of many bows? Hadn't they screamed and begged him to continue?

Hadn't things changed in the space of ten years?

For even the optimistic Marty had to admit that the raucousness of the people in front of him wasn't, in fact, directed at him and that the word 'audience' was something of a misnomer. Half of limbo's clientele were oblivious to his presence and those who had watched his routine had done so with expressions of such vacuity that their mental presence had to be doubted. The most vacant among them – men and women alike – wore heavy make-up and haunted expressions, staring at the world through ghoulish, unseeing eyes. One of them, a creature of indeterminate sex, shouted something in Marty's direction. Marty brightened and, white suit glittering, twirled niftily in response to the plea to 'Get them off!' It didn't occur to him that the strange creature had actually shouted, 'Get off!'

When Marty did get off the stage it was with a heavy heart. He weaved his way through the assembled throng and, as he did so, the music began again. This time it was a slow, rhythmic yet slightly eerie throb that had an electrifying effect on the people on the floor. They began to move as one, but with no indication that they were together or even that they were enjoying themselves. Vacant and unblinking, holding glasses of fluorescent imaginary cocktails and not moving their feet, they bent their knees and, without moving their heads, bobbed up and down.

Marty felt a stab of irritation as he left the dance floor. What was wrong, he wondered, with proper dancing? Why couldn't they continue to enjoy *his* sort of music and celebrate the Bob Fosse moves that he rehearsed with such gusto? People in limbo had no taste. Worse, they were boring.

Marty needed excitement in his life. Companionship. And there was, he reflected as he left limbo, one place he was guaranteed to find it. Humming to himself, he shimmered down to see Jeff.